Anna,
Welcome to the
World of Alfheim!
Hope you enjoy!!
Gary Nilsen

Alfheim

by

Gary A Nilsen

Alexian Books, Inc.

P.O. Box 2140

New York, NY, 10163

This book is a work of fiction. Any references to historical events, real people, or real places are used fictitiously. Other names, characters, places, and events are products of the author's imagination, and any resemblance to actual events or places or persons, living or dead, is entirely coincidental.

For information about special discounts for bulk purchases, please contact Alexian Books, Inc. at info@alexianbooks.com.

Manufactured in the United States of America

10 9 8 7 6 5 4 3 2 1

ISBN 978-0-9835180-4-4

To Alex and Ian, my future…

To Nancy, my everything…

Her skirt was o the grass-green silk,
Her mantle o the velvet fine,
At ilka tett of her horse's mane
Hang fifty silver bells and nine.

True Thomas he pulled aff his cap,
And louted low upon his knee:
"All hail, thou mighty Queen of Heaven!
For thy peer on earth I've never seen."

"O no, O no, Thomas," she said,
"That name does not belang to me:
I am but the queen of fair Elfland,
That am hither come to visit thee…

—"Thomas the Rhymer"
Anonymous, 17th Century

Chapter 1

A BARREL-CHESTED FIGURE SAT BEHIND a massive wooden desk that would have dwarfed an ordinary person. The lighting in the heavy wooden-paneled library was minimal, a single electric desk lamp tilted over a sheet of parchment. Cadwaladr stared at the perfect precision of the letters drawn on the page as if looking through a microscope at something unrecognizable to the naked eye.

"Is there to be a reply?" The voice was timid.

Cadwaladr shifted his gaze to the sound of the interruption.

"Is there any word of the bitch to the north?" he asked.

"No, my lord."

"Pity. I was certain that news of her daughter's death would spark some reaction. Actually, I'd hoped she would die from grief, and yet, nothing but silence on the matter."

"Yes, my lord."

"Seumais seems quite certain the boy shows no signs of knowing the nature of his parentage." He looked at the paper once more, then crinkled it into a ball and tossed it aside. "Still, things are turning in my favor, and no need to take chances. Tell Seumais the time has come to return home. Have him kill the boy and be done with these rumors."

"What if the boy is...well?"

"What if, what if?" He mimicked the trembling voice of the messenger. "Who cares? I will not run the risk of some pretender waltzing into the middle of my plans and ruining things again. I've waited too long."

"Yes, my lord."

* * *

The messenger backed into the darker shadows of the room toward the door. Outside, in the great room, his face regained its normal serenity. A long dark-blue tunic swirled around his ankles as he made for the courtyard of the centuries-old castle. After mounting a dark horse, the color of ebony under the glow of the half-moon, he kicked the animal to a gallop and charged under the portcullis onto the open grassy plain outside the walls.

Chapter 2

Timothy Brennan hitched his backpack over his right shoulder and strode out of the classroom late in the afternoon. Detention was done, and he couldn't wait to get home. The halls of Kingswood Regional High School were quiet, except for the few jocks who filtered out of the locker rooms after practice. Timothy wasn't a jock, nor was he much like the remaining students; they were all like another species to him.

The glass front door nearly ripped his arm off as a gust of wind yanked it open. A swirl of leaves and lunch-size potato chip bags rose toward the roof—a maelstrom of activity that mimicked the angry sky. It smelled like snow.

"Hey Twitchy, boinked any trees lately?" Two guys from the wrestling team were leaning against the wall next to the open gym doors, nudging each other over their impressive wit.

"Assholes," Timothy said under his breath. He pulled his hoodie over his head, as much to fight against the cold as to shield himself from torment, and walked to his car. He opened the door and slid onto the vinyl block of ice that resembled the front seat and turned the key, but the engine started the slow rolls that suggested it had other ideas about firing up. Timothy slammed the palm of his hand against the steering wheel and yelled. His anger over hearing his unofficial nickname compounded the frustration that his car might die right there in the parking lot. A six-mile hike in this weather wasn't a prospect he wanted to consider, and he sure as hell didn't want to call his uncle at work to come pick him up.

The engine sparked and rumbled to a start, idling roughly. He pressed on the accelerator a few times to make sure the valves were getting enough gas; he didn't want the thing to sputter its last breath.

Glancing in the rearview mirror, he saw that the guys had gone back inside. It had been two years since he'd written the English composition in which he confessed that he found solace in the trees of the New Hampshire forests. Some mistakes just weren't fixable. At first, he'd been teased about being a tree hugger, but once the motor tics had started because of his ADD medication, his oddity had skewed far to the left of normal. The joking had taken a meaner turn from enough of the A-list to make life more miserable than sublime.

Timothy yanked down on the column shift and turned for home. It was still hard to consider it home since it belonged to his uncle, and he didn't exactly make it feel like a place you wanted to return to at the end of the day. The short drive to the north brought him to Ossipee, a small town with little going for it except a big lake and beautiful forests. The local economy barely supported the few thousand people who lived there, but Timothy felt that was a notch on the plus side. More trees, less people. The same for the street he turned onto. Four houses you'd barely notice unless you were looking for them.

The driveway was empty, and Timothy fist-pumped the air. His uncle was still at work, which meant he could turn up the heat in the house for a while; his car hadn't had any since the onset of winter.

"Hi, Mom," he said as he shut the door. She'd been gone for six months, but the routine was something he refused to let go. Not yet. He notched up the lever on the thermostat and went straight to his room, dumped his backpack on the floor and stepped over multiple piles of dirty clothes before dropping into an age-worn recliner. He pushed the power button of an old GameCube and watched his favorite character gallop across a field. When he wasn't in the forests, playing Zelda was a surrogate way to escape his mounting depression.

A few minutes of video gaming before homework somehow turned into three hours. A glow lit his room from a pair of headlights outside. His uncle was home. The front door slammed open, then giggling. He had company. He prayed they'd leave him alone.

"Timothy! You home, boy?" The sound of his uncle's voice was enough to make him grind his teeth.

"Yes, Uncle Jim, I'm here." It was too much to have hoped.

"It's hot as hell in here," he yelled. "Did you turn up the bloody thermostat again?"

"Damn." Timothy dropped the game controller on the floor. "I'll get it."

"Grab me a couple of beers from the fridge, will ya?"

A bloated excuse for a middle-aged man was leaning against a dark-haired woman, holding her against the wall, licking and kissing her face. He looked like a dog trying to find the last bit of food in its bowl.

She opened her eyes and saw Timothy looking at them. She poked Jim on the shoulder and said in a loud whisper, "The boy is watching."

"What?" He pulled away from her and she brushed the sides of her short skirt back down her thighs. Timothy wondered how she avoided frostbite below the waist.

"Damn it, Tim, get the beer, and be off with you."

A red flannel shirttail hung over his uncle's belt. It was half-unbuttoned, offering a glimpse of his dingy white tee shirt. He took the bottles in one hand and swept the other back over his head, smoothing his thinning red hair. His beer belly sagged, pulling the eye down toward the half-opened zipper.

"Not working tonight, huh?" Jim asked.

"No, it's Tuesday. I don't work on Tuesdays," Timothy said.

"Oh yeah, I forgot." Jim handed a bottle to the woman. "This is Elaine. Did you do your homework?"

"Yeah." It was a lie, much like their relationship as uncle and nephew. Timothy walked around them and threw a quick nod in her direction.

"Good, don't want you growing up a lazy bum." Jim's voice trailed away as Timothy closed the bedroom door. The last thing he heard was Elaine's comment about how cute his uncle's ears were, and she squealed with laughter again.

He picked up the game controller, but he'd lost the desire to keep playing. The idea of doing homework held his attention for about a minute, long enough for him to have turned on his desk lamp. There, as always, Melanie Marshall was waiting, and all thought of English disappeared.

A single photo was pinned to the corkboard above his desk. It was the only one he'd kept from his photography elective the year before. Melanie was sitting on a bench in the park, nestled against the base of an oak tree. He remembered wandering through the park looking for landscapes to take pictures of when he spotted her. He doubted if she remembered, as least not as clearly as he did, the times they'd played together that one summer, their mothers sitting on benches, reading.

"Do you mind if I take your picture?"

"Sure," she'd said. "Is it for the school newspaper or something?"

"No, just for class."

Melanie turned sideways and fluffed up her hair. Timothy knelt down and manually focused the camera, a full framed shot. She smiled. He pushed the shutter release, once.

"That'll be the best one I take today," he said. Melanie laughed.

"Why is that?"

"Because, you're in it."

"Aww, that's really sweet," she said, reaching her hand out and gently brushing his cheek.

Timothy could still remember his mind going blank, desperately searching for some witty remark. She had looked as if she were waiting for him to say something, but someone had pushed his brain's off switch. She was one of the prettiest girls in school and had been the object of his secret affections since those days so many summers before when they'd played on the swings and shared ice cream.

"Well, I have to go meet my friend," she announced.

"Yeah, sure, of course." Timothy looked over to see a girl coming across the grass.

"See you in school?"

"Yup." He felt like an idiot. "Thanks for the picture." She'd already started across the field and waved her hand, not even turning back around. "I'm such an idiot," he murmured, his words catching up with his feelings.

Timothy turned off the light and crawled on top of his bed. He closed his eyes and thought of her smile. It was a much more pleasant way to drift off to sleep than anything else he could think of. At least in his dreams he could imagine the outcome of taking her picture ending in so many different ways.

Chapter 3

A SKIRT WAS WEDGED BETWEEN the posts of the banister. Unless Jim had driven Elaine home naked, they were up there somewhere. Timothy pushed the image out of his mind and escaped through the front door.

The air was warmer and the car started right up. He managed to find a parking space near the front door of the high school but decided to wait until it was time to go in. He wasn't in the mood for small talk.

A silver Acura pulled up to the curb and three girls jumped out, laughing and talking like they were out for a shopping spree at the mall, but the one who caught his attention was Melanie. The familiar sensation of butterflies taking flight in his stomach brought his mood up a notch. At least until he heard another voice from somewhere behind.

"Mel, wait up." Derek Hollister was jogging toward her. The two girls with Melanie smiled and waved, then moved off, leaving her to him. Derek draped his arm over her shoulders and they walked toward the door. The butterflies crashed and burned; he could feel the acid reflux. Derek Hollister, the school hero, captain of the hockey team, captain of the varsity ski team, all-around jock, and Timothy's worst nightmare. To most everyone, Derek was the charming all-American boy. But Timothy had seen the dark side, how Derek's fierce competitive nature could make him turn ugly. It was a Jekyll and Hyde thing, and just like in the movies, only the victims got to see the face of Hyde.

Last year, in tenth grade, at his mother's urging, Timothy had tried out for the hockey team. He'd barely scraped by the cuts and spent several games warming the bench. At last the coach had sent him in because of an injury. During a crucial power play, Timothy had slipped and turned an almost sure goal into something painful as he fell under Derek in the midst of a fast break. The other team went on to win, and Derek had raged at Timothy in the locker room. The rest of the team fell in behind their leader. The incident would probably have ended there, but the coach had then decided to make an example of Derek's poor-sportsman-like conduct and benched him for two games. The school lost both, and Timothy's life became hell as the team slowly worked their revenge. He knew the whole school didn't hate him, but it certainly felt like it sometimes.

The warning bell rang, and Timothy stepped out of his car. Classes were simply a means to get to lunch period. Chemistry, English, and something resembling a lecture on history went by with Timothy staring out the window at the trees across the highway. The melting snow had frozen overnight, and the wilting branches looked as though an artisan had blown glass around them. Mostly, he was grateful the teacher hadn't called on him to answer anything.

In the cafeteria, he grabbed a hamburger and some fries, then sat at his usual table in the corner of the room. Timothy dug into his backpack, pulled out a new paperback that was a novelized version of one of his favorite video games, and started to read.

A pile of books slammed down on the table. A boy swung his leg over the back of the chair and sat opposite him.

"Dude, good news!"

"Omar, you scared the crap out of me," Timothy said. Omar was the son of a Pakistani immigrant and often picked on for his skin color, especially among the predominantly white local neighborhoods, along with his religion and his nationality. His father owned a small auto-repair shop in town. In their freshman year, Timothy had accidently hit him in the face with a Frisbee, but their individual oddities drew them together in an "us versus them" arrangement, and it worked. They'd been best friends since.

"Sorry."

"It's okay. What's up?"

"My dad found a thermostat for your junker; you get to have heat again."

"Whoa, that's cool. Where'd he find one?"

"In Nashua. He was downstate getting some other stuff, and the yard had a bunch of old parts for your car. Stop by after school, and I can install it."

"I have to work today."

"Oh." He shrugged. "Hey, you going to the game Friday afternoon?"

"What game?" Timothy dipped a couple of fries into a miniscule cup of ketchup and slid them into his mouth.

"The hockey game. What's the matter, don't you have any school spirit?"

"Since when do you?"

"You're depressed again, aren't you? Most of the school's going. You never know, we might get lucky." He peeked over his shoulder as if he were about to share a secret. "Have you seen Jenny? She's kinda hot since her braces came off."

"Thanks, but there's other things I'd rather be doing than watching Derek play hero…again."

"It's not Derek you'd be watching, it's Melanie, and she'd be watching Derek."

"Something like that," Timothy said.

"Seriously, you've got to get past that girl. She's never going to look at you like she does that jock."

"Thanks for the vote of confidence."

"Just keeping it real."

"Yeah, well…someday she'll get tired of him being Mr. Perfect."

"You'll be doing walker races at the old folk's home."

"Are you going out of your way to cheer me up today?" Timothy threw a french fry at him. "Cause you're doing a hell of a job."

"I know you're not big on hanging out, but maybe if you did, you might actually make more friends…girlfriends, too. You haven't twitched in like two months, right?"

Omar was one of the few Timothy had ever confided in about the ADD diagnosis. He'd tried his best to describe that when he felt severe stress or anger, it was like something trying to break out of him. It forced his body to tic, usually a jerk of the head.

"I've been keeping a tight check on it." It was true. He hadn't really gotten angry about anything for a while. It was hard to be depressed and pissed at the same time. Being pissed took energy, and depression made sure you didn't have much of that. The occasional bullying from jockland was easier to keep at bay by not hanging out.

"Just think about it, okay?"

Timothy shrugged. "Okay," he said. It was the quickest way to get past the conversation.

"Cool." Omar jumped up and grabbed his books. "I gotta go see my guidance counselor. She's worried I'm not applying myself." He rolled his eyes. "Like I need to? She knows what I'm doing after school's over. I told her my father's already ordered a new shop sign adding my name."

Timothy wondered if anyone in guidance even knew who he was.

* * *

After school, driving to work took only minutes. Overton's Back Porch Family Restaurant was a local place just off the highway.

He wasn't crazy about the job, but it offered a sense of peace to work at the same place his mother had. Not long after she died from meningitis, he'd asked the owner, Herbie Overton, if he would consider hiring Timothy. Herbie was good like that. Living in Jim's house was so foreign that it was nice to be somewhere familiar, somewhere still connected to her. And the money didn't hurt either. It was good to have some independence. At least Timothy could pay for his own clothing and car.

Getting the hang of the restaurant routine had taken time: learning how to bus tables quickly and quietly, to offload deliveries to the kitchen, to lug beer kegs and soda tanks up from the basement. The nice thing was working with people who seemed to appreciate his company, and he didn't have to deal much with the customers, at least not like the waitstaff did.

Timothy parked on the service side of the building and walked through the back door. Just inside, a stairway dropped into the basement. He grabbed a clean busboy jacket. As he turned to go back up, Herbie stood at the top of the stairs, gazing down, looking relieved.

"I'm glad you're a bit early," he said.

"How come?"

"We have a large group on the way. Most of the ice hockey team and their parents are coming for a pregame party, and we need to set up tables on the back porch."

"You mean the high school team?" Timothy felt the muscles in the bottom of his stomach tense.

"Is there another around here?" Herbie shook his head. "Go help Jasper and then get a backup soda tank ready."

Of all the restaurants around Ossipee, they had to choose this one? Seeing Derek and his friends at school was bad enough, but doing busboy work in front of them?

Timothy considered feigning a sudden illness, but that wouldn't have been fair to Herbie. After all, it meant a good night's business. He sighed and turned toward the back of the restaurant.

The rear of the building, formerly the back porch of the house, was glass enclosed during the winter and opened for outside dining during the spring and summer.

Jasper, a young waiter, though older than Timothy by a few years, was trying to move some of the larger tables around.

"Need some help?"

"Thanks," said Jasper. "We have to set for about forty-five." No wonder Herbie was tense. That was more than the normal total for an entire weekday night. The last napkins were going on the tables when some of the parents began to arrive with their sons.

Herbie accompanied the first group inside. Jasper motioned for Timothy to start filling the water glasses, so he grabbed two pitchers from the sideboard. Out of the corner of his eye, Timothy saw one of the guys nudge his teammate and nod in his direction. He was smirking and whispering something in his ear; they both laughed. Timothy lofted his middle finger toward them after they turned around.

Timothy bit tiny chunks of flesh from the inside of his lower lip. It felt like one of those dreams where you're standing naked in the middle of class with everyone laughing and ridiculing you. He thought of what his mother used to tell him: Don't let the teasing of a few make you think that everyone else is just like them. Ignore them, and they'll get tired of bothering you. Timothy was still waiting.

Jasper and Mary, another member of the waitstaff, had started taking orders once everyone was in and seated. Timothy snuck from the back porch and started helping Herbie fill mugs with soda. He stayed away from the dining area until it was time to clear the dinner plates. He carried a folding stand onto the porch and laid a large tray on top, then began collecting plates. For the first few months, clearing dishes with half-eaten food had nauseated him. The worst was Italian; the sauce got everywhere.

Timothy stacked as many dishes as possible without danger of them toppling. Then, he lifted the tray from underneath, turned, and moved carefully, concentrating more on the tray than where he was stepping. He noticed Derek slide down in his seat. Something blocked Timothy's ankle, preventing him from moving his foot forward. He tried to step over it, but couldn't untangle himself. The weight of the tray shifted forward. He struggled to hold on, but it was too late. With a sense of horror, he crashed to the floor, landing on top of the dishes. Pieces of china and food flew in every direction. His jacket was soaked with tomato sauce, gravy, bits of half-eaten vegetables, and mashed potatoes.

Several of the parents circled him, asking if he was all right, and trying to help him up. When Timothy got to his feet, he turned toward Derek, who was shaking his head sadly.

"You always seem to be falling down," Derek said.

Timothy wanted to hurl something heavy and hard at him. It was the naked dream come alive, and he felt the tops of his ears burning with rage. It was the worst prank he'd ever pulled, by far.

"What's this?" Herbie called as he came running into the room.

"The poor boy must have tripped," said one woman.

Timothy looked at Herbie, wanting to tell him it had been deliberate, but who would believe it? He stormed through the restaurant and out the back door, sitting hard on the short set of stairs, forcing several slow, deep breaths. A tight pressure rose through his chest to his neck. An instant later, his head twitched to the right.

The motor tics were back.

The doctor had put him on Ritalin for the ADD. It was supposed to help him learn and think better, something about the way his brain fired differently from normal people. When the tics started, the doctor had prescribed Zoloft to counterbalance them. It didn't seem to matter either way. Anger brought them on, medicine or not.

"Damn it." Timothy clenched his fists and slammed them down on his knees. Several car alarms started honking in the parking lot all at once, but he took no notice as he stood and started to pace, breathing too fast. He was hyperventilating and getting dizzy. He felt like beating the sides of his head to make the tics stop. He wanted everything to stop. Processing a single clear thought was hard. It was childish, but he wanted his mother's arms around him, just long enough for him to get some control.

Timothy made it to his car without remembering how and drove home. He climbed into bed, covered his head with a pillow, hugging another one closer, and fell into a deep sleep.

Chapter 4

TIMOTHY SLAMMED THE CAR DOOR just as he noticed Omar jump up from the small grassy berm outside the front of the high school. He was afraid someone was going to find out about the events of last night but clung to the wild hope that it would fade away in everyone's memory. He didn't even want to mention it to Omar.

"You didn't happen to check Instagram this morning, did you?" Omar asked as he closed the distance.

"No." Timothy held up his empty hand, reminding Omar that he didn't have a cell phone. "Something I should know about?"

"What about Facebook?"

"No," he said. "What's going on?"

"Oh boy." Omar rolled his eyes. "Some dork on the hockey team posted a video of you taking a header onto a tray of dishes."

Timothy closed his eyes. He felt pressure rising up in his chest, again. A second later, his head twitched to the left.

"I'm sorry, man," Omar said, circling his fingers around Timothy's arm. "If it's any consolation, a lot of people wrote back that he should pull it from his timeline, that it was, like, super mean."

"Yeah, and how many likes were there? How many saw the stupid thing?"

"By the time I left the house, there were about thirty-four likes and about a hundred views. But all the likes were just the guys on the team and some of Derek's buddies."

"Was Melanie on the list?"

"No, I didn't see her on it."

Timothy walked toward the front doors. He was doing all he could to keep his temper down, not wanting to add to the notoriety of his newest social media fame with more body tics.

"It'll be okay. They were just joking around, right?" Omar sounded like he was trying to be the voice of reason.

"Yeah, some joke. Wanna be the punchline sometime?"

Omar stopped talking, and Timothy wanted to kick himself. Omar was the target for his share of mean jokes because of his darker skin and Pakistani accent. Getting mad at him was beyond unfair. "Sorry, I didn't mean that the way it came out."

"Don't sweat it. See you at lunch?"

"Sure."

Timothy tried to move to the back of homeroom as though he were nothing more than a shadow on the wall, but a boy named Keith, who was sitting on the fringe of seats near the door, gave him a big smile.

"Think you got some tomato sauce on your shirt there, Tim."

A couple of students laughed, but a girl halfway across the room yelled at him.

"Shut up, Keith, you're such a jerk."

Timothy slouched in his seat, hyper-grateful that someone had come to his defense. There was divide over the prank, so at least it wasn't one-sided, and that was a nice change.

By lunch period, the event seemed to have lost its appeal and wasn't being discussed, at least in front of Timothy. He dropped a few things onto his lunch tray and wandered to his normal seat in the corner to wait for Omar.

Derek came in and walked toward the middle table. Melanie was waiting for him. He fist-bumped a few of his buddies along the way. Timothy felt his usual irritation, but forced himself to look away. It wasn't in his nature to hate anyone, but Derek was a major exception. The guy had charm. Most of the girls swooned over their fantasies about dating him, and the teachers thought he was the all-American boy. Timothy wished everyone would see the evil streak that drove him into doing pranks like the night before. Derek pulled out a chair and turned it around so that he was sitting with his chest to the seatback and looked straight at Timothy. He said something to Melanie with a grin plastered across his too-handsome face. To Timothy's surprise, she said something sharp in return. Derek looked at her, his smile gone, replaced with something that was a cross between shock and a scowl. He stood and stalked away from the table, turning once to glare at Timothy.

Did she just stand up for me? Timothy wondered. As much as Timothy wanted to believe that, it just didn't seem likely.

"Screw this," he said, pushing his tray across the table. He walked to the back of the cafeteria and pushed through the doors that led to a wide-open field. It was too cold for anyone to be hanging out, but he didn't care. He wanted to be alone anyway. Leaning against the cold bricks, he crossed his arms.

The grass still had that odd greyish-green color with large patches of snow that looked like giant stepping-stones all the way to the line of trees on the opposite side of the field. Timothy couldn't wait for spring, when the rains would turn the grass into a soft green carpet. He loved watching the breeze cut through the blades of grass. It was like watching ripples on the water lapping against the tree line like tiny waves.

A dark shape whizzed past Timothy's face, followed by a sickening thud. A bird flopped to the ground, lifeless. It'd flown straight into the large glass pane of the cafeteria window. He rushed over and knelt next to it, scooping the bird into his hands, not thinking or caring if anyone inside was watching. It was a mourning dove. He rubbed its soft downy chest, its back resting in the cradle of his palms. He couldn't feel a pulse, and the bird's small rounded head limped to one side, its tiny black beak open.

Timothy closed his eyes and lowered his head, still massaging its chest with his fingers.

Images of a bird spreading her wings and flying toward the trees played like a movie in his head. It wasn't like a daydream, soft and fuzzy, but in sharp, Blu-ray, hi-def clarity. He jolted at the intensity of his concentration, which was focused with greater clarity than he'd ever felt. It was like putting a finger into an electrical socket.

Timothy opened his eyes and looked at the dove. She opened hers too, a tiny quivering motion, revealing two small brown orbs. She seemed dazed, fluttering her wings. He spread his hands open like a platform. She flipped over, awkwardly at first, and stood on pinkish talons. He stood and raised the dove higher. She opened her wings to stabilize and then, with a slight tossing motion, he propelled her into the air and tensed, ready to spring if she started to fall. But she took flight, flapping her wings, flying straight for the trees.

The electrical buzz was gone. Timothy looked down at his hands. *What the hell?* For once, he wished other students were there just so he could ask if they'd seen what happened. He'd been sure the bird was dead. Maybe it had just been stunned, but that didn't explain the sharp vision in his head, or the strange pulse that had moved through his body. It was like he'd become a human defibrillator. On second thought, maybe it was better that no one else had been around. The event would probably just have added to his freakishness.

"What the hell is wrong with me?"

He looked one more time toward the trees. For a second, he thought he saw a girl with light hair, but then she was gone. It happened so fast, he might have imagined it.

* * *

The screech echoed through the trees. She rushed to the edge of the forest, uncertain what had happened, just knowing it was serious. The sound was a cry for help. There was injury or worse.

She paused at the tree line, careful now that she was entering a human place. By the side of a building, a boy knelt with something in his hands. Two birds circled high overhead, and the trees shook gently, confirming her instinct. She was ready to launch across the open grass at the boy if he was causing any harm. She hated humans for their insensitivity. They thought nothing of killing for fun. The birds would never have sounded an alarm unless one of their own was in peril.

Just then he stood, opening his hands and lifting them, thrusting a bird into the air. The girl gasped and stepped back. She'd come upon the scene late, but it was clear he was helping. Some humans were capable of kindness, but this was more. All three birds flew back to the trees, and the mood of the forest shifted to one of welcome. The alarm had been more than simple danger; it had signaled possible death. By the look of it, he'd saved the bird or helped it in a way that was beyond a human's capability.

The boy was looking in her direction. She pulled back. There was something different about him, someone she needed to watch.

Chapter 5

TIMOTHY NEEDED TO THINK ABOUT what had happened, and he wasn't about to let some boring class ruin his concentration. Nor did he wish to talk about it, even with Omar. He grabbed his jacket from his locker and walked out of the building before anyone had time to say otherwise.

He drove aimlessly, trying to get a handle on the abnormal way his body had reacted to holding the bird. He wasn't sure which was more disturbing: the pulse that had flowed through his body like some new set of veins that conducted electricity instead of blood, or the vision that had been so vivid he wasn't sure which was the reality—eyes open or closed. Maybe he was a freak. Maybe that's what Derek saw and the reason he hated him so much. Hockey players were knocked down all the time, but he'd reacted so viciously that he'd gotten himself in trouble.

The warmth of the sun shining through the windshield distracted Timothy. He decided to enjoy playing hooky and go to Omar's shop after school.

He drove to a small lake, one not much bigger than an oversized pond, but it was a close and convenient refuge he visited often; it was like his personal reset button. He walked down the narrow dirt path that led to the water and a large oak tree that had grown at such an angle that one of the main branches was horizontal. He pulled himself up and leaned against the trunk. The spot offered a perfect view of the still-frozen water. He closed his eyes and listened to the breeze passing through the branches. It was like listening to the forest whispering its secrets. He'd mentioned that in his freshman composition. It had gone far in setting his reputation as someone a little bizarre, even if his English teacher had commended him on his sensitivity. He no longer cared. It just felt good to find peace in the branches of the oak.

He sat for nearly two hours, oblivious to the cold, watching in silence as the forest stirred. A nervous doe wandered to the edge of the lake and lapped at the top layer of melted water. Timothy wondered if he would be able to approach without scaring her, just to make a small connection with a species other than human. He'd never tried, not wanting to frighten them. This was their realm, and they deserved to feel secure with no fear of becoming a trophy.

Finally, he sensed it was about time for school to let out, so he dropped to the ground and went back to his car. The repair shop was inside the garage of an old gas station. The island was still there, but the pumps were long gone.

A man in his late forties stepped outside, wiping his hands on a dirty rag.

"Timothy, welcome," he said. "Omar mentioned you would come."

"Hi, Aarif, how are you?" He'd had to learn to understand Aarif's thicker accent, but the bigger challenge had been watching how his head rocked from side to side when he spoke, like a metronome measuring the rhythm of his speech.

"Very well, thank you. Come and have a soda. I will fix the car."

Omar showed up ten minutes later and seemed almost agitated.

"You skipped out," he said.

Timothy shrugged, not wanting to go into details. "What's going on?"

"Word around school is that Derek and Melanie broke up."

A mouthful of soda nearly ended up in Omar's face, but Timothy somehow managed to force it down. The person of his dreams might be coming up for air, but now he felt unprepared, clueless about how to make her notice him again.

"I can't believe it," said Timothy, staring at Omar but not really looking at him.

"Tim, look…this might just be a rumor."

"I knew it couldn't last. There was no way someone could put up with Derek forever."

"Dude, are you listening to me? Even if it is true, that doesn't mean she's going to switch lanes for a nice guy like you. Melanie is into the bad-boy type."

"You don't know her," Timothy said.

"Like you do? I mean, really…how many times have you actually spoken to her in the last decade?"

Timothy turned away and sat down on a bench seat from an old car that served as a couch.

"I'm going to see how my dad is doing with your heater."

Timothy swallowed the rest of the soda and let his mind float through the usual fantasies of Melanie as a girlfriend. He thought, for the thousandth time, how it would feel to have her soft arms around his neck and the touch of her lips on his. The fact that every guy would be jealous, and every girl would be wondering what she'd overlooked in him, would pale in comparison to that. Derek would be pissed, but who cared? The playing field would shift, and Timothy would have the home court advantage. As much pleasure as it gave him to think of it, he couldn't help noticing the knots in his stomach. It was a goal so unexpectedly within reach, and yet the likelihood of success was not.

The all-too-familiar pressure hit his chest and his head twitched. His tenuous fantasy blew apart like an exploding grenade. He threw the empty can into the trash and went outside.

Aarif was pushing the hood of his car down, and Omar climbed out of the front seat. He threw a thumbs-up at Timothy and grinned.

"It's like Florida in there," he said.

Timothy forced a smile and walked over.

"That's awesome. Thank you, Aarif. How much do I owe you?"

"Fifteen dollars."

"No way, it had to cost more than that."

"Part was free, just gas back and forth to Nashua."

"Wow, thank you so much." Timothy pulled out several wrinkled bills from his front pocket and handed them over. They both ushered him to the car and sure enough, the interior was the warmest it had been since the last Indian summer in October. Omar slapped the hood of the car.

"See you tomorrow?"

"Yeah, I'll be there," Timothy said.

* * *

Timothy closed the front door quietly. Uncle Jim was in the living room watching the news. Timothy needed to talk to him, but it was important to get a sense of his mood. The sports announcer was discussing a new addition to the Red Sox and spring training. It must have been something good because Jim seemed happy about it. Timothy saw an opportunity to turn the situation to his advantage.

"Can I get you a beer?"

Jim looked at Timothy in surprise, then shrugged, nodding his head.

"There's some pizza on the counter," he said.

Timothy opened the refrigerator. There wasn't much inside but beer, just some orange juice, a half loaf of bread, and a few food containers that were probably more valuable as a science project. Jim wasn't fussy about what kind of beer he drank as long as it was cold. Timothy handed Jim a bottle, then sat in silence until the news was over.

"Uncle Jim, I was wondering if I could ask a favor."

The man's body went rigid.

"What is it?" he asked. Nothing in his tone suggested any possibility of agreeing to one. Timothy wondered if he'd misjudged his mood after all, but it was too late.

"I've started ticking again. Just over the last couple of days," he added quickly. "I was hoping…I thought maybe you'd come with me to get a new prescription for some Zoloft. The doctor seemed to think it would help keep them under control."

The muscles in his uncle's face were working as if he was trying to keep himself from launching into a tirade.

"I'll pay for it of course," Timothy said.

"Drugs," Jim said. "When are you going to get your head out of your ass and start acting like a man? You don't need any goddamn drugs."

Timothy thought of how much beer Jim consumed. Was that any different?

"You know what drugs do? They fog up your head. Did you ever think that maybe when your mother got sick, you might have done something about it? Your head was probably so fuzzy, you couldn't make a good decision. So she died. So much for drugs."

Timothy gasped. There were probably a thousand things wrong with that argument, but he saw none of them. Jim punching him in the face would have been easier to take. Instead, it felt like he'd knocked the wind out of Timothy. He couldn't focus on a single thought except that his uncle had just accused him of letting his mother die.

"You're not getting them, so don't ask again." His uncle picked up the remote and raised the volume a little higher.

Timothy clenched his fists and stood up.

"Fuck you!"

Jim just waved his hand in the air as if to say "whatever."

Timothy barely made it into his bedroom and slammed the door before the pressure in his chest erupted like a volcano. His head twitched violently to the side. An empty glass on his desk shattered, but he had shut his eyes so tightly, he didn't notice. The first tic was followed by the worst attack he'd ever had. He jumped on the bed, covered his head with a pillow, and screamed.

Chapter 6

Word around school is that Derek and Melanie broke up. Omar's words pulled Timothy up from the exhaustion of constant ticking through the night. Somewhere in the background, he heard the front door close and the sound of an engine from outside. His uncle was gone.

It took all his energy to stumble into the shower. The water slowly washed the grogginess away, and he began to think about the rumor. School was his least favorite place on the planet, but for once it would be worth going, just to see if the rumor was true.

He towel-dried his dirty-blond hair and stared at the dark patches under his eyes in the bathroom mirror. Timothy looked as if he'd beaten himself up, and all from the grief of a single accusation. He wanted to take a baseball bat to his uncle's head. As a rule, his thoughts seldom wandered to violence. Lately, though, his uncle was proving the exception. How it was possible that Jim was his mother's brother was beyond him. It was hard to believe that two members of the same family could be such polar opposites.

It was early enough that Timothy had time to clean up the mess in the kitchen. He threw a couple of paper plates, the pizza box, and half a dozen beer bottles in the trash and brought it outside. He was about to go back in when he noticed three mourning doves perched on the fence behind a rusting barbecue. They seemed to be watching him. Timothy took a single step closer, figuring they'd be spooked and fly off, but they hardly moved.

"Hey," he said. For reasons he couldn't understand, he held out his hand. The bird in the center spread her wings and glided toward him, landing gently on his palm. She was the same bird from the day before. He knew it without any further proof other than by simple touch. "How are you feeling?" He looked around, paranoid anyone watching would send for the crazy squad.

The dove raised her beak and cooed as if answering.

"Is this your family?"

The other two birds moved their wings. He wasn't sure if they were answering or signaling the dove that she'd spent enough time already. In fluttering unison, the three lifted away and up into the trees, disappearing from sight.

"Whoa," he said.

Once again, he turned to go in, but a rustling in the trees stopped him. It was just the wind, but he sensed something else, like someone watching. This time, it wasn't paranoia but an innate sense that told him he wasn't alone. He walked several yards into the trees, his eyes scanning for some sign of neighbors out for a walk, but saw no one. He stood quietly, listening, but apart from the breeze, there was no sound. With a shrug, he tried to convince himself that he was just unnerved from the weirdness with the birds.

At school, he didn't share a class with Melanie until second period. Having to sit through chemistry first left him feeling antsy. Deep in thought, he slid into his normal seat near the back of the room. Mr. Caliendo walked in and the conversation died like someone holding down the volume button on the remote.

"Before we start this morning," he said. "We should welcome a new student." He pointed to someone at the back of the class. "This is Aenya. She just moved up from Connecticut."

Timothy gauged his classmates' reactions. The boys' eyes lit up. The girls took notice of her, and then their attention reverted right back to the guys, obviously more concerned with what they were thinking. Timothy turned his head and understood why the guys were ecstatic. She was beautiful, with rich blond hair the color of wheat and powder-blue eyes. Aenya waved, then returned her hand to her lap. It wasn't the movement of a shy girl acknowledging the attention, but rather an elegant, poised greeting. It made her seem older.

When the bell rang, several of the guys made a beeline for Aenya. A few of the girls did too, but most of them made for the door. Before Timothy left the room, he turned to see how she was handling the onslaught, but she was looking straight at him. She offered a slight smile, and Timothy gave a nod in exchange, then he was out in the hall. As he neared the next classroom, he saw Melanie leaning back against the wall, her face lowered. Four girls were smiling and talking in animated ways, trying to cheer her up. He felt elated but checked himself, mindful that it was unseemly to take pleasure from another's misery. It was just the possibility that she was free from Derek that made him optimistic. The frustrating part was that he didn't know what to do about it.

Except for those few minutes in the park when he took her picture, they hadn't spent any time together since first grade. That meant he was going to have to make her notice him in a whole new way. He was so absorbed in his thoughts that he didn't realize the class had gone silent until he looked up to see Mr. Greiner staring at him with his fists on his hips.

"Mr. Brennan, I would appreciate if your daydreaming could be saved for your own time and not here in class."

Timothy felt a tingling rush down his spine and the tops of his ears grow molten hot. "Sorry, I—"

"For the third time, what is the quotient identity of tangent x?"

Mr. Greiner might just as well have been speaking in a dead language. Timothy frantically looked at the board for any clues to how to answer the question. He came up blank.

"I…I don't know, sir," Timothy said, barely above a whisper.

"Uh huh, and do you wonder why you got a forty-six on the last quiz?"

"No, sir."

"Would anyone care to enlighten Mr. Brennan with the correct answer? Yes, Miss Robinson?"

"It's easy, Mr. Greiner, sine x over cosine x."

"Correct." He stared down at Timothy, then turned to resume his lesson, apparently satisfied that he'd done his best to humiliate the boy. Timothy felt like throwing up, but that would have clinched it for the most humiliating event ever.

By lunchtime, he was just starting to feel normal again. He joined Omar at their table.

"The heater working okay?"

"Yeah, it's amazing. It's like the first day in months that I didn't have to speed to school to get warm again," Timothy said.

The cafeteria doors opened. Melanie and her entourage went to their table in the middle. She sat down, her shoulders sagged, and she laid her forehead on her arms. All four girls pulled out tissues. She was obviously crying.

"Derek is such an asshole."

"You just noticed?" Omar said.

"She doesn't deserve to be that miserable, especially because of someone like him." Timothy felt Omar's eyes on him and he looked at his friend. "What?"

"That's my question. What are you thinking about?"

"She needs to know that guys can be nice, that not all of us are dicks."

"And you want to volunteer."

"You know how I feel about her."

"I know what you think of her, but I also think you've got it all wrong."

"You don't know her."

"Neither do you." Omar was leaning partly across the table to add emphasis.

Melanie got up and rushed to the doors, like she was trying to run away, like she needed to be alone. Timothy knew something about that kind of need. He also knew how a caring presence could turn agony into something much less painful. He stood up.

"Tim, don't."

"You have to strike while the iron is…" The thought suddenly raised an image of his mother. Someone had said it on TV once, and his mother had shuddered. "What an awful expression," she'd said. He remembered her comment was curious at the time; it was as if someone had cursed in front of her.

"How stupid would it be if I looked back someday and realized I never tried?" Timothy asked.

Omar opened his mouth to say something, but Timothy started walking. He pushed through the doors and saw her standing halfway down the hall, leaning against the wall, her arms crossed tightly in front of her, as if trying to hold herself together. He approached her as he would a sleeping lion.

"Hey, Mel."

She looked up at him. It seemed to take a second for her to recognize him.

"Hey." The word came out more like she'd formed her lips around a sigh than actually speaking a word.

"Listen, I heard…well, I heard that you guys ran over a rough spot."

"Ha!" She shook her head.

"You know, sometimes it's cool to take a break." He wasn't sure where he needed to move the conversation, but it was too late to stop now. "I thought maybe it would be fun to do a movie or something."

She looked up at him, her eyes still moist from crying. Smiling, she raised her hand to his cheek, just like she'd done the day of the picture.

"That's very sweet of you, Tom."

Before he could find a way to correct her, Melanie's friends came through the doors like a rescue posse. She quickly put her arms around herself again and stood up taller.

"I don't think that's a good idea," she said. "Sorry." They swarmed her and formed a protective shield, looking at Timothy as if he were a bug, like he had assaulted her. They led her back into the cafeteria, leaving him standing in the hall with his mouth open.

Timothy's legs felt like rubber; every square inch of his body tingled as if a million tiny ants were crawling over his bare skin. Terrified of collapsing in the middle of the hallway, he took halting steps into the boys' room. At the sink, Timothy splashed tepid water over his face. He caught his reflection in the shiny metal of the towel dispenser and couldn't reconcile the expressionless image with the turmoil churning his insides. He hated that face. Timothy balled his hand into a fist and drove his knuckles into the stainless steel.

"Whoa," said one of the two other boys in the bathroom. "Chill out, dude."

Timothy glared at the boy, wanting to say something, but his thoughts failed to yield words; only hurt and self-loathing registered. He yanked the door open and stepped back into the hallway.

Her entourage was working overtime. With a burst of clarity, he recognized Melanie for the first time. She wasn't the sophisticated prom queen. She was frightened of being ordinary. It was Derek's popularity and being his girlfriend that gave her the social status she enjoyed. Those girls were probably her friends only because they hoped for a chance at Derek. It was pathetic.

Worse still, he recognized himself for a fool. He'd built an unrealistic image of a girl based on a summer of playing and sharing ice cream cones, but the mistake was his. He'd fed his dream to the point of recklessness. Omar had tried to warn him. He'd been in love only with his image of her and not the person she was. Why? Because she was pretty? Because she had an awesome hairstyle, or lips he longed to kiss?

"I'm a moron," he said.

He spun on his heels and walked straight out the side doors and around the building to the parking lot. Tears of frustration blurred his vision as he pulled out and started driving. He stopped at a fast-food place and bought a hamburger. After one bite, he closed the box and tossed it into the back seat. It was enough to make him nearly vomit.

The sky was starting to turn dark as he pulled down a dirt road that led to an old covered bridge no longer used for vehicular traffic. He parked and shut off the engine. Feeling stiff after driving for nearly three hours, he stepped out of the car and crunched through frozen patches of snow onto the wooden platform of the bridge. Leaning his elbows on the railing, he peered down at the water rushing below.

Depression, as dark as the river, clouded his thoughts. There was no white water, only blackness, deep and swollen from the heavy snowfalls of the past three months. It wasn't a very grown-up thing to think, but he missed his mother. Those thoughts, now tainted with guilt, came often. His uncle had firmly planted the seed that Timothy was partially responsible for her death. If that weren't enough, he was a poor student, evidently talentless, lived with a troll of a relative, and was exceptionally stupid where girls were concerned. He felt sorry for Melanie. He imagined that the foundation of her perfect life was built on something like terror, fearful that she could lose her standing at the whim of a shithead like Derek. No wonder she was distraught. He wondered how long it would take one of her BFFs to claim Derek.

Timothy ran his hands through his hair, ignoring the cold. He hadn't bothered to grab his jacket before walking out of the building, and he didn't want to go home. It wasn't a home, anyway. It was a place to take a shower and sleep. Home had been with his mother. She'd loved him. Timothy doubted whether Jim had any idea what the word meant. He drank beer and brought desperate women home to sleep with. Love and warmth had exited his life six months ago in a dimly lit hospital room.

Timothy had read once how a person standing at the edge of a cliff felt compelled to wonder what it would be like to jump, to experience the fear of falling from a deathly height, that the compulsion was almost irresistible. As he looked down at the water, he thought of slipping into it. He'd never have to see Jim's face again; he'd never have someone like Mr. Greiner humiliate him in class or Derek trip him in front of a crowd of people.

What girl would ever want to date a loser like me? The idea of how much energy it would take to consider other girls darkened his mood further. What could come of it, anyway?

He closed his eyes and listened to his favorite sounds: the breeze through the branches, the gurgling sound water makes as its surface causes friction with the air above it, small animals foraging through the underbrush. This was home. This was where he belonged.

With a tiny bit of effort, he could make all the anxiety go away. In just seconds, he could be pain-free, and the thought didn't even scare him. It felt good. It felt right. It was the compulsion to leap off the cliff, and there was no conflicting emotion to resist. He didn't know anything about drowning, but how difficult could it be? A simple breath to let the water into his lungs? Not so bad.

Timothy slid his leg over the railing and stepped onto a narrow ledge of wood. Holding on, he moved his other leg over so that he stood facing the water. He took a last deep breath, filling his lungs with cool night air. The moon had risen just above the tree line, lighting the forest with a silvery glow and reflecting off the water ten feet below him. He leaned forward, one foot stepping onto nothingness. A slight pause, and his fingers slipped from the bars.

Timothy plunged below the surface of the water. A thousand tiny needles of pain stabbed him as the frigid water attacked his skin. He'd given no thought to how cold it would be. He gasped. A trickle of water slipped down his throat, and his air passage shut down involuntarily. He choked but couldn't take a breath of relief. The strong current was pulling him along, and he somersaulted as he started to float toward the surface. When his face broke into the air, he tried to take a breath but still couldn't. The laryngospasm wouldn't release. He pushed down on the water with his hands to keep his face up, but his arms were growing weaker as his body tried to conserve its blood flow to protect his lungs and brain.

He opened his mouth, and his sealed lungs fought for control of his body, forcing him to gulp and swallow several mouthfuls of water. He started feeling dizzy and slipped under again. He kicked weakly with his legs, but the effort was too much. With one last push, he broke the surface, his vision blurred from lack of oxygen. His last thought before blacking out was how beautiful the stars looked; then his eyes rolled back, and he sank into the depths of the river.

Chapter 7

It smelled like chicken soup. Timothy pulled the aroma deeper into his nose. There was more, a smoky scent like wood burning, then the sound of crackling and bubbling.

He didn't want to open his eyes. He'd suffered a terrible dream where he couldn't breathe, so the simple matter of inhaling and exhaling was peaceful, a relief from the torment of his nightmare. Then the memory of jumping into the river hit him. Fear and anxiety dug in their claws, urging him to open his eyes to see where he was, but he loathed the idea. He was warm and dry and breathing. If he opened his eyes, that comfort might disappear, and that would be worse than anything he might see.

He wasn't dead. He couldn't decide if it was a blessing or a disappointment.

Curiosity won out. He cracked his eyelids, but only a little.

The room was dark, lit only by a fire in a hearth a few feet away. A round black cauldron hung by a chain over yellow flames and fiery embers. Steam danced up and away into the flue.

Peering into the gloom, he could make out a ceiling that looked made of straw. He moved slightly, and the bed rustled, like the crinkle of leaves. A cocoon of the softest wool surrounded him, and his head rested on a downy pillow. He moved his hands down his body, relieved to find that he was clothed. It wasn't a hospital room, that was certain, but it was like no other place he could remember. He was afraid to make a sound, like a kid wary of a monster, lurking, ready to eat him the minute he woke.

He thought how ridiculous that was and eased the woolen blanket aside. He felt sluggish and achy, like he had the flu. A cough made his head throb. It was another clear indication that he wasn't dead. Death was supposed to be pain-free.

"You mustn't move too much," a voice said from behind.

Timothy spun around.

"Ow," he said. Every muscle in his body screamed.

"Like I said."

Aenya, the new girl from school, was sitting cross-legged on a wooden bench, her hands resting in her lap. The firelight illuminated her blond hair, and her face bore the same smile he'd seen in class.

"You're safe," she said. Her voice was therapeutic, as though she'd reached into him and plucked all the anxiety away.

"Where am I?"

"My home."

"How did I get here?"

"I brought you." She sounded so matter-of-fact, like she'd answered a silly question.

"But, I…" He shook his head, trying to fight his way out of a stupor.

"You were drowning."

"I know, that was the idea. Who pulled me out of the water?"

"I did."

"By yourself?"

"I'm a little stronger than I look," she said, the amused expression returning to her face.

"Why?" The list of reasons he'd decided to kill himself ran through his mind. Now, he was going to have to face everything he'd wanted to get away from.

"You needed saving."

"I needed dying."

"No, you needed healing. You could have done it yourself, but you chose the wrong way." She made it sound like he'd simply turned right instead of left. There was no declaration of judgment on her face.

"You can't heal yourself," he said.

"Of course you can. It's difficult to do since one usually fails to recognize the need for it, but you sought the wrong solution."

"That's ridiculous," he said.

"You healed the dove."

"How do you know about that?"

"I watched you."

"She was just stunned."

"She was near death."

"How could you know that? You weren't even standing next to me."

"Her family."

"Okay, this is too weird." He shook his head again, but it hurt too much. "What do you mean her family?"

"The birds she travels with, forages with."

The two other birds on the patio. The memory was stunning.

"There is more to you than you realize," she said. "That's why you needed saving."

Timothy had no idea what she was talking about; she seemed to like riddles.

"At my house, the three of them, were you there for that as well?"

"Yes," she said, then laughed. "They came to express their appreciation."

He held up his hands to ward off anything else she might say.

"When she flew into the glass, her companions were distressed. I knew they needed help, but you were already there."

"So, what you're saying is...you can talk to birds." He was beginning to think a lunatic from some horror novel had saved him. He looked around for a sledgehammer and contemplated making a run for the door, but his body felt too sluggish to attempt it.

"Well, not in the way you and I are speaking, but communication happens in other ways. I know how hurt you were by the other girl, just from how you walked away, by the look on your face, by the emotion emanating from you."

"You saw that too?" The tops of his ears began to burn. The reminder of Melanie's rejection made his chest tighten, and his head twitched to the side.

Aenya stood. In fact, she nearly floated from her seated position and reached with both hands toward the sides of his head. At first, he felt dizzy. The air around her hands shimmered like heat, but then her soft palms, warm, not hot, closed against his skin. An electrical pulse much like the one he'd experienced with the dove coursed through him, only with much greater power.

The memory and the anxiety disappeared. The instant relief was overwhelming, like having the world's worst migraine suddenly vanish. It made him feel weak enough to collapse. He started to fall backward, but Aenya swept him into her arms and cradled him. His eyes closed, and he melted into her.

"Wow," he whispered. "How do you do that?"

She answered with a gentle caress, her fingers fanning through the hair on the back of his head. It was an experience he didn't want to end. Too soon, she pulled away, holding his shoulders in her hands.

"Better?"

"Yes."

"Are you hungry?"

"Now that you mention it, is that chicken soup? It smells amazing." Eating had just been a necessity to get through the day. For the first time in months, it seemed like something to enjoy again.

"It is indeed," she said. "Come."

Timothy walked stiffly to a rectangular wooden table just past the hearth. She moved about lighting candles. Glancing around, he realized there were no lamps; in fact, there was nothing electrical at all: no plugs, no television, no kitchen appliances. He was waiting for it all to make sense.

Aenya ladled soup into a beautiful china bowl and placed it on the table in front of him.

"This place is like something from a fairy tale," he said.

She hastily turned toward the fire, pulled a round loaf of bread from a small oven above the main hearth, and put it on a matching plate.

"Do you live alone here? Where are your parents? How come you don't have power?"

She held up her hand and smiled. "Shall I answer them in order?" She tore a small piece of bread from the loaf. Steam rose, sending a remarkable buttery scent of yeast and wheat across the table.

"My parents are dead, and yes, I live here alone." She took a bite. "I've lived here awhile. I was just reluctant to go to school."

"I can relate to that," he said. "But I've lived here all my life, and I don't remember seeing you in town. By the way, where are we exactly?"

"We're near the river by Lake Ossipee."

"But that's miles from the bridge. And there aren't any roads that close to the mouth of the river."

"Don't worry, your car is parked at the end of Deer Cove Road."

"You drove my car here, too?" Her answers just caused more confusion. "Deer Cove Road is a ways from the river. Someone must have helped you get me here."

"As I told you, I'm a little stronger than I look." She motioned to the bowl of soup. "Eat."

She was being evasive. Maybe she was shy and didn't like talking about herself. But it was weird: her answers, her house, everything. Timothy took a spoonful of the broth, blew on it, and sipped it.

"Whoa, this is delicious."

"Thank you."

He couldn't stop wondering how she had just happened to be near the bridge when he jumped in. It had to be ten miles from the lake. He opened his mouth to ask, but she reached across the table and put a finger on his lips.

"My turn," she said.

"For?"

"What of your parents?" she asked.

He put the spoon down. Thinking about his dad was easy, but his mother was a difficult subject.

"I don't remember much about my father, but the memories I do have are good. He was a schoolteacher and an artist. Mom said he loved kids, and that teaching allowed him to do everything he enjoyed and get paid for it at the same time. His real passion was drawing and painting. I still have a few of his pieces. He died of a heart attack when I was five. I don't think Mom ever got over it."

"And your mother?"

Thanks to his uncle, he wasn't sure he could talk about her at all. He took a deep breath. Aenya reached across the table and put her hand over his. More electricity, less intense, but the raw part of thinking about her was gone.

"Mom died about six months ago. She got spinal meningitis and passed away in the hospital. I let her die."

"What? Who told you that?" Aenya sounded shocked, almost angry.

"My uncle. I went to live with him after. He blames me, and I guess he's right. I knew she needed medical help, but I didn't get it, and she died."

Timothy thought Aenya wanted to say something, but she seemed to hold back, biting her lip.

"It's one of the reasons I did what I did last night. It was last night, right?"

"Well...actually, it was the night before."

"I've been out for two days?"

"I sort of kept you that way," she said. "You needed to heal. You know there is a thing called secondary drowning?"

"What's that?"

"If water gets inside your lungs, even if you survive the drowning, they can absorb the water, still making you drown. Also, bacteria from the water can eat away from the inside and kill you just the same. I had to make sure you were going to be okay, and you needed to rest."

"How do you know stuff like that?"

"You pick things up along the way." It still sounded like she was sidestepping something. "What did your mother do?"

"She worked in a restaurant to support us. Before Dad died, she used to stay home with me. I remember as a kid hanging on the couch, reading books and watching movies. There was one she liked called *Peter Pan*. It has this fairy named Tinker Bell, but my mother used to joke about it, saying they never got it right. I have no idea what she was talking about." Timothy noticed that Aenya's eyes opened wide. "What?"

"Nothing," she said, shaking her head. "So, your last name is Brennan, isn't it?"

"Yes."

"Were either of your parents born in Ireland?"

"As far as I know, my mom was born here, my dad too, I think. Why?"

"Just curious."

"Why do I have the feeling there are things you're not telling me?"

"What makes you think so?"

"Because you're communicating without words."

"You know your name roughly translates to 'sorrowful poet'?"

"It does? What about Aenya, what does that mean?"

"My mother told me it's a Gaelic word that means 'kernel,' which came from an old English word Cyrnel, a word for corn. When I was little, my hair was yellowish, so she named me Aenya." She sounded sad.

"What happened to your parents?"

"Eat more soup," she said. "My mother and father brought me from Ireland when I was a girl. He was a soldier, and like your mother, mine looked after me and took care of my father. He died in the war. My mother went on for years, but she was never the same. It broke her heart. She died much younger than she had to. All my healing powers were useless."

"So some people can't be healed." He wondered which war she meant but didn't feel comfortable asking. It was probably the Gulf War or maybe Afghanistan, and it was probably still painful.

"Some," she admitted.

"Then what makes you think I can be?"

"I think that's enough for one night, don't you?"

"I've only scratched the surface."

"You should get another night's rest before school tomorrow."

"School?" Just the thought of going back there was terrifying.

Aenya reached across the table and seized his wrist. This time she closed her eyes. There was that shimmer again when her fingers connected with his skin. The relief was immediate, but he felt instantly sleepy. "I don't want to go to school," he tried to say, but his words were slurred.

She came around the table and lifted him from the bench. He had to be dreaming; there was no way a girl her size could pick him up like that. It seemed effortless. Then he was falling into a warm, misty place.

Her lips brushed his forehead. "Good night, my fair little elf."

Chapter 8

Aenya watched Timothy sleep. It wasn't an easy rest for him: his face contorted as dreams carried him to places she could only imagine. She could feel the darkness of his thoughts even under the veil of slumber. Her mother had succumbed to such a state.

She knelt by the side of the cot and gently brushed the hair from his ear. The top edge swept upwards to a small point. It wasn't so noticeable yet, but that would change.

He rolled onto his back with a troubled sigh, and she touched her palm to his chest. The lines creasing his forehead relaxed and smoothed out.

He was an enigma, and she wasn't quite sure what to do. He'd said both his parents were dead, which would explain many things, but what of his uncle? Certainly he would have offered his love in exchange for the one Timothy had lost. She was sure the boy had no idea what he was. And the healing of the bird, that was beyond all explanation. No one of his kind would have such power.

Aenya glanced at the window as dawn light came. Maybe the best thing was to get him back to his life and then watch. She wanted to understand what was causing him such grief. He clearly felt bad about his mother, but she was certain there was more.

The embers in the fire were still hot. She slid a cast-iron pan over the heat and started to cook eggs. It wasn't long before the smell brought him fully awake. She couldn't keep from smiling. At least his appetite was good.

"How did you sleep?" she asked.

"Pretty well, I think," he said with a yawn.

"Good, then you'll be well rested for school."

"You're really set on that, huh?"

"Come and eat."

Timothy ate in silence, gazing out the window. His attention seemed fixed on the landscape. A bird was perched on the rim of a birdbath in the garden, chipping at the thin layer of ice.

"Do you want to stop home for clean clothes?"

"No," Timothy said. "These were just washed."

"Very funny."

When it was time to leave, she handed him his jacket. He took it and then paused.

"I thought I left school without this," he said.

She didn't see much point in explaining how she'd gone for it, thinking there might be a possibility he would need it. Moving his car had been a much bigger challenge. She led him onto a forest path away from the cottage.

He stopped to look back. "Looks like something out of *Snow White*." The thatched cottage stood out from the backdrop of pine and white birch trees. The structure had a yellowing tinge as if someone had spread butter over the rough stone surface. A tendril of white smoke spiraled into the branches above.

"I thought you'd be able to see it." If she'd needed any last bit of proof, that was it.

"Well, yeah. My head might not be screwed on quite right, but my eyesight's pretty good."

It took some time to reach the quiet country road where she'd left the vehicle. She noticed how easily he moved through the trees, not like most of the townsfolk who tramped through the forest like bears. He was stealthy, as though accustomed to the patterns of foliage and underbrush.

Aenya slid into the passenger seat of Timothy's car and shuddered. She hated automobiles. She hated the horrific smell of the exhaust, how it fouled the air. She hated the steel and iron. But she kept her face expressionless, not wanting to add anxiety to the drive. He had plenty of that already.

As they walked from the parking lot to the doors of the high school, she observed several of the students' attention settle on Timothy. She also noticed that he was seeing it as well. She felt the lightest sensation she'd gotten from him yet: nervous but happy.

Walking through the halls of a school wasn't something she'd done in a long time, and it felt strange being inside a building like that again. It was claustrophobic, but she attributed that more to the occupants than to the bricks and mortar.

After taking seats side by side in the classroom, he leaned closer to her.

"Would you like to sit with us at lunch?"

She looked at him. Overall, he was a good-looking boy, and his eyes were expressive and sincere. She could feel his question held more. She also detected a hint of fear, as if worried she might say no.

"Us?"

"Yeah, I usually hang out with my friend, Omar. He'd love to meet you."

"Sure," she said. "That would be…cool." She thought that was the right use of the word. She hoped so.

"Awesome."

Mr. Caliendo stepped to the front of the class and announced the beginning of a segment on the laws of gas. She slid down in her chair, crossed her arms, and agreed with how Timothy hated being there, too.

* * *

Timothy went straight to the cafeteria when class was over. He dropped his backpack on the chair and looked around for Aenya and Omar, but neither had come in yet. So many had watched him walk in with her, he knew they'd be curious to see if something was going on between him and her. It was important to look casual and not like he was waiting desperately.

He went to the salad bar and grabbed a tray, quickly tossing a few items in a bowl. The doors of the cafeteria crashed against the masonry and Derek Hollister stalked toward Timothy.

"What's this I hear about you asking Melanie out, twerp?"

"Relax," Timothy said. "It was just a harmless invitation to—"

"Who are you telling to relax?" Derek slammed his fist up under the tray, sending a spray of grape tomatoes, cucumbers, and lettuce raining down on the nearby tables. "You watch your step, or next time that'll be your face."

"Leave him alone." The voice came from behind Timothy's right shoulder. It was quiet, female, but tonally threatening.

Derek looked past Timothy with a look of shock, as if surprised to find someone standing there.

"What did you say?" he asked.

"You heard me," said Aenya. "Leave him alone.'"

"Listen, little girl, you should keep your nose out of my business."

"Having to repeat myself leaves me feeling irritable." She stepped in front of Timothy.

"You're a feisty little bitch, huh? I kind of like that, but you're new here, so I guess you don't know who I am."

"Don't trouble yourself," she said. "I know exactly what you are, so I'll suffer my irritability and tell you a last time: leave him alone."

Derek grabbed her wrists. "I don't care if you're a girl, you need a lesson in manners."

"Have a care and let go, that's your one and only warning," she said.

"Oh yeah? I'm scared of a little girl. I'm not like your pathetic boyfriend who runs away when a girl gives him some shit."

Aenya pulled her wrists free as if they'd been held by nothing stronger than toilet paper. She moved her palms toward Derek's chest as if to push him, but her hands never connected. It was as though she'd compressed an invisible balloon of air against him. Derek went flying backward. He landed ten feet away on the small of his back and slid along the vinyl tiles, knocking over several chairs. Everyone in the cafeteria stood like statues, staring. Timothy heard several gasps as Derek stopped sliding and shook his head, pushing a chair off of himself.

She walked straight for the cafeteria doors. Timothy felt everyone's eyes shift to him. He didn't know what was worse—whatever revenge Derek would start planning or how bad it was that Timothy had just been defended by a girl. He went after her.

When he opened the doors, he expected her to be a few steps ahead, but she was at the school's side entrance, fifty feet away. How did she do that?

"Aenya!"

She stopped moving. Timothy started to jog down the hall. Another cafeteria door opened and a teacher reached out to grab him.

"Mr. Brennan, you're to come with me to the main office."

Timothy never broke stride.

"Mr. Brennan, did you hear me?"

"How did you do that?" he asked when he caught up to her.

"Do what?"

"Well…the push, for one thing. And how did you get down the hall so fast?"

"Oh, that," she said. "I'm sorry, Derek just made me angry." She opened the side door. "And I walk fast when I'm angry."

The teacher was still standing there, fists planted on his hips, talking to two other faculty members and nodding in Timothy's direction. *The hell with this.* He followed her outside.

"Where are you going?" he asked.

"To your car."

"Are you cutting?"

"I'm done here."

He was walking as fast as he could without breaking into a full run, but keeping up with her was almost impossible.

She disappeared around the corner of the school and by the time he did the same, she was leaning against the side of his car another hundred feet away. She needs to join the track team, he thought.

"When you say…you're done, did you mean done for the day, or done-done, like you're not coming back?"

"I've learned what I needed here."

"Do you want me to drive you home?"

"Let's go to your house," she said. "You've seen where I live."

He wasn't sure he wanted her to see where he lived, but it was better than staying at school. He started the engine and pulled out.

"I'm not sure if I'll ever be able to live it down; you defending me, I mean. But thanks."

"You're welcome. Derek is a typical human jerk and needed to be brought down a notch or two." Timothy glanced at her over her use of the word "human." What a strange way to put it.

As they drove, Timothy pointed out Omar's father's repair shop and Herbie's restaurant. She seemed interested, but maybe simply out of politeness. She spent more time looking around the car—at the gauges, the ceiling, the radio buttons, the way the seats felt. She glanced over her shoulder into the backseat a couple of times. On the way to school, she'd spent most of the trip looking out the window.

"Sorry the car isn't all that great, it's pretty old."

"Depends on your perspective," she said.

"And this is the street I live on." As soon as he made the turn, he saw his uncle's old Corvette in the driveway. There were two different-colored panels and a large crack in the fiberglass over the rear tire. It was bad enough she had to ride in an antique car, and that the house was something of an embarrassment, but having to meet Jim? There was smoke rising from the car's vibrating tailpipe. "That's my uncle's car. I guess he's about to leave."

"Don't say anything about me to your uncle," she said.

"Well…okay."

The front door opened; Jim stepped outside and stood there, as if waiting for Timothy to get out of the car.

"Hi, Uncle Jim."

"Where the hell you been?" he asked.

Timothy had given no thought to explaining his absence for two days. "I was sleeping at Omar's," he said, as if Jim could have cared. It would've been less surprising if he'd asked why he was back.

"Uh-huh." Jim glanced at the car and nodded in that direction. "Who's the broad?"

"She's a friend from school." Calling her a broad was infuriating, and Timothy wanted to punch him. It was becoming a frequent craving.

"What's she doing here?"

"We're working on a school project."

"I see. Well, I have to go to work. No funny business with you and her, got it?"

"Of course not." Like there was a chance of that happening, he thought.

Jim grumbled and got into his car. When he pulled out, Timothy reached into his and turned off the ignition.

"Come on in."

"He could see me, huh?"

"Well, you were sitting right in front of him." Timothy wondered why she asked weird questions like that.

Aenya followed him inside. It was the first time he'd ever had a girl visit. He gave her a quick tour, saving his room for last. As they walked down the hall, he remembered just how messy his room was. He was afraid that after she saw it, she'd never want to see him again.

"I guess you could use some help organizing things," she said.

He laughed, but it sounded a bit shaky.

"So your uncle is your mother's brother, right?"

"Yeah, though sometimes I don't get how it can be. My mom was nothing like him. Uncle Jim is crude. My mother was sophisticated and gentle."

"You loved her," she said.

"She made all the difference." That realization seemed to grow stronger every day.

Aenya squeezed his forearm, then searched around the room. She glanced at the video-game console and frowned as she picked up a jewel case. On the cover was a picture of the hero with a small white fairy-like creature circling above his head.

"Who's this?"

"Oh, he's the champion of the game, and the fairy is like his guide."

Aenya laughed and shook her head, handing him back the case. She looked at the desk and spotted the picture of Melanie and only nodded.

Aenya sat on the bed, fluffed the pillows behind her, and rested against the headboard. It was the kind of vision guys dreamt about. He couldn't believe she was there, leaning against his pillows. He knew he'd never wash that pillowcase ever again.

"So tell me more about your mother."

"I don't know what to tell you. Sometimes, she was more like my friend. I know that sounds strange. I have ADD, which makes it hard to have, like, normal friends. She understood me, and we spent a lot of time together after school and during the summers when she wasn't working."

"You said she died from meningitis, right?"

"Yeah, it was so sudden."

"Was your mom seeing anyone before she got sick? Was there anyone new in your life?"

"No. My uncle was hanging around more often, but I figured he was just trying to be more of a brother. I don't think she liked him much, though."

"No, I'm pretty sure she didn't."

"What makes you think so?" Timothy asked, wondering where that came from.

"Let's just say I have some sense of what he's like."

"It's not hard to hate him. It killed me when he said Mom's death was my fault. The worst part is that he's probably right. Mom got sick pretty quickly, and I kept telling her maybe we should get a doctor, but she kept saying that she just wanted to rest, that she'd be fine."

"Your mother's death wasn't your fault."

"No, he's right, I should have gotten her medical help much sooner."

"Your mother would not have been helped by that kind of medical attention."

"What do you mean? How can you know that?"

"Timothy, your mother didn't die of meningitis." Aenya locked her eyes on his. "Your mother was murdered."

Chapter 9

Aenya regretted the bluntness of her statement as soon as the words left her mouth. Timothy staggered back and found his seating on the arm of a leather chair. She moved quickly to the foot of the bed. He looked crestfallen, and his anxiety thickened the air in the room. She took his hands.

"I'm sorry," she said. "I didn't mean to upset you."

"What do you mean...she was murdered?" He looked dazed, but she could feel his reaction fading with her touch. Then he pulled his hands free. "Aenya, stop doing that!"

"What?" she asked.

"It's not normal. People don't just touch other people and have all their anxieties disappear. I mean, hugs are great and all, they make you feel better, but that's nothing like what you do." As he talked, she sensed the floodgates about to burst. "And then there's all the rest. It's just too freaky. There's no way you jumped in the water and pulled me out by yourself, and teenagers don't live in fantasy cottages in the middle of the forest by themselves. And last night, I'm pretty sure you picked me up like a stuffed toy, and I must outweigh you by, like, fifty pounds." His mood was moving from anxiety to anger. "I just don't understand. Nothing about you makes sense."

"There are some things you need to know about yourself and your mother." Aenya paused, holding eye contact. "And me."

"Like what?"

She took his hands again. He tried to pull away, but she held them firmly.

"Don't be afraid," she said.

"Why should I be afraid?"

"You shouldn't be, but you are. It's because you don't understand." She kept her voice soft and level as she pushed her energy into him until his anger and fear dropped to a manageable level.

"Then tell me what it is I don't understand."

She searched for a way to do something she'd never done. It was unfair that his mother or father had never been straight with him, or even his uncle. She didn't feel equipped to deal with this, but her heart went out to him knowing that he was suffering on so many levels.

"Do you remember when you told me about the movie your mother liked, but that they always seemed to get the part about Tinker Bell all wrong?"

"Yeah." Timothy was frowning. He shrugged and tried once more to pull his hands back, but it was more important than ever to control his senses. She used her greater strength to hold on.

"It's because she knew that fairies aren't tiny little creatures with wings."

"What are you talking about?"

"Your mother knows that because she was one."

"What? Was what? A fairy?"

Aenya nodded and held on. Timothy laughed.

"Right, so what does that make me? You're going to tell me I'm a fairy too?"

"Of course not, only girls can be fairies. You're an elf." His face went blank and for a second she felt nothing from him, as if everything inside had been erased. "Look at me, Timothy. You will know that I'm telling you the truth."

It took two or three minutes and her full attention, forcing her thoughts into him and holding his hands tightly. She finally sighed with relief when his eyes began to register understanding and acceptance; it was like opening the shades and letting the sun into a dusky room, though she almost felt like she'd cheated. She knew he would never have come to believe it if she hadn't forced it.

"You are, too, aren't you? A fairy, I mean." His voice was soft.

"Yes," she said. "But we've been known by many names. We consider ourselves fae, and more specifically, I belong to the Sídhe."

"And I'm an elf," he said like he was convincing himself.

"You are."

"That sounds crazy."

"I'm sure it does and I don't know why you were never told. There is only one reason I can think of."

"What?"

"Do you remember studying genetics in biology? There are different possible outcomes based on your parentage. If one of your parents had been human, then there was a chance you could have been, too. They might have been waiting to find out which way you'd turn before telling you."

"If I'd been born a girl, then I would have been a fairy?"

"Sídhe," she corrected. "Only if your mother had been one. Sídhe are born of the union between an elf and a sídhe. There are also female elves. A male and female elf will only have elfin children no matter the gender," Aenya said.

"You don't know my parents. How do you know what they were?"

"I'm only assuming your mother was of the sídhe based on what she said to you, but she could have been elfin. Your father is another matter. Either way, you're not human."

"How did you find that out?"

"What you did with the bird was pretty much out of the range of human capability. Elves too, for that matter, so I knew you were unusual to start with. I followed you for a while. Of course, I was there when you tried to…well, there was no way I could let that happen. The proof came when you woke up in my cottage and you saw me."

"How could I not?"

"Humans can't see me if I choose not to be seen. We can't hide from fae creatures. Same thing with my cottage, too. Humans would not have been able to see that, either."

"Oh my god, that means Jim is an elf. That's why you told me not to mention you to him. You were testing him."

"Exactly."

"But how can he be an elf? He's such an asshole."

"Trust me, there are assholes in every species."

"So, how does this all come down to the fact that my mother was murdered?"

"Your mother would not have succumbed to a simple human disease."

"It's not a simple disease, it's lethal."

"Only to a human."

"And what, the sídhe are immortal?"

"No, we're mortal. We just live longer than humans, and it takes a bit more effort to kill us."

"What about an elf?" Timothy asked.

"Elves are stronger than humans and they live longer also, but they're more susceptible to physical trauma than the sídhe."

"When you say longer, how much longer?"

"A sídhe's lifespan can reach between eight hundred and a thousand years or so."

Timothy's eyes widened. "And elves?"

"Maybe between five and eight hundred years."

"I must be dreaming," he said. "So…so who would have murdered my mother? And why?"

"I'm not exactly sure. It's one of the other reasons I think your mother was sídhe and not elf. We're a smaller set of the species, kind of like a minority, so we've been the target of humans and some elves for a long time."

"That sounds kind of racist."

"You could say that. We used to cohabitate with humans, though it's been a couple thousand years since. When Christianity spread through Europe, the religious zealots were convinced we got our power from the devil and they started to hunt us. They found an ally in some of the elves who resented us interfering with their affairs. Like I said, we've been known by many names—witches, gnomes, sorcerers, goblins, banshees, leprechauns...some of us left our homeland and came to this one."

"So you're thinking a warrior elf killed her? She wouldn't have hurt a soul." Timothy's anger started to rise, but Aenya didn't attempt to interfere with it this time. The squashing of all emotion wasn't healthy either. "And why would she have hidden everything from me? Maybe she was waiting to find out if I was going to be human, but she wasn't. She was my mother, it wouldn't have mattered what she was. It's not fair."

"There's a possibility your mother's existence was discovered and..." Aenya let the thought go unsaid.

"What about you? Doesn't that mean you're in danger, too?"

"I guess, but I keep to myself. I've interacted with humans from time to time just to keep up with the world. It's always enough to drive me back to the forest. For the most part, elves and the sídhe cohabitate with no difficulty at all."

"Except for the racist ones. So how old are you, anyway?"

Aenya had been waiting for that. "I was born in Ireland in 1820."

"You're two hundred years old?"

"One hundred ninety, thank you," she said. "So that makes me something of a teenager, just like you, in relative terms, of course."

"You mean that makes me a human teenager, but an elfin infant."

"You don't look like an infant." She couldn't keep from smiling. "We grow to adult appearance, much like humans do, in about twenty years. After that, the signs of aging take a lot longer. As you can see, I still look like a human teen myself."

"So now what? What am I supposed to do?"

"I don't know. I realize how difficult this is for you. Under normal circumstances, your mother and father would be raising you in elfin culture, but you don't have anyone to guide you. Your uncle's not the best candidate, as far as I can see."

"Is he a danger to you?" he asked.

"Not that I can tell. Although he doesn't know I'm sídhe specifically, so I can't say for sure."

"I thought you said he could see you."

"He can, but with my long hair, he wouldn't know whether I'm sídhe, elf, or human."

"You mean by the shape of the ears."

"Hadn't you noticed it by now?"

"I thought my uncle's ears were just weird. What do you know about him?"

"He's a bit of a redcap," she said.

"What's that?"

"An elf who can be quite dangerous, capable of extreme violence. I get that sense from him, even though I've only seen him once."

"He's never been warm and fuzzy." Timothy shook his head and stared into space as if trying to make sense of it all. Aenya couldn't imagine what it must feel like to have your world instantly turned inside out.

"What about school, my job?" he asked.

"School is something to consider finishing, especially if you choose to continue dealing with humans. Your job, well, I think there are more important things to consider."

"I don't care about school," he said. "I need to find out who killed my mother and do something about it."

"I think so, too," she said.

"Will you help me?"

Aenya felt a twinge of fear creep back inside him. She let one of his hands go and brushed the hair away from his forehead.

"Of course," she said.

"What do we do next?"

"I think it's time we look at your mother's things."

Chapter 10

TIMOTHY PULLED ENOUGH OF THE clutter away from his closet door that he and Aenya found a large-enough section of carpet to sit on. He reached deep inside and pulled out the four boxes he'd saved from his mother's house. There hadn't been time to collect much after she'd died. Jim hadn't seemed interested in dealing with it. He'd called the landlord to say she'd died, that Timothy was coming to live at his house, and that he'd arranged for a cleaning crew to dump most everything. As soon as Timothy had moved his belongings, he'd gone back and emptied the contents of his mother's closet into the car: three boxes, a jewelry case, and three of his father's paintings.

He'd pushed everything into a dark corner at the back of his closet, knowing a time would come when going through them would be more comfortable. Somehow, the task didn't seem quite as depressing with Aenya sitting next to him.

Timothy opened the jewelry case first. Its contents included cufflinks and a wedding ring, which must have been his father's; his mother had been cremated with hers. He recognized several of the earrings she'd worn, but there was also a beautiful necklace he'd never seen. It was a choker with delicate Celtic knots in gold filigree. It seemed weightless in his hand.

"Your mother would have worn that on her wedding day," Aenya said. "It's really lovely. The knots show no beginning and no end; two lives entwined for eternity."

He slipped it back inside the case. They were both dead now; so much for eternity. He wondered why his mother had never shown it to him. Maybe the memories had been painful for her, too.

The first box was a disappointment. His name was on it, but it turned out to be a collection of baby clothes. The tops of his ears got warm. He closed the box and pushed it aside.

The next had hundreds of pink and white Styrofoam peanuts that spilled over the side as he sank his hands inside. He pulled up an old wooden box in the shape of a chest. It was fashioned with carvings of intricate circular lines, like branches of ivy crawling over the sides. The brass latch had no lock, and Timothy opened it.

Something rolled in soft leather and tied with a red silk cord rested inside. He undid the bow and let the leather unfurl. There was a crinkling sound: a protective layer of wax paper. His mother had obviously cared for this piece of curled parchment, golden brown with age.

"There's writing," he said, flattening the parchment on the floor.

"It looks like a letter," Aenya said.

He felt disappointment. The writing was very strange, in some kind of language he'd never seen.

"Maybe someone at the library can help us translate this."

"No need," Aenya said. "I can read it."

"What language is it?"

"Elfin." She traced the first few words with her finger. "What was your mother's name?"

"Wendy."

"It's addressed to someone named Owein." She started to read aloud. "To Owein, my beloved daughter. It grieves me, or it pains me, that you must take leave of us to travel to the world beyond the western sea. I place blame on your brother Seumais for his…" Aenya stopped reading, a frown creasing the skin at the top of her nose. "Your uncle's name is Jim. Seumais is Celtic for James. Your mother must have taken a name that sounded like her own, but wouldn't draw attention."

"Why did you stop reading? Is that a bad thing?"

She picked up again. "I place blame on your brother Seumais for his alliance with Cadwaladr, who has caused so much suffering. Seumais has brought much shame upon our family. I take solace in that you will be safe from those who wish you harm. I would journey with you, but my place is here, with your father. It is our duty to stand against Cadwaladr. The unwarranted burden of seeing after your brother falls to you in exile. But you must always remember and honor the bloodline of Aylwen that is within you..." Aenya gasped and looked up at Timothy, then back down and read, "no matter where you are. May fortune carry you home to us one day, and may we all meet in Alfheim. It's signed Tuathla, December 1686."

"Wait, what? You're saying my mother was alive in 1686?"

"I would say from long before that," Aenya said, her voice low.

"Why did you gasp? What does all that mean?"

When Aenya looked up, her expression was no longer one of simple curiosity. Her gaze shifted to Timothy. She looked concerned.

"I think this letter makes some things clear."

"Okay, good. Like what?"

"Give me a second," she said. "It's hard to explain. You don't know anything of our world, but I think I see why it's been kept from you."

"Stop sounding mysterious, and just tell me."

She took a deep breath.

"For one thing, it seems you're descended from Aylwen."

"Who's—"

"Shhh." She held up her hand. "A very long time ago, there was an elfin realm called Alfheim. It's rumored to have been a truly magnificent place, elegant, a place of learning and peace. It existed long before the first human civilizations. Aylwen was its queen. She was wise and greatly revered, especially by the sídhe."

"And the letter says I'm related to her?"

"The letter claims your mother is of her bloodline. First, Tuathla, your grandmother, is a powerful figure in her own right. Second, it's against our laws to claim the bloodline if it's not true. So it seems you're not only an elf, but a prince."

"I'm sorry, Aenya, but this is a lot to get my head around. A couple of hours ago, we were sitting in class. Now I find out my mother was like four hundred years old and my ancestor was some queen." Timothy ran his fingers through his hair and clamped down on the sides of his head as if trying to keep his skull from exploding.

"Not just some queen." Aenya almost sounded offended. She chewed the side of her lip. "Do you know the ancient stories of Jerusalem and King Solomon?"

"You mean like Bible stories?" Timothy asked.

"Yes. After Rome invaded Israel and virtually destroyed everything, it became the desire of all the Jewish people of the world to recreate a place on the land that was holy to them. About two thousand years later, the State of Israel formed. Alfheim is kind of like that for fae people."

"It's like a lost kingdom," he said.

She nodded. "What's in the last box?"

It was heavier than the rest. He opened the flap and looked inside.

"Books." They looked like textbooks, and he assumed they were his father's. One was wrapped in cloth. It was leather-bound and appeared quite old. Timothy gently fanned the pages and saw it was written in Elfin, too. He handed it to Aenya.

"It looks like a diary."

"My dad's?"

"I'm not sure. We can look at this later."

"Do you have to go?" Timothy was alarmed. His world had just gone *Twilight Zone*; if she left him alone with all of that, he was afraid he'd go insane.

"Yes, but you're coming with me. I need to get you away from here. There are others who will know more than I do, and I just don't have a good feeling about your uncle."

Aenya carefully wrapped the letter back inside the wax paper and leather, then grabbed a half-empty backpack from the floor and dumped the contents onto the bed. She slid the jewelry case, the letter, and the book into it and tossed it to Timothy.

"Here, put some clothes in there, too."

Leaving his uncle's house sounded great, no matter the reasons. He shoved some underwear, socks, and a couple of thermal shirts inside and zipped it up. She had already stepped into the hall.

"Come on," she said.

Timothy shrugged into his jacket and followed her outside. He reached into his pocket and pulled out his keys.

"Put them away, you won't need them," she said.

"We won't get far on foot." It was probably fifteen miles to the lake near Aenya's cottage.

"We won't be on foot, and we don't need a car. I can't stand those things anyway, they foul the air. Take my hand."

He didn't mind that idea at all.

She looked at him and then up at the sky. A second later, their feet had lifted off the ground and they were moving quickly upward. In midair, he twisted and threw his arms around her.

"Don't be afraid, I've got you," she said, holding him close.

"You've got me, but who's got you?" He could hear the panic in his own voice.

"Did you forget that fairies can fly?"

"Tinker Bell had wings."

"And your mother said they never got that part right, remember?"

He made the mistake of looking down. The treetops grew smaller and smaller as the wind rushed past his face.

"Oh shit!"

Chapter 11

THE DROP TERRIFIED TIMOTHY MORE than the takeoff. The fading light and the ground rising at roller-coaster speed made the earth look like a giant black hole ready to swallow them.

He walked on wobbly legs to the door of the cottage, amazed at how quick the trip had been. It was much faster than using roads with lights and stop signs. His heart was still pounding as he sat at the table. Aenya started lighting candles and then built a fire in the hearth.

"What now?" he asked.

"You're safe here. Tomorrow we'll go up to the White Mountains. I'm friends with an enclave of elves there."

"We'll be flying again?" He wasn't sure he was ready for that.

"And some walking." She pulled the cast-iron cauldron from a hook by the fireplace and handed it to him. It took all his effort to keep from dropping it.

"This thing weighs a ton. How strong are you, anyway?"

"I don't know. I lifted a pregnant cow over a fence once."

"I thought you said elves were stronger than humans."

"You will be. You're only seventeen, remember? There's a pump outside, to the right."

"Do the sídhe have something against indoor plumbing?"

She smirked and made a shooing motion with her hand. A few cranks of the pump were needed to crack the ice and prime it, but then several steady gushes quickly filled the vessel. He had to use both hands and several stops to get it inside. She took it in one and re-hung it on the hook, then swiveled the arm over the wood that was starting to burn.

"I thought I read somewhere that iron was poisonous to… well, creatures like you."

"That's one of the many things humans get wrong about us. It's only part of the truth. If iron gets into our bloodstream, then yes, it's poisonous. It's like humans and mushrooms. They can handle them all day but if they swallow the wrong kind, they'll die."

"I have about a thousand questions, you know?"

"No doubt."

"Can elves fly?"

She laughed. "No, I'm afraid they can't." For some reason, despite the fear, he felt a wave of disappointment.

"So how come the sídhe can?"

"I suppose it's like asking why females have babies and males don't. They're just not built for it."

"What other differences are there between elves and humans?"

She sat across the table to wait for the water to boil. He was still reeling from everything that had happened in the last hour or so.

"Humans are frail, for one thing, and they don't seem to have much intuition. Sometimes, it's hard to hold it against them since they clearly lack the clairvoyance of an elf."

"Is that like seeing the future?"

"No, it's like seeing things with more clarity. Call it having more...awareness."

"Like the way you understood the birds," he said.

"Moods and emotions travel. I'm sure you've heard someone say that a room has a good vibe, but there's so much more. Even plants absorb and emanate energy. The stronger the emotion or thought, the farther it will travel. During the Civil War, the wind was almost too painful to endure. There was so much suffering and devastation, whole forests shook with anguish."

"It's still hard to believe you were alive that long ago."

Aenya went to a chest along the wall and opened it. She pulled out a very old photo that was crinkled and yellow with age. It pictured a man dressed in a dark uniform with brass buttons and brevet stripes on his left arm. He was handsome with piercing dark eyes, a clean-shaven jawline, and a trim mustache. Timothy had seen pictures like it in history books.

"Who is this?"

"My father. His name was Heulfryn. Well, that was his elfin name. Humans knew him as William. He was killed on June 17, 1864, during the assault on Petersburg. He fought with the New Hampshire 2nd Regiment."

"I'm sorry." Timothy wasn't sure what else to say. Was it possible to grieve still, after a hundred and fifty years?

"My mother never got over it." Aenya didn't mention whether *she* had. "She died about five years later."

"Have you been alone here ever since?" Timothy couldn't imagine that kind of isolation. He enjoyed solitude, but hers was on a whole different level. She placed the photo back in the chest. At first, he thought it was her way of avoiding the question. She took a basket of vegetables and started cutting them into the water.

"I suppose I could have found others of my kind to live with. Like I said, I have friends to the north. I could have gone back to Ireland, but this was my home. Some even take the company of humans, much like my father and your parents, but I don't really care for them. The forests and the animals became my companions. After a while, I found I didn't need anything else."

She put a round wheel of cheese on the table with a knife and a small loaf of bread. A few minutes later, she scooped out the potatoes and carrots from the cauldron and sprinkled them with salt and pepper.

"Why did your father fight in the Civil War? It certainly didn't have anything to do with elves."

"No. On the voyage over, he befriended some of the humans on board. So when they went to fight, my father offered to go with them. My mother told me that he'd seen enough of the injustice of elves and humans trying to kill the sídhe, so when he realized the darker-skinned humans were being treated so badly by the rest, it didn't take much to convince him to fight for them."

"So elves aren't above being cruel to their own either." The concept surprised him.

"It's rarer among our kind, but it exists. Cadwaladr, the elf your grandmother mentioned in her letter, is one of the worst. My mother told me stories of him and how ruthless he could be. He'd gone to war with others in one of the woodland realms in Ireland. Your uncle's history with him was the main reason I wanted you out of that house right away."

"You think I'm in danger also?"

"It seems logical that you might be."

Timothy fell silent as he ate. The quiet crackling of the fire and the lingering smell of Aenya's cooking was completely at odds with the discussion. He studied her face and couldn't help feeling drawn to her. She was pretty, but it was more than that. He sensed none of the shallowness of someone like Melanie. In just three days, Aenya had saved him twice, once from drowning and once from Derek. At the first sign of trouble, Melanie would have whimpered away.

Another idea was starting to take shape. Being elf and not human was probably a major reason why he never seemed to fit in with the kids at school. Omar had been his only real friend, mostly because of their mutual need to survive the routine of getting through the day.

"It's snowing," she said, breaking the silence.

Timothy went to the window. There was a quarter moon in the sky, enough to light the fresh dusting of snow on the ground. He took his coat and opened the door.

"Where are you going?" she asked.

"Just outside, it looks so pretty."

"I'll come with you." She swirled a long, russet-colored cloak around her shoulders and pulled the hood up over her head.

The smell was cold, almost sweet. The branches were still, and snowflakes clicked as they touched the ground and crunched under Timothy and Aenya's feet as they wandered near the birdbath. The light from the windows cast shadows around the bushes over a canvas of white.

Aenya stopped and turned her face upwards. A gentle breeze ruffled the fabric surrounding her face. She closed her eyes and sniffed the air. Timothy moved closer to the tree line, wanting to put the light behind her, to frame her in silhouette.

"I think I may have made an error in judgment," she said, her eyes still closed.

"What do you mean?"

"It would have been better not to leave your car parked in front of your uncle's house." There was tension in her voice.

"Why?"

"He suspects."

"What?"

"Shhh." She held up her hand and pulled the hood back from her head, turning to one side, listening to the quiet.

A sharp rushing sound broke the silence, followed by a clap against the tree next to Timothy. It sounded like someone had thrown a hard-packed snowball. Bits of bark pelted his face. A second and third barely missed him, and only because he'd staggered to the side.

"Timothy, run!" His blood turned cold at the sound of panic in her voice. "Now!"

He darted headlong into the trees, not knowing why or what he was running from. The sound of scurrying came from behind, and from more than one creature. The silence that came with the snowfall made whatever they were sound close and gaining. Tiny branches whipped his face, the stings more painful from the cold. Timothy held his hands out, trying to shield himself from what he couldn't see, praying his feet wouldn't catch on the underbrush.

Off to the left, he heard a yelp and a thud; whatever it was had been injured and silenced. Fewer were following, but still more than one. What were they? Hearing them, feeling them close behind, but not seeing them in the dark was terrifying. His chest was pounding, and his lungs screamed as frigid air filled them. He increased his speed as he hurtled through the trees.

There was a clearing in the trees, and alarm bells went off in his head: the lake. He didn't know if it was still frozen, but if it wasn't, he'd be trapped between the trees and the water. If it was, there was no telling how strong the ice would be. He might escape onto it only to break through the crust and drown. Talk about going full circle. Turning to his right, he veered down an incline. His footing gave way, and he fell to his side, sliding down the hill, grasping at the brush. Timothy fought to regain his feet, spinning around and cracking his face against the base of a tree; the taste of blood filled his mouth.

Something growled from ten feet away. Timothy found his footing just as the bark of the tree next to him exploded. He took several steps away from the sound, but the underbrush was thicker than farther up the hill. He had no choice but to turn toward the lake. He hitched left as a deep moan echoed through the trees. Now only one set of footfalls were coming for him.

He broke through the trees and pounded across a twenty-foot beach and onto the ice. The dusting of snow offered some traction, but it was still slippery. He risked peeking over his shoulder, desperate to see what was chasing him, but there was nothing. Had it stopped? He took a chance and turned around. A short, heavyset figure stepped from the trees and stood on the bank. It raised something like a bow and pointed it in his direction.

He spun on the balls of his feet and started to run. It was a ridiculous idea; he couldn't outrun an arrow. He hoped that the dark and whatever distance he could put between them would make it more difficult.

A sound echoed across the lake, slight at first, then longer and louder—cracking. Timothy tried to stop, but his feet slid out from under him, arms swirling to keep some balance. He went down hard on his back as several dark lines spread from his body like a spiderweb. The ice was giving way. Sliding to a stop, he expected to sink into the icy depths of the lake any second. Trying to kill himself in the river had taught him the shock of cold water, and he was terrified of feeling that again.

A fluttering noise came from somewhere above. He strained his eyes in the darkness, trying to find it.

A black shape was hurtling toward him, growing larger by the second, its sides rippling in the wind, hands reaching toward him like death come to snatch its victim. He yelled just as it swooped and grabbed him.

"Got you."

"Aenya?"

"Were you expecting someone else?"

Timothy laughed hysterically as they soared up and away from the lake into the swirling mist of snow.

Chapter 12

Timothy's feet brushed the edges of the thatched roof as they landed in front of the cottage. Aenya practically shoved him through the door and began moving about at such speed that he barely kept her in focus.

"We have to hurry," she said.

"What was that? Who were they?" His voice was strained. Bullied at school was one thing; being chased and shot at was quite another. "Aenya?"

"Grab your pack." It was still resting next to the door. He slipped the straps around his shoulders. She moved behind him, unzipped the main pouch, and shoved something inside. Before he could blink, she blew out the rest of the candles in the center of the room. Then they were back outside.

"Aenya, please tell me what the hell is going on."

"Later."

She wrapped her right arm through his left and they soared into the air. He thought he saw movement in the small clearing outside her door, but then they were over the darkness of the forest and gone.

Her eyes looked focused in concentration and her jaw clenched. Though he chalked that up to urgency, he still thought something was wrong.

"Are you all right?"

She didn't answer.

They flew close to the tops of the trees for about ten minutes before passing over a four-lane road just near the highway. There was a gas station and a fast-food restaurant on one side and a Holiday Inn on the other. She brought them down on a grassy section along the side of the entrance to the motel.

"We need to rest for the night," she said, sounding winded. "We'll go the rest of the way in the morning."

He didn't follow as she began to move up the pavement.

"We're staying here? Aenya, I don't have any money," he said.

"I put some in your backpack. I need to sleep." She'd hardly broken stride to mention it. "When we get inside, just tell the clerk your car broke down, and it's being fixed across the street."

He thought it was more likely the clerk would think they were there for something else altogether. "How should I explain you? Like, you're my sister or something?"

"He won't see me."

"Oh, right." He still didn't get how she could make it so humans didn't see her if she wanted it that way. As they entered the lobby, an older couple passed in front of them. The woman smiled, not even glancing at Aenya.

"Can I help you?" asked the clerk.

"Ah…I need to rent a room for tonight. My car broke down and they're going to fix it over there," he said, pointing out the door.

"Oh, that's too bad. Fill out this form, and we'll need a credit card and ID please."

Timothy pulled out his wallet and slid his driver's license across the counter.

"I'm afraid I don't have a credit card."

"We'll require payment in advance then."

"How much?"

"It's one hundred eight dollars."

Timothy put his pack on the floor. When he unzipped the top, he saw a brick-sized wad of hundred-dollar bills banded together. He gasped and then quickly made a coughing noise to cover himself. He pulled two bills free and pushed them at the clerk, who finished typing something into his computer. He returned what looked like a credit card. He must have noticed Timothy's confusion.

"That's your room key," he said. "You're in 210. Just walk down the hall to the elevator. When you reach the second floor, turn right and the room will be down the hall on your left. Will you need a wakeup call?"

"No, thanks." Timothy turned away from the counter. Aenya was sitting on the arm of a couch across the room. They rode up in the elevator, and he had some difficulty figuring out how the key worked on the door. He didn't understand why a normal key wouldn't have done just as well.

She sat heavily on the side of the bed, her chin dropped to her chest, as if drained of all energy. He thought maybe flying with him was harder than it looked, but when she slid the cloak off her shoulders, he gasped for the second time that night. The top half of her sleeve was soaked in blood.

"Oh my god, you're hurt." He rushed to her, not sure what to do. He remembered that you were supposed to put pressure on a bleeding wound. "What happened?"

"I must have gotten in the way of one of their arrows."

He ripped at the fabric of her sleeve. Her arm was punctured with several small holes; rivulets of blood rolled down it. He pulled a towel from the bathroom rack and soaked it with warm water, then washed her arm and wrapped strips torn from a pillowcase around it.

"We should get a doctor."

"A doctor won't be able to help."

"Why not?"

"Because it's elfshot."

"What the hell is that?"

"Something poisonous. It's deadly to us if not treated in time," she said. "I have a feeling it was used on your mother."

He wished she hadn't said that. The thin sheen of sweat on her forehead made her look much like his mother in the hours before she died. Aenya lay against the pillows and closed her eyes. Blood was already seeping through the cotton strips. He wondered if he should call the front desk just to ask how far it was to the nearest hospital. At least they might stop the bleeding.

"Stop worrying," she said, her voice faint. "There's nothing you can do for me right now."

"How do you know what I'm thinking?"

"Your concern is emanating violently. I'll be fine."

"That's what my mother said. She didn't turn out so fine."

"Get some rest, please." She turned her head and took a deep breath through her nose, then drifted off to sleep.

Timothy slid onto the other side of the queen-sized bed and tried to close his eyes, but the tension was too much. He rolled onto his side, facing Aenya, and thought of his mother.

Why hadn't she told him the truth? Why hadn't she ever told him that they were part of another race of beings? Had he known, he could have gotten the help she needed instead of watching her die. What had his mother been protecting him from? It was troubling that he might never have all the answers.

Chapter 13

Timothy woke to the sound of Aenya slipping into her cloak, faint light filtering around the edges of the curtains.

"We should be going."

She seemed to have gained some energy back, but he didn't like the color of her face as she pulled the curtains open to the balcony. It was ashen grey, as if all blood had drained from her head. His sense of alarm doubled, but this time she didn't say anything about it. The room faced the back of the hotel and overlooked a small parking lot. She pulled the collar of his jacket up around his neck, and smiled, weakly.

"I'll get us to the border of the White Mountains," she said. "From there, we'll walk the rest of the way."

"That's got to be twenty or thirty miles."

"We'll make it." She slid her arm around Timothy's and looked upward; then they were sailing over the top of the motel and the people walking in the parking lot. They didn't even glance in the pair's direction. Timothy realized that if she could hide an entire cottage from view, he wouldn't be much of a challenge.

The signs of urban development slipped away as they skimmed above rural landscapes with increasing pockets of woodland. Roads yielded to streams and rock-faced walls, cars to moose and deer.

He kept glancing at her, his concern growing with every mile. Her expression had shifted from looking tired to grimacing in pain. As they touched down on a grassy meadow, just yards from the edge of a vast forest, she yelped and staggered. He slipped his arm around her waist, and she leaned into him for support. That scared him more than arrows shooting at him.

"We need to enter the forest there," she said, pointing at a path through the trees with a trembling hand. "It's a mile or two in."

"Where exactly are we going?"

"There's a small village of elves." She spoke with difficulty. Whatever was happening to her was happening faster.

He tightened his grip around her waist and half-carried her into the trees. A stream trickled over a small waterfall. Under other conditions, he would have stopped to enjoy its beauty.

She was losing strength with every step she took, faltering over mere twigs and stones. Her breathing was becoming ragged and short. After a mile or so, she slumped to her knees, trying hard to draw breath, as if she'd just run a marathon.

"How much farther?" he asked, trying to keep the sound of panic from his voice.

"Not…much…"

There was no time to waste. He scooped her up and rushed down the path. She managed to put her arms around his neck and laid her head on his shoulder.

The density of the woodland increased with the depth of the forest. Even if she could have flown the rest of the way, she would have found it harder to land.

"Hello there," a voice said from within the trees.

Timothy froze. At first he saw no one, then, from behind a thick oak, an older-looking man stepped onto the path. He was wearing a pair of brown corduroys, a cream-colored cotton shirt, and an unbuttoned vest. His white hair was wavy and long, and his chin sprouted several days' worth of beard.

"We need help."

"For certain." The man took another step closer, and a look of shock transformed his face. "Aenya?"

"Yes, sir," Timothy said, afraid she would find it too hard to speak. "She needs your help. It's elfshot."

"Who are you?"

"I'm Timothy." Somehow, that didn't seem enough. "I'm… I'm an elf."

"I can see that, lad," he said, pointing to his own ear. "Here, give her to me." He took her limp body. "Come, quickly."

They moved at a much faster pace and soon entered a small clearing. The trees around a group of cottages formed a canopy over the circle of ground in front, and thin tendrils of smoke rose from each chimney. The man entered the middle cottage and moved up a sturdy wooden staircase that circled to the second floor. He laid Aenya down on a bed.

"Gwen, bring your herbs!"

Aenya's eyes fluttered open. She tried to smile, but it was a weak attempt at most. With enormous effort, she lifted her arm and pointed at Timothy. Her lips were trying to form words. "Ayl…" she said with great effort. "Aylwen." Her eyes closed, and her arm dropped to the side.

"Why does she speak of Aylwen?" the man asked. He pulled open her cloak. "Gwen, are you coming?"

"I'm of her bloodline; I think she was trying to tell you that." The information seemed so unimportant, Timothy's voice trailed off in a whisper.

Just then, a woman of nearly the same size and build as the man rushed into the room carrying a leather satchel. She moved to Aenya's side and removed the strips of linen Timothy had tied there.

"Oh dear," she said. "I'm afraid this has gone very far." She opened the bag and pulled out a thick green leaf. After unrolling it, she scraped a thick, dark ointment from it and began to work it into the wounds on Aenya's arm.

"Will she be all right?" Timothy asked.

The man shrugged his shoulders and shook his head. "Hopefully the medicine will take hold. What happened?"

"Last night." Timothy wanted to explain, but he realized how little he really knew. "We were outside and suddenly she told me to run. Something was chasing me, but I have no idea what. I ran onto the ice to escape. The lake was frozen, and Aenya flew down to save me. They were aiming at me, but they hit her."

"Come, lad. There's naught you can do here. Have some biscuits and tea while we wait for the salve to do its work and you can tell me more."

Timothy wanted to tell Aenya that he'd be right downstairs if she needed him, but she seemed out of it. He followed the elf down to the main room. It was similar to Aenya's cottage: a few pieces of wooden furniture and a table, an open hearth for cooking, and the smell of bread baking over the fire.

"I'm Donlan," he said. He reached for a teapot sitting on the table, poured the rich amber liquid into a thick mug, and put it in front of Timothy. "And that was me wife, Gwen."

Timothy was relieved to have gotten there, but praying it was in time. It was just too much like the last day with his mother. He slumped onto a chair by the table.

"So why would someone be chasing ya? And with the intent to do you harm, no less."

Timothy shook his head.

"Mr. Donlan, I'm afraid a lot of this is new to me."

"It just be Donlan. And this mention of Aylwen, you say you're of her bloodline. Serious offense if it not be true, but if Aenya says it is, then it must be so. There be no finer lass than she. Headstrong, mind ya, but a true heart just the same."

Timothy had never heard anyone speak like him, except in movies. His Irish accent and cadence were so much thicker than Mary's at the restaurant. It felt as though they'd left the state for a foreign country.

"How do you come to know her?"

That was a question he didn't want to answer, or at least not the full version. "We live near one another, and she recognized me as an elf. She…introduced herself. I hadn't known I was… well…an elf."

"And your parents?"

"My mother was fae. We think my father might have been human."

"So she was waiting to see how you'd turn. But you said *was*. They're dead?"

"Yes, sir. My mother died a few months ago. Aenya thinks she might have been murdered, and that my uncle may have had something to do with it."

Donlan frowned.

"And how is it she figures you for Aylwen's bloodline?"

"From a letter of my mother's. It was from my grandmother. Aenya wanted to bring me here, to some people…or rather elves, who would know more."

"Aye, I think that was wise."

Finally warm, Timothy pulled his backpack off and slid out of his jacket. Donlan put a plate of hot biscuits on the table, each coated with a thick slab of butter. He couldn't decide which was better, the smell or the taste, as they melted in his mouth.

Donlan settled into a thick chair, pulled a long white clay pipe from the pocket of his vest, struck a match, and drew a mouthful of thick smoke from its slender stem. They sat quietly for at least an hour. Timothy was glad for the silence; it was like sitting in the waiting room of the hospital, and he wasn't in the mood for small talk.

Finally, Gwen came down the stairs and into the room. Her shoulders sagged. She shook her head, casting her eyes to the floor.

"I'm afraid the poison has run too deep. I can do no more."

"What?" Timothy said. She might have been speaking gibberish for all the sense it made. He jumped from the chair and brushed past her, clambering up the stairs. Donlan followed behind.

Aenya was motionless, her limp arms resting alongside her. There was only the tiniest rise of her chest.

Donlan crested the stairs, took hold of Timothy's arm, and held tight.

"Let her be." His tone was gentle.

"But—"

"There's naught to do," he said. "There's no cure for this, let her be at peace."

"No!" Timothy yanked free and ran to her side. He sat on the edge of the bed. "Aenya, can you hear me?" There was a swirl of fear and helplessness; it was just like watching his mother die all over again.

"Aenya," he whispered, "you promised to help me. I need you." There had to be something he could do; he couldn't allow her to die like this.

Then he realized how stupid he'd been. What if he tried on her what he'd done for the mourning dove? She was a hundred times bigger and had poison in her blood—she wasn't just stunned from running into a window—but what if the kind of energy that had woken the bird worked on her, too?

He put a hand over the bandaged wounds of her arm and cupped the other around the curve of her cheek. He squeezed his eyes closed. If this worked, he could have saved all this trouble. Then again, maybe it wasn't something that elves could do, or she might have suggested it. After all, she'd fixed his anxiety how many times now with a simple touch. Maybe this was something only the sídhe could manage.

"I need you to come back to me." A clear vision of an open grassy field burst into his imagination like it had with the dove; it felt as though he were standing there. A soft breeze caressed his face. He wasn't alone. Aenya stood beside him, her eyes cast toward the sky. He felt the pulse as he had before, but it was far more powerful. He trembled as if trying to lift a great weight, and his chest felt like someone had ripped it open, allowing searing-hot gushes of blood to boil out of him. He thought he might have cried out. He knew he wasn't bleeding; it was the energy vibrating in his chest. It was hard to breathe, but the vision continued, as though contained in a protective bubble, a counterpoint to the violent sensations in his body. The only sound was rushing wind—was it the breeze in his vision, or was it the sound of his own blood pounding inside his veins?

Whatever part of his brain that wasn't focusing on her told him to let go. The longer he held on, the weaker he felt, but it wasn't time. She needed more; he sensed it. Someone was calling his name; it echoed inside his head. He didn't respond, afraid that breaking his concentration would hurt her. It wasn't Aenya's voice anyway. The vision began to blur, like a mirage dancing beyond the rising heat of a desert. He cracked one eye open, just a slit, and he saw her skin glow with a translucent, pinkish warmth. He tried to refocus and saw the color gradually draining away, changing, as if cooling to a shade of icy blue. Sensing it was a good thing, he closed his eye once more, afraid to lose sight of her on the grassy field.

"Aenya." He didn't know if he said her name aloud, or if it was the vision-self calling to her, but she turned to him, lowering her face from the sky, searching for his. She was radiant, alive. Her lips were forming words, but he couldn't hear them. The roar in his ears was deafening, like a jet engine passing just feet over his head. She reached for him, her face blurring, her features morphing. The smile was shifting to a look of concern as she mouthed words with greater care. "Let go," she was saying. "Let go."

Timothy opened his eyes; hers fluttered, then opened, too. He choked back something between a laugh and a sob and all but collapsed on top of her from exhaustion. It took every remaining ounce of strength to hold himself up.

"Aenya?"

"Timothy," she whispered. She touched his arm, then lowered her hand to her chest. She had fallen instantly back to sleep, but she was alive.

Timothy glanced over at Donlan; his face was a mask of astonishment, or maybe it was fear? He backed to the stairs, turned, and ran from the room.

He couldn't hold his head up. Walking was out of the question. Still, he wasn't convinced she was healed. He slid his arms around her and, resting his head on the pillows, fell into total darkness beside her.

Chapter 14

Aenya sat with Donlan, watching Timothy sleep. It seemed to her that she'd done much of that in the last few days, but this was different. Six days ago, she'd thought he was just an unusual human. Now, the boy resting in front of her had done something impossible. He'd brought her back from the brink of death that was beyond anyone's reach. She knew he was frightened and confused, depressed and full of guilt. Something made her want to stroke his hair and obliterate all his anxiety. But that would take more than a simple touch. There was more to him yet; otherwise, someone wouldn't have tried to kill him.

Timothy jumped and opened his eyes.

"Hey, sleepyhead," Aenya said. His eyes found her, and he looked relieved.

"You're all better," he said. His voice croaked as though suffering from laryngitis.

"All better," she confirmed.

Timothy looked at Donlan, who was staring at him as he would an untethered and dangerous animal.

"I guess the medicine did a better job that we thought," Timothy said.

"Bollocks. The medicine played little part in all of that."

"I think he has some of the healer in him," Aenya said, trying to soothe Donlan's ruffled nerves.

"Aye, no doubt. Tell me of your father, lad."

"Like I said, he was a teacher and an artist."

"And I'd bet me soul that's not all. Do you remember much of him?"

"He died when I was little. I only have a few things of his."

"Like what?"

"Some of his art, a few of his books." Timothy looked at Aenya. "Didn't you put that old one in the pack?"

"I did," she said.

"What sort of book?"

"We thought it might be a diary, but we didn't have time to read through it," said Timothy.

"Would ya mind if I take a gander at it?"

Timothy shook his head. Donlan stood and turned for the stairs.

"I'll send Gwen with some food. You'll be needing your strength back, the both of ya."

Aenya moved to the side of the bed and slipped her hand in Timothy's. She felt him stiffen and watched him blush. His eyes dilated, and she felt his thoughts whether he knew them himself or not. They were flattering in a way.

"What you did was incredible," she said.

"Did you feel any of that?"

Though she hadn't been fully conscious, the experience had been intense. She'd felt him touching her, his hand on her face. The searing sensation that moved through her body from the places where his fingers had touched her was like wildfire burning out the poison. And then coolness, like she'd slipped into a stream on a hot summer day. Still uncertain whether she'd been awake or asleep, she'd seen Timothy. His face had been contorted in pain and only seconds from collapse. She told him to let go, knowing that if he didn't, it would kill him. Only when he finally released her did she realize the power that had seized her body. The aftermath had been a sensation of weightlessness and exhaustion.

"Yes, I felt it," she said. She tried to explain it and ended with an admonishment that if he ever did something like that again, he needed to let go the second he'd given enough. "What about you? How do you feel?"

"A little tired, like I've been drugged," he said. "What's up with Donlan? He seemed pissed off or something."

"He's very curious about you. He knows most of the fae folk in this part of the world, yet he knew nothing of your mother and father. He thought that was odd. I mean, he wouldn't have had cause to know your father, maybe, but he was surprised that another member of the sídhe lived so near without him knowing."

"You didn't know of her either, and you lived just miles away."

"I know. I told him, and that only adds to the mystery."

"What about my uncle, does Donlan know of him?"

"That's a bit more interesting. He doesn't know him, but he was aware of an elf who'd been banished from Ireland because of his loyalty to Cadwaladr. Then again, Donlan wouldn't have sought his company."

"So, Donlan was the one you said I should meet, the one who could help me learn more about my kind?"

Aenya nodded. "He's been here a long time, too."

Gwen arrived with a tray holding two steaming bowls of stew, a loaf of dark bread, and two mugs of mead. She had to explain to Timothy that it was like beer, but made from honey and maple syrup. He wrinkled his nose at first, but then seemed to enjoy the sweetness. They were both ravenous. Aenya told him stories about growing up in New Hampshire in the 1800s and 1900s while they ate.

Donlan popped his head above the last stair.

"Aenya, I'd have a word with you." Just as quickly, he was gone.

"Wonder what that's about. I'll be back. You get some more rest." Apart from blushing when she held his hand, he still looked pale.

As she sat across from Donlan at the table, he held up the book and slapped it against his palm. "It's all in here."

"What is?" asked Aenya.

"It's a diary all right, but also a history of his father's family."

"Timothy will be so excited when you tell him."

"I'm not going to tell him. At least, we shouldn't just yet."

"Why?" She felt a chill. *What could be so bad?*

"Timothy's father was elfin, not human, and he had other children. Six…other…children, all sons."

"So, he's a seventh son." She shrugged. It wasn't common, but there was nothing terrible or abnormal about it.

"Aye, but he's not just the seventh son. His father's and grandfather's line dates back more than a thousand years. Timothy is the seventh son of a seventh son."

Aenya drew a sharp breath and looked at the stairs, hoping Timothy hadn't heard her. The rarity of such a birth was beyond measure. She wracked her brain trying to remember anything she had been taught about it. She could only recall it had something to do with Aylwen in some way.

"Now you see how it was that he could heal you," Donlan said. His words prompted her to remember the myth that a seventh of a seventh would have incredible healing power. She couldn't recall a specific instance in their history when it might have happened before, but she knew her education wasn't the most thorough.

"Think, Aenya, what that could mean."

"What are you thinking?" she asked, sensing that he was driving at something more.

"In elfin lore, the seventh of a seventh would have unnatural abilities."

"I know that."

"So imagine the union of such an elf with the bloodline of Aylwen. It would produce a son unprecedented in history. Such a boy might be key to the restoration of Alfheim."

"Oh!" She felt the blood flush from her head.

"Do you see now, lass?"

"It's no wonder he was kept hidden, why his mother kept it to herself. His father must have come from Ireland because he knew there'd be those who'd try to prevent him from fathering another son."

"Precisely," Donlan said.

"Timothy must be protected at all costs."

"You must take him from here. You have to get him to Sídhlin. He'll actually be closer to danger, but there are many more who will shield him."

"His uncle, Seumais, do you think he knows the truth?"

"No. If he did, he would have killed Timothy long ago. I have a feeling that neither his mother nor his uncle knew his father's true history."

"It was Seumais who was responsible for the attack the other night, I'm sure of it," Aenya said.

"His instinct must have told him something was wrong when Timothy disappeared with you, and he decided to take no chances."

"I don't know how he knew where to find us," she said. "We should leave right away."

"There's one more thing," Donlan said. "There's a family tree diagrammed in the diary." The elf scratched his head. "It shows Cadwaladr was the second born of the fifth son. He's Timothy's cousin."

Chapter 15

As soon as Aenya crested the top of the stairs, she knew Timothy had overheard most, if not all, of the conversation.

"Were you going to tell me?" he asked, his arms crossed over his chest.

"Of course," she said, not sure if she actually would have. There was a look of anger and maybe hurt in his eyes. "To be honest, I might have waited until I had the chance to understand all of this better."

"So my father was an elf, and I have an entire family of brothers out there somewhere."

"Timothy, it's not that we planned to keep this from you, it's just that all of this is so new and the information is incredible and—"

"Aenya, please promise me something," he said with a note of firmness. "It looks like everyone has kept a lot of secrets from me. I don't want anyone doing that anymore. From now on, just tell me or include me when you have these little talks with people. Okay?"

She nodded. "That's fair. I promise you'll know what I know."

"Thank you."

His rigid posture deflated, and he sat back on the bed, going from angry bear to the shy boy once more. She didn't understand why that made her want to rush over and hug him, but it was also clear that underneath that vulnerable look was someone who was capable of ferocity and desperate action. She thought it would be wise to remember that.

"So, what's all this seventh son stuff?"

She didn't know where to begin. It was frustrating if not challenging to keep finding ways to describe things so that he would readily understand.

"Listen, don't take this the wrong way, but the birth of a seventh of a seventh is an event like the birth of Christ or something."

Timothy looked at her, his mouth twisting into a grimace of incredibility.

"Next you'll be telling me I can walk on water."

She shook her head. "No, I think given your history with water, you will definitely not be walking on it."

"So, where is it you're taking me?"

"It's called Sídhlin, one of the last woodland realms and the largest in Europe. There are other realms in the oak forests of England, Poland, and Russia, but Sídhlin is the only one that's enchanted. It's completely hidden from humans."

"We're going to Europe?" He sounded shocked. "I've never been away from New Hampshire."

"Ireland, actually." She picked up his backpack and slipped his father's diary back inside.

"Do you really think my mother had no idea about my father?"

Aenya wasn't quite sure how to answer that. She'd never known his mother or father, so it was difficult, under the circumstances, to understand what their motivations had been.

"We may never know," she said. "I think if she'd understood the significance of your birth, and your father's bloodline, she would have taken greater precautions to protect you and to educate you. She also knew her brother's allegiance to Cadwaladr, since it's what forced them to America in the first place. So if she knew, I'm sure she would have put you beyond his reach. It seems she thought there was a chance you would turn out human, so I think your father kept his secret to keep you both safe."

"Do you think we'll find my family in Ireland?"

"I'd say the odds are pretty good."

"So how are we getting there?"

"We're taking a plane, of course." Aenya laughed. "You don't expect me to fly you across the Atlantic, do you?"

She straightened up the bed and had Timothy rewrap her arm with fresh bandages. They were going to travel light. She didn't want to risk stopping at her cottage and certainly not Jim's house, just in case. He tied off the last piece of the gauze and grabbed her wrist to keep her from getting up.

"I don't know about all this stuff you and Donlan were talking about, but I don't want you to forget that whatever it is you have planned, I want to deal with those who had something to do with my mother's death." She felt his eyes boring into hers.

Sometimes it felt like he was a totally different boy than the one who jumped into a river. She covered his hand with her own.

"I know, Timothy. I won't forget."

By the time they walked out of Donlan's cottage, he and Gwen were waiting. Gwen's face transformed with a maternal smile, and she embraced Aenya.

"Bless ya both," she said. Donlan pulled her into him and squeezed hard for a few seconds, then let go. He put a rolled parchment into her hands, which she slipped into one of the pockets of her cloak. Then Donlan turned to Timothy and clasped his hand firmly.

"Now listen to me, young Tim. I've taken the measure of ya and can say I'm proud to have been of service. You listen well to my lass here, and she'll keep you on the straight."

"Thank you," Timothy said. They studied one another for a time, and then Donlan pulled Timothy into a tight embrace, too. Aenya saw that Timothy looked embarrassed and bewildered at first, but then she recognized something in the tears that welled up in his eyes. He'd never had a father's affection, and it was clear that he was getting a small taste of what he'd been missing.

"Now off with ya both, and may we all come together in Alfheim."

* * *

Aenya brought them to within a half mile of a bus depot in Concord. Timothy had to jog to keep up with her as she made her way to the terminal. He was amazed how she demonstrated a level of efficiency he doubted he'd ever have. Within minutes, she'd checked timetables, purchased tickets, bought snacks, and herded him outside to the bus that was about ready to depart for Boston.

"I've never been on a bus that wasn't painted yellow," he said.

"Neither have I."

"And I've never been on a plane before." He felt shy admitting that.

"Neither have I."

"But you came from Ireland."

"I did, but if you recall, that was before there were such things as planes. We came by ship."

"Duh," he said, feeling stupid. "Come to think of it, don't we need passports and stuff?" He knew they had plenty of money, though he didn't like the fact that she'd be using her money to pay for his ticket to travel to Ireland. That had to be expensive.

"Let's just say that I don't plan to follow the usual travel formalities. We're going to borrow some space on the aircraft. No one will know we're there."

"I should have figured."

Two hours later, they stood in front of Terminal E at Logan International Airport. There was a certain excitement watching taxis and limos pulling to the curb and people jumping out with their luggage, bundled against the cold wind. Timothy had always thought how awesome it would be to step onto an airplane and go somewhere exotic.

Inside the terminal, Aenya started reading the signs. "Ah," she said, pointing upwards. "Arrivals. Come on."

"Arrivals? I thought we were departing."

"Donlan said there are huge lines going through security, and since we don't have passports or tickets, he suggested we go to the gates by walking against traffic. We'll make our entrance through the exit. There's no security in that direction. Once passengers leave to go to baggage, they're not allowed back in. Since no one will see us, we don't have to worry about that."

"You think you can teach me how not to be seen?"

"Probably not," she said. "You have your talents, and I have mine."

As predicted, the security people watched as scores of passengers filed down the hallways away from the gates and toward the luggage carousels, dragging their carry-ons behind them. Timothy and Aenya walked past and entered a long corridor with numbers posted on either side. He looked all around, noting every detail, and almost bumped into her when she stopped. He followed her gaze to a monitor that listed all the departing flights.

"That's the one we want, Boston to Shannon, Gate 6. It leaves in an hour and a half."

"Good, we can get something to eat."

"You're hungry again?" She rolled her eyes.

"What? I've had only a bag of chips since this morning. I'm hungry."

"Well...I suppose we might as well."

Within sight of their gate was a pub-style restaurant, and Timothy wolfed down a burger, fries, and a Coke. Aenya satisfied herself with a salad. He watched the hundreds of people milling about the concourse, waiting for their boarding time with impatience.

"Once we get to Ireland, then what?"

"We'll go directly to Sídhlin. I have a letter from Donlan to his nephew and wife. He said they'll help look after us till we get settled."

"You make it sound like we're moving there permanently."

"I don't know what to expect." She twirled her fork through the last few shreds of lettuce. "We'll meet the elfin council and tell them what's going on."

Across the corridor from the gate they'd be leaving from was a waiting area for Gate 7 with several rows of seats. A scruffy-looking man with a long tweed coat and a rust-colored button-down vest sat looking in their direction. His eyes locked on Timothy's. The scruffy guy held his gaze for several seconds before looking away, almost too casually.

"Aenya, we're not enchanted at the moment right?"

"What do you mean?"

"I mean, other people can see us?"

"Yes, why?"

He didn't want to sound paranoid. "Just wondering. Do I have to be standing right next to you for people not to see me?"

"No, not right next to me, but you can't wander too far off, otherwise the enchantment fades."

"Then how do fairies keep a whole village enchanted?"

She laughed. "Well, the cottages don't get up and move, do they?"

Scruffy was watching again. This time, he turned his face away faster. "We haven't tried that yet, have we? I mean, putting an enchantment on me and letting me stray a little bit."

"No, why?"

"I was thinking of using the men's room before we board. I'd like to try it while being invisible, just to see what it's like. I could start learning how to move around people who can't see me. It would be good practice for the plane."

"First of all, it's not that you're invisible. It's just that others can't see you. There's a difference."

"But the effect is the same."

"Pretty much."

"Then I'd like to try it."

She gave him a strange look and shrugged her shoulders, as if indulging a child with an ice cream cone.

"Where are the bathrooms?"

He pointed to the signs on the wall in the corridor. "Like fifty or sixty feet away."

Aenya pursed her lips and glanced around to see who might be looking in their direction. She concentrated, moving her hand as if she were wiping down an unseen wall. "Okay."

"That's it? You mean I'm invisible?"

"You're not invisible. People will look right at you. They just won't process the fact mentally."

"Right...if you say so…I'll be back in a minute."

He slid from the booth and walked right past the hostess. A woman, barreling down the walkway with an oversized carry-on, nearly collided with him. He realized how precarious not being seen might be, though he couldn't imagine the scare he'd give someone who bumped into him without being able to see him.

Out of the corner of his eye, he noticed Scruffy follow his progress. Timothy tensed; he was elfin. He'd never asked Aenya how common elfin folk were. For all he knew, they might be all over the place. He entered the men's room, found an empty stall, and bolted the lock, not sure what to expect.

Three or four men came and went. There was flushing, the sound of water splashing into the sink, the roar of the hand dryers blowing hot air. Then he was alone in the bathroom and figured it was about time to get back; the flight was due to board in a few minutes.

A soft squelching noise came from the left, near the door, followed by another, then one more. The hem of a long tweed coat appeared just under the bottom of the stall door. Timothy held his breath, afraid to make the slightest noise.

"Well now, Mr. Brennan." The voice was very English Cockney. "I 'ope you're not 'aving too much trouble in there."

He didn't know what to do. It had been a dumb idea.

"Come on out, we'd like to 'ave a word with ya, and I 'ave a message from your uncle."

His spine tingled. If Aenya had been right, that his uncle had been the one behind the attack, then this situation was not good at all. Timothy stood, took a deep breath, and slid the lock, letting the door swing inward.

"Now there's a good lad," the man said. He had a smile cold enough to freeze a hot coal. "We'd like you to come with us."

"Who's us?"

“Me mate, just there outside the door, sort of keeping an eye out, you know? Your poor uncle’s been ’alf beside ’isself with worry.”

“I’ll just bet he has,” Timothy said. Something in the man’s condescending tone made Timothy want to smash his face. He wondered if this guy had been part of the group who’d chased him through the forest. He might have been the one who shot Aenya.

“You can tell him I’m just fine and in a lot better company.”

“Is that a fact? I’d venture a guess that poor old Jim would be ’eartbroken to ’ear you tell of it.”

Timothy went to push past Scruffy. “Tell him I’m not particularly concerned with his ’eartbreaks.”

Scruffy grabbed at his arm, and Timothy bolted. A broad-shouldered hulk with black hair and ugly brown teeth filled the doorway. “And where do you think you’re going so fast?”

Timothy did the only thing he knew that would bring down the small giant: he shot his foot up and connected with his groin. He had the fleeting satisfaction of seeing a look of shock and pain register on the man’s face just as Scruffy grabbed him from behind. His arm locked around Timothy’s neck like a vise, lifting him off his feet.

“You stupid little runt, I’m gonna snap your scrawny neck and ’ave done with ya.”

The pressure he put behind Timothy’s head was intense; he saw tiny points of light swimming in front of him. Scruffy’s partner was rolling on the floor. He moved to his knees and pasted one meaty paw on the wall tile as he tried to get to his feet.

Timothy gazed into the mirrors above the sinks and saw the look of murder in Scruffy's eyes. He braced the bottoms of both feet against the edge of the counter, and shoved as hard as he could. They fell backward and down. The stall door slammed against the partition as they landed on top of the toilet bowl. Scruffy moaned, and Timothy could breathe again. He took several gulps of air and started to choke as he stumbled back toward the exit.

The other man growled and turned in his direction. Timothy was never going to get past him. His face was a mask of fury. For the second time, he lashed out with his foot, connecting with the man's chin. His neck snapped back, and Timothy jumped past him into the angled entryway. He landed badly and had to lean against the wall to steady himself. A hand grabbed hold of his ankle, and he sprawled on the tile floor, his head sticking into the hall. Timothy kicked hard and managed to pull free, scrambling to his feet and into the walkway between gates, choking. Several people turned their heads at hearing someone yelling in the bathroom. Timothy was frantic about getting to Aenya; he needed to warn her.

Then she grabbed him. "What's going on?"

"We have…" He started to choke again. "We have to move, now. I'll explain later, but we have to get on the plane."

They rushed toward the gate just as the flight crew was passing through the door to the jetway.

A yell came from behind. The large black-haired man limped out of the men's room, holding Scruffy by one arm. People jumped out of the way. Aenya must have summed up the situation. Her brow furrowed. She held one hand out toward them. A concentrated, translucent ball of shimmering air shot across the corridor and slammed into the larger man, knocking him back into the wall of the men's room. They both slid to the floor, unconscious.

Aenya pushed Timothy in the direction of the door the flight crew had used, and they rushed down the narrow jetway onto the aircraft.

Chapter 16

TIMOTHY COULDN'T TELL IF AENYA was angry, but the vibe emanating from her felt like it. They stood in silence behind the last row of first-class seats watching the hatch to the plane. It wasn't until all the passengers had boarded, the flight crew had closed the door, and they were backing away from the terminal that she relaxed.

They walked farther into the aircraft and found two open aisle seats next to each other just as a flight attendant was checking the overhead compartments, oblivious to their presence. A young woman was sitting by the window in Aenya's row and an older couple in Timothy's, all staring at the scenery rolling by. Aenya whispered, "Sleep." In seconds, their eyelids fluttered and closed.

They watched a short video about seatbelts, flotation devices, and oxygen masks that he'd only seen in movies. It was exciting sitting on a real plane. The rumbling vibration as it accelerated down the runway got his heart pumping, but Aenya sat composed as though she'd done this before. He thought it must be nice knowing if the plane stopped flying, she still could.

"Now, would you mind telling me what happened back there?" she asked once the plane leveled out.

Timothy wriggled his ears and jaw, trying to deal with the cabin pressure. He told her how Scruffy had been watching and his feeling that something wasn't quite right. Then he admitted what he'd said and how they'd tried to kill him.

"So your idea was to walk into a trap without so much as a hint of what you were getting into without telling me. Is that what you were thinking?"

"Stupid, huh?"

"Stupid doesn't quite cover it."

"I can take care of myself, you know." That she thought of him as a helpless kid was annoying. Maybe it was old-fashioned, but it bugged him that he needed a girl to rescue him.

"Timothy Brennan," she said, turning an angry face toward him. "Have you remembered nothing I've told you? You don't have the knowledge or the tools to take on an elf who is set on killing you. It has nothing to do with whether you think you can take care of yourself. It's just you have no idea what you're facing...not yet, anyway. Furthermore, if I'm supposed to be level and honest with you, then I expect the same in return. Understood?"

It was hard to argue with her on that, but the lecture stung just the same. There was so much to learn. Timothy wondered if elfin children went to some kind of elf school, but that sounded ridiculous. He thought of what she had told Donlan, that he needed to be protected at all costs, like he was some fragile commodity. Timothy didn't see what the fuss was about, but then, there had been two attempts on his life, so someone did.

"Listen, just to make sure, the people sitting around us can't hear us, right? I mean, it would freak them out if they heard voices and didn't see where they were coming from."

"No, the same way they can't see us also means they can't hear us."

"Okay, good to know." He wanted her not to be mad. "At least we found out you were right about my uncle."

"Yes." She sighed. "Are you all right, though?"

He summoned his best smile. "I'm fine. My neck hurts a little, but that will go away."

"You're lucky to be alive," she said. It wasn't a scold. She returned the smile. "I'm sort of impressed, actually."

His ears burned, but this time he didn't care. It was enough that she seemed pleased in some way.

"They'll know we're going to Ireland, won't they?"

"I'm afraid so. They'll be waiting for us."

If she was worried, she hid it well. He admired her constant self-control, except for those moments when she was frustrated with him, or when someone was threatening him. Derek's assault in the lunchroom came to mind. How long ago and far away that all seemed, yet it had only been a couple of days.

Aenya fiddled with the buttons on the armrest and pushed a silver one, which made the seat recline by a few inches. She closed her eyes. Timothy studied her face, tracing the soft curves of her cheeks. She was beautiful. But the beauty went through her, not like with Melanie, who was only pretty on the outside. Her blond hair fell away from her face, and he noticed for the first time that the top of her ear ended with an upswept point.

Her hands rested in her lap with that same feminine, almost regal look he'd first seen in class the day she'd been introduced. He wondered what she would do if he reached across the aisle and slipped his hand into hers, but was too afraid she'd pull away. Timothy satisfied himself with just looking at her every now and then.

He sighed and pulled at the magazines sticking out of the pocket in front of him. One was an in-flight volume that featured articles on what to see and do in Ireland, travel distances, onboard entertainment choices, and maps of the airports Aer Lingus used. There was a map of Ireland with the names of cities and counties. He wondered where they were going once they landed. He turned to ask Aenya, but she'd fallen asleep.

One of the magazines had an ad for a Middle Eastern aircraft company. The plane in the picture had Arabic writing on the side, and he thought of Omar. *He must be wondering where I disappeared to*, Timothy thought. So would Herbie and the crew at Overton's. It was depressing to realize they'd be the only ones who'd care that he was missing. Uncle Jim was simply trying to kill him. That was cheery. Timothy wondered if it was possible that Jim had been the one to hurt his mother. If so, then sitting on a plane to Ireland almost seemed the wrong choice. It felt more like he'd been swept along by circumstance than by actively deciding to leave New Hampshire behind. Whatever this Sídhlin place was, he hoped going there would help him get to the bottom of his mother's death so he could deal with it. Whoever had caused it was going to pay, of that much he was certain.

* * *

A small ding woke him. Light was sneaking under the bottoms of the window shades. He felt stiff.

"The captain has turned on the fasten seat belt sign as we begin our final approach into Shannon," a soft-spoken flight attendant announced over the speakers.

"Good morning," Aenya said. "I think it would be best when we land to move into that small lavatory over there so everyone can exit the plane before we do."

Timothy glanced at the people she had put to sleep.

"You think we should have gotten them up for a potty break or something?"

"They'll be fine," she said. "Nice and rested for their vacations. A bit hungry maybe, but rested."

Twenty minutes later, the plane touched down with a resounding bump.

"Let's go," she said.

He unbuckled his seatbelt and led her the short way down the aisle to the lavatory tucked right behind row twenty.

"Is anyone going to notice the door swinging open by itself?"

"Not a chance," she said, pushing him inside.

They didn't bother to close the door, which would have been suffocating. The plane took forever to reach the terminal, but it finally jolted to a stop, and another bell sounded. All the cabin lights came on at once. People catapulted from their seats and reached to the overhead compartments to get their luggage.

It was obvious when the front hatch opened, because the passengers suddenly seemed more anxious to move up the aisle.

Timothy felt a sudden sense of dread. Something was wrong. Aenya gripped his arm.

"What is it?" she asked.

"I don't know. I just got this feeling we shouldn't get off the plane."

She was sitting on the toilet cover, studying him.

"Interesting," she said.

"What is?"

"I think your little scuffle in Boston has focused some of your elfin wits."

"What does that mean?" he whispered.

"Most elves have that measure of clairvoyance I told you about. It's interesting to find your talent beginning to emerge."

"Great, I'm just full of surprises."

"So it would seem," she replied. "I sensed it also, so let's assume yours is accurate too. I studied the exit plan for the aircraft last night; there is another hatch in the rear."

As the last passenger cleared the aisle, Aenya and Timothy moved in the opposite direction. Two flight attendants were working in the galley at the back. Aenya waved her hand.

"Walk forward," she said.

She pushed him into a row of seats as the two attendants obeyed a suggestion they weren't even aware of. Once Timothy and Aenya were alone at the rear of the aircraft, she studied the door, reading the instructions for emergency opening. She took hold of the handle and swung it down in an arc. The door pulled in and then pivoted outward. There was a puff of air as the seal was broken, and a rush of cool morning air brushed past them.

"Somehow, I don't think the flight crew is going to be happy about this." Timothy glanced over his shoulder to see if the two attendants had come to their senses now that the door was open, but it wasn't them who worried him. "Ah…Aenya, are we still invisible to the flight crew?"

"Yes, why?"

"Then we have trouble, and it's coming right at us."

She looked past Timothy, and her normal composure slipped.

In the instant between the elf releasing an arrow and Aenya pulling Timothy out of the way, his mind framed two questions: first, how had the elf gotten through the rush of people exiting the plane, and second, how had he managed to get a longbow past everyone?

In a heartbeat, Aenya had him airborne and flying over the top of the plane, away from the door opening and the elf's line of sight.

"I'm getting tired of being attacked every few hours," Timothy called into the wind.

"You'll be safer once we get to Sídhlin," Aenya answered. "It's about seventy miles south."

It was soon obvious that she hadn't fully recovered from her wound and keeping them aloft was taking its toll. It was a wonder she'd done so well the day before, flying from Donlan's to Concord.

"Take us down, Aenya, and I don't want any arguments. Neither one of us is going to be all right if your strength fails." She thought about it, then nodded, as if resigning herself to the truth. He had won his first argument with her, but the satisfaction evaporated when he heard a sharp whistle and looked down. She was making for the top of a train as it wound through the trees, and it was moving a lot faster than they were.

Chapter 17

LANDING ON THE GROUND WAS one thing; touching a surface that was moving at sixty miles per hour was quite another. Timothy's feet hit the top of the car first, and the momentum yanked Aenya's hand from his arm. She simply flew up a foot and then elegantly stepped onto the narrow steel walkway along the spine of the car. He slid over the edge and just managed to grab a ventilation stack before plummeting to the ground. His legs were dangling and brushing against the branches of the trees that whipped past.

She sat cross-legged on the steel grating in front of him.

"Well?" he yelled into the wind.

"Well, what?"

"Are you going to leave me hanging here?"

"I thought you said you were tired of being rescued."

He pulled himself toward the stack and brought his knees under him. Then he crawled to the middle of the car and sat next to her. A few days ago, his worst dilemma, apart from the teasing at school, an uncle who was a dickwad, and a girl who had issues—none of which related to him—was a car heater that didn't work.

"Thank you."

"Don't mention it." Aenya sniffed at the air. "It's changed."

"What has?"

"The air. It's not as…crisp as I remember it."

"Global warming?" He brushed the legs of his jeans, which were covered with a layer of grime. "Don't they ever wash these things?"

She laughed and he found himself unable to keep from doing the same.

"Okay, what now?" he asked.

"Three trains, then a quick hop to Sídhlin."

"Maybe we could ride inside the next train?"

"What, and miss this view?"

He had to admit riding on top of the train was actually kind of fun. True to its reputation, Ireland was as green as he'd heard. Vast tracts of forest and open fields spread far in all directions, with small towns and villages scattered over the countryside. Meandering walls of stone broke up large parcels of land, and he thought they were much more charming than a bunch of chain-link fences. Aenya looked happy to be back in her original home. He never imagined there would be a place as beautiful as New Hampshire, but there was something mesmerizing about Ireland.

The first train had taken them east. The next went south and, finally, they switched to one moving west toward Killarney. It was late afternoon when Aenya stood up.

"Time to go, we're almost there," she said.

They flew from the train, and it seemed that within minutes they were crossing over a large body of water. On the far shore of the lake, they touched down on a rocky outcropping. They were level with the treetops that stood between them and the lake.

"We've come to Sídhlin," Aenya said.

"It's here?" Timothy was confused. He wasn't sure what he was expecting, but at the least a village like Donlan's. "Where is everyone?"

"There." She pointed down. "Remember, we're woodland creatures. We live in the forests."

"You've been here before?"

"Not that I recall."

He gave up trying to understand how she knew what she knew. It was just easier being her shadow.

A narrow path led into the forest, and the world transformed. The canopy of tree branches formed a ceiling high over the woodland, while moss and pine needles made a velvet carpet underfoot. Where the sun did manage to penetrate the treetops, it shimmered in golden rays like spotlights on the forest floor. A breeze rippled through the leaves and whispered in his ear, like the wind was trying to share a secret. They walked past a small pond with lily pads floating on the surface, and ferns growing at the water's edge dipped their leafy fingers into the pool.

"Enchanting, isn't it?" Aenya smiled. "Come on."

Timothy nodded and eagerly followed, wanting to see more. He felt disoriented, certain they'd been walking in the direction of the lake, but there was no sign of the water. He figured the path must have gradually moved in a different direction. The deeper into the forest they walked, the thicker the trees became, and the darker it grew. Peering into the twilight, he noticed tiny twinkling lights, like sparkling diamonds against a dark-green backdrop. They were fireflies. He thought they came out only in summer, but there were thousands of them. They swarmed like a river of light cascading over rocks and downed trees and through notches of Siamese tree branches, then up again like a wave breaking on an unseen shore, spreading wide in a dazzling display of buttery-yellow radiance. He stood transfixed until Aenya gently took his arm and guided him farther down the path.

It was so storybook-like, Timothy expected the Cheshire cat to appear and to see a little girl run by in chase of a rabbit. He was about to ask Aenya if she'd ever seen anything like this, but she stopped quite suddenly.

On the path ahead of them, where a small break in the tree cover allowed a ray of sun to penetrate, stood a single figure. His hands were clasped in front of a silken robe of azure blue with a thin golden rope tied around his waist. His dark-blond hair was long, brushed back from his face, and cascaded below his shoulders. He was motionless, like a statue, or more like an actor who'd taken his position on stage as the lighting crew focused on him.

Aenya bowed. "I am Aenya of the Sí."

"I am Aran." His eyes shifted.

"This is Timothy, heir to Aylwen," she said.

Aran registered no expression, but his eyes didn't leave Timothy for a full minute, and then he bowed slightly. Timothy wasn't sure what to do, so he bowed in return.

"You are welcome here," Aran said. He turned with the same kind of grace Aenya had. Timothy wondered if he'd ever be able to move with that much poise. He doubted it.

"Is he an elf?" Timothy whispered as Aran started to walk down the path ahead of them. "He's a lot different than Donlan."

"That's because he's in the service of the elders," she whispered back. "It's an honored position and his robes signify his status. His greeting makes our entrance to Sídhlin more official. In our country, he'd be like the White House chief of staff."

How does she know this stuff? Timothy figured it wasn't the time to ask.

They walked again for some time, and the forest thinned as the path grew wider. In the distance, Timothy thought he heard laughter, like the sound of children playing. The ground was sloping upward and as they came to a crest, they entered Sídhlin. His jawed dropped open and he couldn't hold back a gasp.

A cluster of the most enormous trees he'd ever seen towered above the forest floor. Each of the trunks must have been forty feet in diameter, with stairways that snaked up and around, far into the highest branches. Determining their exact height was impossible, but the measurement was in hundreds of feet. The stairs reached landings every so often where dwellings nestled against the trunk, held in place by cantilevered braces. Interior lights brightened the diamond-paned windows, which twinkled in the dimness of the forest. Enough light from the sky penetrated the canopy to bathe the forest in a greenish-blue glow.

"It's beautiful," he said.

"This is the oldest part of the forest," Aran said. "There is no other like it in the world."

"I had heard stories from my mother," Aenya said, "but even I am astounded."

Timothy saw something like sadness cross Aran's face. He was peering up into the trees, as if he, too, stood in wonderment. There was little doubt that seeing them inspired awe, no matter how many times you looked at them.

"Over the millennia that our kind has dwelt here, the number of Primal trees has dwindled. These are the last. Most of us live in dwellings on the forest floor," he said. "Come, we still have a little ways to go."

For the second time, Timothy tore his attention away from the spectacular scenery and followed, though he kept straining to look back. He wanted to wander through them, but had to settle for the hope that he'd be allowed to soon.

The path led to a large circular building made of stone. The ivy-covered walls rose straight to the height of two stories, flared outward to form an eave, then curved toward the center in the shape of a dome ending with a pointed cap. There was an opening with no door, and he could see through the building to the forest beyond. Though it was dark inside, he could make out the surface of a polished round table with twelve heavy wooden chairs spaced around it.

He followed the paths around the building with his eyes. Within the trees and set back from the paths that branched off were smaller stone structures of similar design that blended with the forest. They looked like upside-down acorns and as much a part of the background as the foliage. Some had long extensions to one side, built of timber, and covered with thatched roofs.

Aran led them inside the building with the table, and Aenya produced a rolled parchment. He read the document carefully. At one point, he stiffened, his face registering surprise, and his eyes went from the page to Timothy. Then his poise returned just as quickly. He handed the scroll back to Aenya.

"Please remain here. I will return shortly and send word to the elders of your arrival."

"He seems a bit stiff," Timothy said as the elf moved out of earshot.

"Yeah, maybe a little." Aenya smiled.

"What exactly did Donlan put in that letter?"

She started to say something, but then seemed to think better of it. "It has instructions to his nephew to make certain you're taken care of and why. Clearly, Aran understood the importance of it."

Timothy nodded and looked around. The structure was like a meeting hall, and the large polished table dominated the room. Several ornate iron sconces hung on the walls, and a large chandelier with a circle of thick candles was suspended over the center of the table.

"I'm guessing this is where the elders get together."

"Probably," she said. "But very often, meetings are held by the oaks."

"Oak trees?"

"There's an ancient oak where festivities and gatherings are held, especially during the moons."

"You've never been here, how do you know all this?"

"Have you ever been to Broadway in New York?"

"No."

"But you know they do plays there, right?"

"Yes, but—"

"Be patient, you'll learn," she said.

An elf with the appearance of one in his thirties rushed toward the entrance. He was wearing soft leather leggings, a rough-textured linen tunic, and brown boots. Everything here looked medieval but struck Timothy as completely normal, given the surroundings.

As he came into the building, he smiled and held out his hands to both Timothy and Aenya.

"I'm Ailill, Donlan's nephew. Welcome to Sídhlin. I'm honored to be of service."

Timothy stumbled over the pronunciation of his name, which sounded like Al Yil, but he seemed not to notice.

"I'm Timothy."

"Come, my wife, Derval, will prepare rooms for you."

"I hope this doesn't put you to too much trouble," Aenya said.

"Not at all. We have plenty of room and consider this our privilege."

As they followed the cheerful elf, they soon walked clear of the forest and onto a sprawling pasture. "They're preparing the fields for the spring planting. We still do some trade with humans, but we prefer to grow most of our own things."

"Aenya told me that Sídhlin is concealed from humans," Timothy said.

"Oh yes, there are several of the sídhe who live amongst us who keep the forest enchanted."

"What happens if a human enters?" Timothy was worried that they might meet a violent end for trespassing.

Ailill smiled. "They just feel a bit disoriented and find themselves back outside the forest, no harm done. We trade some of our fabrics and jewelry at the local human markets, but that's about it. It's best to keep our distance these days."

Timothy was anxious to understand why, but thought it best to save questions of that sort until he was a little more at home. With every new discovery, he felt a growing sense of impatience to know everything right away.

Rounding a curve in the dirt path, they came to a magnificent cottage nestled in the trees. The main structure was three stories high and built of stone block twice the size of normal brick. The sloped roof of dark slate overhung the walls, creating an eave two feet deep. A single-story addition was attached to the main house, and where the two joined, an enormous chimney rose to a height several feet above the rooftop. Heavy wooden framed windows, again with diamond-pane glass, extended from the front of the cottage, each with their own slate roof. It appeared very English in design from pictures Timothy had seen, so it was apparent that the line between human and elfin architecture was somewhat blurred.

They followed Ailill through an arbor and up a short stone path to a heavy wooden front door, which stood open. Elfin homes seemed to come with wonderful aromas. Both Aenya's and Donlan's cottages had been the same.

Standing in the middle of the room was a woman of Ailill's age. She was dressed in a full-length tunic of the same ivory-colored linen as her husband's shorter one. A thin rope belt circled her waist. The light-colored fabric was in sharp contrast to her dark-brown hair, but her eyes were stunning, like two glistening emeralds that sparkled as a smile crossed her face. Timothy couldn't help the sudden intake of breath as the warmth of her presence reminded him of his mother; he felt an instant affection for her.

"This is Derval," Ailill said.

She stepped forward and embraced Timothy in a way that immediately confirmed him as a member of her family. He had the sudden thought that he was going to enjoy being an elf. She hugged Aenya, too.

"Welcome to our home. I think you'll find it comfortable here."

Timothy was at a loss for words, but managed to summon a nod and a smile.

"We didn't have time to call our son, Oillin, to come meet you, but he'll be here before too long. You both must be hungry."

"Timothy is always hungry," Aenya said before he could respond.

He looked at her with a grimace, but she just mimicked it right back. They all sat at a long table with carvings of leaves and acorns along the edges.

"This is beautiful," Timothy said, running his fingers over the intricate pattern.

"Thank you," Ailill said.

"He is one of the realm's best craftsmen." Derval sounded proud of her husband. "He is often called to do woodwork for the elders."

Afraid that he might wind up saying something stupid, Timothy thought it best to tell them he was new to everything.

"I think you should know, that…well…I became aware that I'm elfin and not human only a few days ago, so I hope you'll be patient with me as I learn."

Derval laid a plate of steaming-hot cakes made from pumpkin and sprinkled with sugar in front of him. She squeezed Timothy's shoulder and said, "We are here to help you in any way we can." Ailill's expression was more serious.

"I don't want to give you cause for alarm, but you must be careful who you speak with for now. Sídhlin is very peaceful, but not everyone who lives here can be trusted. It's sad to think this, but there are some whose loyalty remains with Cadwaladr. They are a minority, but they are here just the same. Until the elders figure out the best way to protect you, I think it would be wise to be careful."

"I know. I've already had some experience with this," Timothy said, looking at each of them. "Thankfully, Aenya has been looking out for me."

"Except for the little potty incident," she said. She kept her eyes on the food she was eating, but he could tell she was enjoying a little amusement at his expense.

He heard someone running outside; then a boy around his age burst into the room.

"Sorry, Mother, I was just playing..." His speech tapered off when he realized there were strangers in the room.

"Ah, Oillin, I'm glad you've come home. We want you to meet Timothy and Aenya. They are friends of Uncle Donlan's and they're going to be staying with us for a time."

Timothy immediately felt defensive. For most of his life, meeting other boys had involved some kind of snickering or something unpleasant, but Oillin walked right up to the table with a big smile and took Timothy's hand. The bad feeling evaporated as quickly as it had come.

"That sounds great," he said. Then he held out his hand to Aenya, which she took in greeting. Timothy sensed he was going to like this boy, except for one thing—he didn't like the look in Oillin's eyes as he met Aenya's gaze.

For an hour or so, as daylight faded to twilight, they shared the events of the past few days. It was the right thing to do, especially in light of what Ailill had said. By offering safe harbor, the family might be taking a risk, and not telling them didn't seem fair. Aenya had almost died trying to help him, and he couldn't allow something like that to happen again, not to a whole family.

"Why don't we show you to your rooms so you can get some rest?" said Derval.

"Thank you," Timothy said. The idea of putting his head down sounded great.

"Come on, Aenya, I'll show you where you'll be sleeping," Oillin said, hopping up from his chair.

"Sure, thanks." As she got up, she threw Timothy a glance as if to say goodnight. A devilish grin played across her face, like she was impressed with Oillin's attentiveness. Timothy wasn't.

Derval held out her hand and guided Timothy up the stairs to a small but cozy room on the third floor. She pulled back the blankets, revealing thick, fluffy bedding that was so inviting he couldn't wait to jump in. She leaned forward and kissed him on the cheek.

"Thank you," he said. "For everything."

"I hope you'll be happy here."

When she left, Timothy pulled off his shirt and jeans and slid under the covers. His head melted into the warm, downy pillow; the bed was as soft as a cloud. For the first time since his mother died, he felt as though he were going to sleep in his own home.

Chapter 18

Aenya sat on the edge of the bed and looked over the forest through the open window. The waxing moon hung above the treetops, casting a silvery glow. Oillin had been very sweet in making sure she had everything she needed, and she'd sensed his reluctance to leave her, but she was grateful for the quiet.

It was hard to believe she was in Ireland. She'd never imagined there would be a reason to come back home. No, this wasn't home; New Hampshire was, now. Her mother's stories had been fascinating, but beyond that, Aenya had felt no urge to investigate them further. That had changed in only a matter of days. Timothy was every reason to take a deeper step among her own people. Still, she felt out of place. She'd been taught fae etiquette, but her self-styled isolation left her feeling unprepared for the reality of living in the woodland realm. Her mother, Donlan and his enclave, and one or two others were all she'd ever experienced on a regular basis. She'd come to despise humans, so living in her cottage and communing with the forest had become her way.

Sídhlin had the largest number of fae creatures of any of the world's realms, and she sensed getting to know them would be important. There was no way of telling what difficulties and challenges Timothy was going to face; it was up to her to be there for him, and that meant inserting herself into the culture. On the other hand, she worried that she might wind up not being useful to him.

She took a deep breath and flew out the window, following the path. Stepping onto the grass, she sniffed the air and caught the scent of oak off to her left. The forest was full of oaks, but the one she sensed was far older and larger than the rest. She knew it would be the sacred one and followed her nose.

She came to a clearing, and a number of sídhe had gathered on the open field in front of a massive tree. A multi-tiered fountain made of stone was in front of it, and water trickled from each bowl to the next lower one. Several of them were dancing and cavorting with a swarm of fireflies, flying in patterns and making shapes and figures against the backdrop of the stars. The golden glow was warm and inviting, and Aenya couldn't help but smile at their childlike play. It was easy to understand why humans thought fairies used pixie dust. But they never got anything quite right, even the ones who still believed in fae fold. Though human misconception did make it easier to move among them.

"Hey there, we see you peeking. Come and join us." One of them flew straight at Aenya and stopped just a few feet from her. "I'm Darina," she said as she pulled Aenya to the fountain, where the rest grouped around her.

"This is Éabha, Gormflaith, Éadaoin, Iúile, and Líle," she said, pointing to each, and in turn, each welcomed Aenya with an embrace. It was more of her kind than she'd ever seen together at one time.

"So what do you like to play?" Éabha looked eager for Aenya's answer. She'd been one being chased by the fireflies.

"Play?" Aenya asked.

"Sure, what games do you like?" Iúile asked.

"I'm afraid...actually, I don't know any," Aenya said, feeling at a loss.

"Oh, then we'll have to teach you some," said Darina.

"Let's go spook some tourists," said Éadaoin.

"No!" they shouted.

"You must forgive Éadaoin, she's a bit mischievous." Iúile said, giving the errant sídhe a frown. Aenya knew from her mother that taunting humans, while not truly evil, was something to be avoided. It was one part of their behavior that humans got right, but it hadn't been practiced much over the past couple of centuries, or so she'd been taught. They were clearly members of the Sǣlie Court.

"Fine," she said, crossing her arms and pouting.

"We saw you come today with Aran and that boy," said Darina, changing the subject.

"That's Timothy," said Aenya, uncertain just how much she should and shouldn't say about him. "He's come from America."

"Is he your brother?"

Aenya laughed. "No, but he only just found out he's an elf."

"Oh, that sounds like fun," said Éadaoin, cheering up. "Let's do some pranks on him."

"No!" they shouted again, including Aenya.

"Ugh! You're so boring." Éadaoin went right back to pouting.

"Do you desire him?" Gormflaith asked in a quiet voice.

"Gormflaith, that's rude, don't you think?" said Iúile.

"I was just asking."

"He's kind of cute, but I'm not sure I'd go so far as to say I… desire him," said Aenya. If only they knew just how complicated the situation was, she thought. "He's still a bit confused about things, and I thought this would be a good place to introduce him to his kind."

"No mother or father or relatives?"

"Just an uncle," she said, "but he's…" Aenya struggled to find the right word. "They're not exactly close."

"There's something important about him, isn't there?" Líle finally spoke.

"Don't mind Líle," said Iúile. "She's the serious one amongst us."

When Aenya didn't answer, the other fairies all turned to her, obviously intrigued.

"The mood of the forest shifted when you arrived," said Líle. "It felt…cautionary."

Aenya suddenly wished she'd stayed in her room. Ailill had warned them not to say too much, but this had to be different. As far as she knew Sǣlie Court sídhe were seldom capable of treachery or deceit, but like Timothy, she was on new ground and was afraid there might be gaps in her understanding. The sídhe were not above prejudice, but their actions would never be deliberately evil; that was the notoriety of Unsǣlie Court sídhe. She thought part of the truth would be better than none.

"Timothy is of Aylwen's line."

All six fairies gasped.

"So the rumors were true, then?" Darina asked. "The story was that Tuathla's son and daughter were sent to the new colonies. Which of them was Timothy's parent?"

"Owein," she said.

"Thank goodness. Because we also heard that the son was one of Cadwaladr's followers and that he'd been exiled."

"That was the uncle I mentioned."

Líle was staring at Aenya intensely. "And what else?"

"The truth is, Seumais, his uncle, tried to kill him, and we believe Cadwaladr was behind it. I'm doing all I can to protect him." Aenya watched Líle to see if that had satisfied her, but judging by the expectant look on her face it hadn't. "I'd rather not go into all the rest just yet."

Líle nodded, apparently willing to let it go for now.

"I'm a little tired," said Aenya. "This has been a very long day. It was wonderful to meet you all."

They took turns hugging Aenya good night, but when she turned to go, Líle put her hand on Aenya's arm.

"When you're ready," she said in a lowered voice, "tell us the rest, and we will gladly help you. I trust your reasons are sound and that he must be protected. Cadwaladr is evil. We will stand for you both."

Aenya felt a wave of emotion. Perhaps coming to Ireland was going to be better than she'd thought.

Chapter 19

Someone had left a change of clothing, only it was like nothing Timothy had ever worn. There was a linen tunic, like the one Ailill had been wearing, a pair of soft tan-colored leggings that were supple and light, and boots that felt more like a second layer of skin.

Downstairs, Derval was alone. She said that Ailill had gone to his workshop and Aenya had been invited to meet with one of the elders. Oillin had tagged along, and that opened a pit in Timothy's stomach.

"Thank you for the clothes," he said, trying his best to hide his concern that her son was...what? Making a move on Aenya?

"We thought it would be best for you to blend in. Aran told us that he would come for you in a little while, too."

"Will Aenya be back to go with me?" Timothy felt embarrassed as soon as the words left his mouth. He didn't want to appear like he needed someone to hold his hand. He was nervous about moving around in their world, but no one needed to know that.

"I suspect the elders will want to meet with you alone."

"What are they like?"

"They're elves of great wisdom and highly respected."

The fact that they were referred to as elders was a bit creepy. Aran appeared almost at the same time Timothy finished breakfast. He bowed as he entered the cottage.

"I have been asked to accompany you to Bardán."

Timothy thanked Derval for the meal, and she gave him an encouraging smile, which did make him feel better.

They moved into the forest beyond the large stone meeting room and onto a different path. They passed several elves, who all nodded with politeness. He wasn't sure if their greetings were because he was a new face or because he was walking with Aran.

"My friend, Aenya, told me that you have a pretty important job here," Timothy said, searching for a way to strike up a conversation.

"I serve at the pleasure of the Elder Council."

"What kind of stuff do you do?"

"I am tasked with keeping the council informed of any new developments in Sídhlin and with helping to keep their functions running smoothly," Aran said with a degree of stiffness. "In short, I do what is necessary and when it is necessary."

Timothy didn't think it was much of answer; more like the kind of excuse he'd give a teacher as to why he hadn't done his homework. It said something without saying anything. Of all the elves he'd met, including his uncle and Scruffy at the airport, Aran gave him a prickly feeling.

"I bet your parents are really proud of you," he said. "Are you married?"

Aran looked as though he'd simply not heard the question. If anything, the side of his jaw was working, like he was grinding his teeth.

"I do not possess a wife."

Timothy decided to avoid any further questions.

"Please." Aran had stopped and raised his arm, indicating a dwelling larger than the meeting hall and made of stone. He motioned for Timothy to enter.

Alone.

It took a minute for his eyes to adjust to the dimness inside. Dark wooden tables, woven rugs, and heavy tapestries decorated the room. One depicted a regal-looking woman cloaked in blue and gold and standing beside a thick tree with one delicate hand placed over her heart, the other grasping the hilt of a sword whose point rested on the ground. Intricate braids of long blond hair swirled to the back of her head while the rest cascaded over her shoulders. Light from several thick candles, wax bubbling over the sides, cut through the gloom but created a hazy atmosphere. A medium-sized fire crackled in a stone hearth. Leather-bound manuscripts and loose pages were piled on every flat surface.

A figure rose from a brocaded chair near the fire. He was tall and dressed in a dark robe that flowed from his shoulders to the floor. His hair was also dark, but long and peppered with grey, just like his short-cropped beard.

The man's eyes bored into Timothy, as if making an appraisal.

"Good morning, I'm Timothy Brennan," he said, desperate to break the silence.

The figure nodded, apparently finished. "I am Bardán, a member of the Elder Council." He pointed to a second chair. "Please, sit."

Bardán's aura of power was intimidating. Timothy understood why Derval would respect someone like him. He wondered if all the elders were so striking.

"I was told you wanted to meet me."

Bardán nodded again. Timothy got the idea that he never spoke until he was ready to say exactly what he wanted.

"I have spoken with Aenya. She was very kind in relating your short history together and enlightening me about you. It seems fortunate that she interceded when she did."

Timothy wasn't sure if Bardán was referring to his suicide attempt or her protecting him from his uncle. He prayed it was the latter and that she hadn't mentioned the former.

"I still don't understand everything that's happened," Timothy said. "A few days ago, I was just a nerdy human teenager."

"Clearly, you were never a human teenager of any kind, but we must help remedy your lack of understanding. In fact, I intend to make it my personal undertaking. I think as you learn more, you will come to appreciate who you are and why it's important that we keep you safe. Donlan and Aenya made a wise decision to bring you here."

"There are so many questions."

"And for as many as we have answers for, you shall have them."

"May I ask one now?"

Bardán opened his hands as an invitation.

"I listened to Donlan and Aenya talking about me, especially the part about being a seventh son. I just don't get why that's worth killing me."

The elder raised his eyebrows, pursed his lips, and let out a slow breath. Timothy thought maybe that was too much for a first question.

"You are the seventh of a seventh. That has happened in our history only one other time that we know of." He stood up. "Come here." He put his hand on Timothy's shoulder and turned him to face the tapestry of the woman. "You're of the bloodline of Aylwen," he said, pointing toward the woman whose eyes seemed to be gazing right at Timothy. "That is your ancestor. She was married to Arthur, the only other seventh of a seventh. Together, they created and ruled Alfheim for nearly a thousand years. You are born of her line with a father of a different house who was also a seventh. The fact is, we don't know what power you may possess, but the culmination of such powerful family blood is extraordinary. Either way, it threatens what some have attempted to achieve over several hundred years. Killing you is an expedient way of not having to find out if you're a threat or not."

"You're talking about Cadwaladr," said Timothy.

Bardán nodded.

"I also heard Donlan say that we're related."

"Yes, through your father's line. Family relations are not always peaceful or sacrosanct, as you well know. I suspect there is a lot more to learn about you. From the unfortunate incident of Aenya's wounds, we know that you have extraordinary healing powers. Did you see her aura as she lay dying?"

At first, Timothy wasn't sure what he meant, but then he remembered how her skin had glowed pink and then cooled, fading to blue.

"Yes, I did."

"That is the power of clairsentience," he said. "The ability to sense things by touch—you see what your hands communicate to your brain. That is a power very few possess."

"Does that mean I can cure anything?"

"In truth, I don't know."

Timothy's thoughts turned dark. If he'd known that when his mother was dying, he could have saved her.

"Yes, you might have saved her," Bardán said. Timothy gasped that the elder had virtually read his mind. "You must learn to live with it. If you let it overshadow your thoughts, it will defeat you in the end. You cannot change the past. Her death was tragic, but you must build on it."

"Just what is Cadwaladr trying to do?"

"He wants to create a new Alfheim, one based on his own vision. It does not include the sídhe or elves who do not support him. He hopes to create an elite society and interfere in the affairs of humans for his own gain."

"That's very original," Timothy said. "He sounds like some kind of elfin Hitler or something."

"The search for power has always been a narrow-minded task, and humans aren't the only creatures susceptible to it." Bardán reclaimed his seat by the fire. "It's curious that you should come to us during the time of the fourth moon, the Alder Moon."

"I'm sorry, sir, I don't know what that means," Timothy said. "It sounds like some kind of druid thing."

Bardán smiled. "I'm sure you will find many similarities between elves and humans. There was a time, long ago, when humans wanted to be more like us. Many of our traditions were absorbed into human culture. The ancient druids, as you mentioned, were very serious about it, not like the pretenders of today. The word druid means 'the knower of oaks.' However, the Alder Moon is associated with the discovery of one's own potential—so it's auspicious that you come at this time."

"Aenya tried to tell me about our relationship with trees."

"Yes, but it's more complicated than that. I mentioned before your gift of clairsentience, but most of us have what's called claricognizance, an ability to sense things like feelings and thoughts that are carried by the energy of the trees. To put it in human terms, it's like knowing if someone is sad or happy just by looking at his or her expression. It's also important for you to know that we depend on trees, especially oaks, for our survival. We need proximity to them every bit as much as we need to breathe air. This is why we live in oak forests. We suffered terribly a few hundred years ago when the British consumed vast forests for building their fleets. We worked very hard to preserve as much as we could."

"It was hard to believe Aenya at first. I mean that there were such things as fairies and elves."

"Why? Humans don't doubt that Neanderthals existed, do they? Humans are too egocentric."

"You seem to keep up with humans pretty well."

"They have a useful expression: keep your friends close and your enemies closer. I don't like to think of them that way, but it's safer. There are normally nine elder council members, and one of them studies human affairs."

"Is that what you do?"

"No. I am honored with two tasks, as we are, at present, short a full council. I am the keeper and protector of the ancient texts you see here, and I am the forest keeper. I make certain our natural home is free of disease and rot, and I see that humans refrain from interfering here. We have the help of the sídhe. They enchant the realm to keep humans from entering."

"Ailill mentioned that yesterday."

"They are a good family. You will learn much from them." Bardán stood. "Well, I have some things I must attend to. You and I will spend more time together. For now, only Ailill's family and the Elder Council must know who you are. It will be safer for you that way."

"It might already be too late," Timothy said, reminding him that Scruffy and his friend had tried to kill him at the airport. "They know I'm here."

"I know, but the fewer of us who know, the better. The elves loyal to Cadwaladr don't reveal themselves. They know we do not tolerate that kind of racism, that they would be expelled from Sídhlin, and it would be a brazen attempt to harm you here."

Bardán led Timothy to the door. He felt the elder was a man he could trust. As the door closed behind him, Timothy's heart leaped at the sight of Aenya leaning against the base of a tree, waiting for him. He looked quickly in each direction; there was no sign of Oillin.

"I missed you this morning," he said, trying not to sound too needy.

"Aran came by really early to tell me that Bardán wanted to meet me. I remember my mother talking about him, and he actually remembered both my parents."

"Where's Oillin?"

"He went to see some of his friends. It appears everyone is preparing for a wedding tonight. That should be fun."

The image of Oillin dancing with Aenya didn't sit well with Timothy. Dancing simply wasn't his thing, and he regretted never taking the time to learn how. His lack of talent would leave an opening for Oillin.

"What do you think of him?" Timothy asked casually.

"He's cute," she said. It wasn't the answer he was hoping for.

"Cute like how? Like puppy dog cute or…"

"He strikes me as a good elf. I think you should make friends with him," Aenya said.

"We'll see." Timothy's instinct was to like him, but he just wasn't happy with what Oillin probably had in mind. His personality reminded Timothy of Omar. "I don't suppose there would be a telephone somewhere in Sídhlin," he asked.

"I doubt it."

"What is it with you—I mean, what do *we* have against modern conveniences?"

Aenya glanced at him. "What do we need them for?"

"Things like TV and electricity and cell phones...it helps keep everything connected."

"Maybe a little disconnect is healthier."

Timothy grunted. He still wished he could pick up a phone to call Omar.

Chapter 20

TIMOTHY WAS BEGINNING TO THINK Derval was a frustrated tailor. She'd laid out a tunic in shimmering black that fastened in front with thick golden loops and matching gold cloth buttons. The fabric was thin but warm and felt like silk. It brushed the tops of soft black boots. Two slits ran down the sides of the tunic to enable walking, and underneath was a pair of black linen slacks. As Timothy finished buttoning, Oillin came in with a length of golden rope. He was wearing an almost identical tunic, but in deep crimson.

"Mother asked me to bring this to you," he said. Without a word, he circled the rope around Timothy's waist and tied an intricate knot. "You're all set. I'll meet you downstairs." Timothy looked at the knot and wondered if he'd ever be able to master it.

He walked around the room to get a feel for the clothing. He'd spent most of his life in jeans and tee shirts. This was definitely a change and way outside his comfort zone. At home, getting dressed up was unthinkable.

Everyone was waiting in the kitchen near the door, but Aenya stood apart. Her beauty forced a hitch in his breath. She was wearing an ivory-colored shift in coarse linen with a powder-blue sash around her waist. It matched the color of her eyes.

Soft white fur cuffed the sleeves and a cloak of the same blue color closed across her chest with an intricately woven golden broach. He thought he was seeing her in true sídhe form for the first time, though she looked more like royalty. When she smiled, he knew he wanted to be the only one she would ever look at like that. If dressing this way met her approval, then bring on the tailors.

"You look very handsome," she said.

"Thank you, you too," he said. "I mean, you look beautiful, not handsome, is what I meant." He felt his ears start to burn, again.

She laughed.

"We should be going," Derval said.

It was twilight as they left the cottage, following yet another new path. The walk was short; the trees gave way to a grassy field that encircled a great oak tree. Its trunk was at least ten feet thick. Gnarled branches spread in all directions. A large stone fountain stood in front of the tree, and water cascaded over several tiers to collect in a low wide pool.

Elves and sídhe gathered from all directions. Within minutes, several hundred had assembled around the fountain. A harp began to play soft music; the notes were mournful but beautiful, mimicking the natural rhythms of the trees and the breeze. Most of the elves and fairies stood silently, waiting for the wedding party.

The nearly full moon was just breaking above the trees, blending with the growing darkness, casting a silvery halo. Even from the back of the crowd, Timothy could see the moon reflected in the water of the fountain; the ripples projected a flickering light against the trees.

From behind, a long procession of elves carried heavy-looking two-foot candles. An old elf with a dense white beard led a young couple dressed in matching white tunics. The bride was wearing a choker similar to his mother's. An image of how beautiful Aenya would look wearing it popped into his head. It also made him wonder what his mother had looked like on her day. He had attended one wedding with her, when Mary, from the restaurant, had invited them to her daughter's ceremony. He thought how it must have been strange for his mother to watch a human wedding when her own would have been so very different. He wondered if she had felt as out of place then as he did standing next to Aenya now, watching a procession of elves emerge from the trees.

The couple held hands as they neared the fountain. The candle-bearers formed a wide circle around the wedding party, knelt on the ground, and forced the spike at the base of each candle into the earth.

The old man turned to face the gathering and drew a silver goblet from within his robes. Then he raised his arms in the air.

"This water has been blessed with the light of the Alder Moon. May its reflection ever shine in the hearts of Cavan and Mairin. May their union be as strong as the branches of our hallowed oak." The man plunged the goblet into the pool of water and pulled it back up. The droplets of water from his arm glistened. He handed the cup to Mairin, and Cavan closed his hands over hers. She drank first and then he followed; together they poured the rest of the water to the ground between them. As everyone laughed and cheered the couple embraced and kissed.

"They get right to the point, huh?" Timothy whispered to Aenya. Mary's daughter's wedding had gone on for hours. In the end, they were just as married but without all the endless prayers and speeches. Aenya laughed, and they watched the throng move inside the ring of candles to congratulate the couple.

More candles lit the tables covered with food and drink, the sound of pipes joined the harps, and couples began to dance in circles around the candles still planted in the ground. Aenya took Timothy by the arm to one of the tables and put a cup in his hands.

"Here, try this, but don't drink too much."

He sniffed at the pale liquid; it smelled like flowers. It coated his tongue and burst with flavors of apple and pear.

Aenya was about to say something, but Oillin came bounding up, grabbed her hand, and dragged her into the middle of the circle. They faced one another, joined both hands, and began to dance. His blatant attention was annoying. Seeing them together felt like a stab in the gut. Timothy turned away; he really didn't want to watch.

He wandered to the tables and sampled the meats and cheeses. He'd already gotten used to the fact that elves were excellent cooks, and they had outdone themselves for the wedding. Every dish he tried was better than the last—and the breads were amazing, steaming with a buttery flavor.

Following Bardán and Ailill's advice to keep a low profile, he tried his best to avoid eye contact, yet he noticed several watching him as if trying to figure out who he was. He smiled a lot, nodded, and kept moving. He wondered if he was being a little too paranoid, though having been a target made it difficult not to look at everyone with suspicion.

Timothy was facing the edge of the forest when the tree branches started blowing about as if caught in a gale-force wind. He expected to see things flying from the tables, but nothing moved except the branches. There was no wind. Seeing but not feeling what his senses wanted him to was disorienting. Everyone grew quiet, and the music stopped. The ground shook, and low thunder rolled through the clearing.

Timothy heard horses snorting from within the trees. A second later, fifty mounted elves burst onto the field. They were armed with bows. A rugged-looking man on a massive dark horse passed through them and into the open.

"Cadwaladr!" The name passed through the crowd in harsh whispers. Aenya moved instantly to Timothy's side.

"Don't be afraid," she said. "He wouldn't dare try to harm you here."

His thoughts raced to catch up.

"I'm not afraid," he said.

One of the riders stopped alongside Cadwaladr, pushed his hood back, and pointed straight down at Timothy. He gasped as he recognized his uncle sitting high on the horse.

Cadwaladr, clothed in dark leather and a heavy cloak, swung his leg back and dismounted, stepping onto the grass. The powerfully built elf walked toward Timothy. Aenya made a move to step in front, but Cadwaladr held up his hand.

"Do not be so presumptuous," Cadwaladr said with a hint of anger. "After all, you must agree this is a family reunion. Isn't that right, Seumais?"

His uncle grinned and laughed.

"I am your cousin, Cadwaladr, Earl of McCrohan, and you," he said, "must be the elusive Timothy Brennan."

"I wouldn't be so elusive if you weren't trying to kill me."

"Kill you?" Cadwaladr looked dismayed. "Why on earth should I wish to do that?"

"I don't know, maybe for the same reasons you had my mother murdered." Cadwaladr's eyes narrowed. Those closest to Timothy shrank back. They clearly knew who the warlord was, but not the boy who'd spoken so rashly. "My lord, this is not the best time and place." Cavan stepped forward. "It is our wedding celebration, and I would beg you to withdraw with your men."

Cadwaladr's eyes bored into Timothy's. "I understand that you possess certain talents. Is this true?"

"What if I did?"

Cadwaladr turned to his men and pointed at Cavan. A mounted elf raised a bow, nocked an arrow, and shot it straight into Cavan's chest with a sickening thud. He collapsed to the ground amid the screaming. Bright red blood blossomed across the chest of his white tunic. Mairin burst from the group, throwing herself to the ground beside her husband. He started to convulse as he grasped at the shaft of the arrow.

A group of elves surged toward Cadwaladr, but his heavily armed guard raised their bows and aimed at the wedding guests.

Timothy could see the cold fury on their faces, made all the more impotent in the face of sudden death. A small group dashed into the forest.

"For his sake, I hope you do." Cadwaladr was looking at the dying groom and spoke with about as much concern as if he'd merely swatted a fly. "Elfshot, in certain concentrations, can bring death quite quickly."

Timothy rushed to Cavan's side. He was sure the poison coursing through his body was the real threat, more than the arrow sticking out of his chest. Cavan's eyes were already glazing over. Mairin tried to push him away, but Aenya held her from behind.

What if the physical trauma of the arrow, in addition to the poison, was more than he could handle? Timothy set his hands on the groom's chest around the shaft of the arrow and closed his eyes. A vision formed as easily as flipping a switch. He felt the now-familiar pulse start to flow, and all sound was gone but for his own breathing and the rush of blood in his ears.

In the vision, Mairin stood a short distance away in a forest clearing and thick clouds blocked out the sun. She wrung her hands, and fear distorted her face.

"Cavan, in a minute I will need you to stand with me, you can do this. Mairin is waiting for you, she needs you." Once again, he wasn't sure if he was speaking out loud or just in the vision. A pinkish glow around Cavan's face and neck phased from a dark shade to a lighter one and back again. It was rhythmic, like a heartbeat. The color was much darker than it had been with Aenya. The poison had to be far more potent. He closed his fingers around the shaft and pulled gently, feeling it loosen. When the tip came clear, he tossed it aside and pressed his hand over the wound, tightening his grip on the man's shoulder. He closed his eyes again. Cavan's breathing started to ease from a rapid pant to a shallow intake of air. Still, the balance of life had not yet tipped in favor of survival. Timothy knew the bridegroom would die if he let up for even a second. In the vision, he reached down and tried to lift Cavan. He was heavy, but he struggled to his knees and gave Timothy a questioning stare, as if to ask whether he was really going to make it. He staggered to his feet, leaning against Timothy, trying to steady himself. Mairin swept him into her arms.

Timothy opened his eyes to see the pink fading. It occurred to him that in the vision, Cavan had managed to stand even though, in reality, he was still on his back. He wondered for the first time if the visions were actually of the future. There was so much about what he was doing that he didn't yet understand. He felt Cavan's forehead. It was cooling, and his skin was turning the translucent blue Aenya's had when she turned back from death. Timothy was still afraid to let go. He started to feel the same weariness and remembered Aenya's warning, but this time it felt more manageable. The next time he opened his eyes, Cavan's flesh was normal, pale, but the aura was gone. Timothy let go and fell to one side. Aenya helped him up.

"Cavan, Cavan…" Mairin called between sobs.

Timothy watched for a sign that he was past the danger point. Cavan opened his eyes and saw his wife. A weak smile played across his lips. There was a collective gasp among the guests as she helped him to a sitting position.

With Aenya's help, Timothy turned to face Cadwaladr.

"Are you satisfied with your little demonstration?" Timothy had never witnessed anything so coldblooded as what Cadwaladr had ordered. He wanted to throw himself at his cousin and choke the life out of him.

The sound of a horn blew in the forest. Seumais brought Cadwaladr's horse closer.

"My lord, we must go."

Cadwaladr glared at Timothy, then turned and swung up into the saddle.

"That was impressive, boy. We will talk again." He pulled his horse around, and they galloped into the trees just seconds before a detachment of Sídhlin's elfin army arrived from the other side of the forest.

Mairin pulled Timothy into a hug. "Thank you," she whispered. "Thank you."

With the threat gone, several elves rushed forward to help Cavan off the field. Most everyone else had moved farther away, their faces contorted with shock and fear.

"Are you okay?" Aenya asked. She rubbed Timothy's back with her hand.

"A little shaky, but I think my body is starting to get used to this." He knew as the words left his mouth that it was a total lie. The power of what he had just done washed over him, especially knowing that it might easily have gone the other way. He started to feel a pressure in his chest, but he forced it back down.

"So much for keeping a low profile," she said, trying to lighten the mood.

"Ya think?"

Oillin moved toward them, but without his usual happy-go-lucky expression. Timothy could tell he wanted to say something, but, like most, he was speechless.

"I guess the party's over, huh?" Timothy said.

Aenya laughed. "Ya think?" The laugh was more a sound of relief than amusement.

A group of armed elves moved around them, and the one in charge stepped forward.

"We will see you safely to your dwelling."

Timothy nodded his thanks.

As they turned to go, Aenya stopped, lifting her face to a breeze that came from the trees. She sniffed the air and then turned to Timothy with a smile.

"She comes."

"Who…who's coming?" He wasn't sure he wanted anyone else showing up.

"Your grandmother, she's on the way."

Chapter 21

CADWALADR STORMED THROUGH THE GREAT hall into his private library, tossing his riding gloves violently to the floor. Seumais followed on his heels.

"I thought you told me the boy was no threat, that he was insignificant," Cadwaladr shouted.

"My lord, in all these years, he never showed signs of being anything but a runt. I didn't know about his father's lineage or that he was related to you. That's all new to me."

"Well, he didn't look so much like a runt tonight, did he?"

Seumais had forgotten what Cadwaladr could be like in a rage. He was terrifying, volatile, and lethal. The intervening centuries had dimmed his memory of the ruthless battles they'd fought. Seumais had become soft on beer and women, but that would change quickly now that he'd returned to the fold. He was still reeling from Timothy's demonstration. He would not have believed it possible had he not witnessed it. He should have poisoned the brat at the same time he had his sister. If he survived the next few minutes, he vowed never to make that mistake again.

"What are your orders, my lord?"

Cadwaladr sloshed a wine glass full of dark amber liquid and took a long slow gulp. He sat behind his massive wooden desk and leaned back, apparently deep in thought. Seumais didn't move and dared not take a seat for fear of appearing too familiar, especially with his lord in such a foul mood.

"You failed to kill him before he left his country. Now, he'll be fully protected in the forest. Send word inside that I want him watched every minute and at the first opportunity, he's to be eliminated. We'll deal with Tuathla next." Cadwaladr laughed. "It might actually work in our favor for the people of Sídhlin to have seen the boy. Now they'll be twice as demoralized when both are dead. They'll be ripe for submission."

"I think you're right," said Seumais, wanting to foster the return of Cadwaladr's good mood.

"It's time to assemble our allies. Send word to Poland and Russia. I want a thousand elves here within the month. This time, Sídhlin will crumble."

"I'll get the messages ready at once," Seumais said. He hurried from the room before Cadwaladr decided to do something worse.

Seumais was just as furious in his own way. Owein had never told him about the boy's father. The elf had appeared much older than his sister, and Seumais remembered thinking it was odd that after almost four hundred years, she had finally decided to get married, and to someone she'd practically just met. Then she'd convinced him that Timothy was nothing special. In fact, she'd played up his special needs. Seumais fumed, thinking of her duplicity.

He'd spent the greater part of his life living in a country he despised all because his own parents had taken a stand against the elf who was destined to become the greatest leader of their race. It would forever be an embarrassment that his sister and mother were Sídhe. To rid the world of them would leave Cadwaladr virtually unopposed. The sídhe had thwarted the rise to power that the elves deserved. It was unthinkable that humans dominated the planet, but until Cadwaladr was successful, humans would just keep taking more and more land and destroying trees. The elves had to cleanse their own kind before they tackled the larger question of putting down the humans. They had come so close in the last war.

Cadwaladr was right. Tuathla's time was ending. Without her to keep the elfin resistance intact, they would roll right over the residents of Sídhlin. Timothy was just a slight wrinkle in their plans. When she died and they killed him, the elfin world would finally realize that Cadwaladr was a leader against whom opposition was futile.

Seumais smiled in the dark as he strode through the halls to the computer center. The time spent in exile was worth it now that it meant he was going to be at the front wave of the change in history.

One elf occupied the brightly lit center and seemed absorbed in surfing the Internet. He sat up as Seumais entered. Cadwaladr hated technology as much as any elf. In fact, all email messages had to be transcribed onto parchment before he would read them, but he was smart enough to realize the advantage instant communications gave him over other elves.

"Cadwaladr wants a summons issued to his allies in Russia and Poland, immediately. I think we might see what our Welsh brethren are up to as well. He wants a commitment of a thousand within the month."

"Right away," said the tech.

Seumais left the room as quickly as he'd arrived. His other order was one he'd see to personally, and it would involve the slight risk of entering Sídhlin quietly to deliver it. *Your days are numbered, Timothy.*

Chapter 22

Timothy's head pounded, and it pulled him out of a deep sleep. He wondered if doing the healing thing drained him in some vital way, that maybe someday he'd run out of whatever it was he had. He closed his eyes and put his hands against his temples, trying to send a pulse through his own head. Nothing happened. So, curing deadly arrow wounds was a piece of cake, but headaches, not so much.

He smelled breakfast cooking downstairs. Rising as fast as his head would allow, he dressed, thinking about how his grandmother, a women he hadn't even stopped to consider was still alive, was on her way. Aenya knew this just from sniffing the air. Apparently, that was another sídhe talent.

The minute he stepped into the main room, Ailill and Oillin stood from the table. Derval put her ladle down and turned toward him, clasping her hands in front of her and lowering her eyes. Aenya remained seated and gave a barely perceptible shrug. The corner of her mouth twisted upwards as if to say, "I have no idea what's up with that."

"Good morning," Timothy said, moving towards Aenya. Ailill stepped away from his chair at the head of the table and motioned for Timothy to take his place.

"That's your seat, I'll just sit here," Timothy said, pulling out a chair next to Aenya.

Ailill looked lost and glanced at Derval, who shrugged, like Aenya, and he sat back in his seat.

"Everyone seems a little uptight this morning," Timothy said. "Did I do anything wrong?"

"Wrong?" Oillin asked. "You've got the whole realm in a twist. You performed a miracle and you ask if you did something wrong?"

"Oillin! Don't be disrespectful," Derval said. Her harsh tone registered just above a whisper. Oillin scooped a wooden spoonful of warm oats and shoveled them into his mouth.

"Bardán sent a note this morning. He'd like to see you, if you are willing," Ailill said.

"I thought he might," Timothy said. Derval placed a steaming plate of eggs and bacon in front of him. "Is there any news of Cavan? Is he okay?"

"He's resting, but his actual wound is fully healed. They said there's hardly a trace of it."

"I was up and flying the day after Timothy healed me. I think the concentration of poison was much stronger on the arrow that wounded Cavan," said Aenya.

"His aura was much darker, too."

"What's that?" Oillin asked.

"It's sort of a..." Timothy wasn't sure how to describe it. "It's just something I see when someone is hurt, I guess."

Everyone returned to eating, but the silence wasn't comfortable. It was hard to pinpoint, but the room's energy had changed.

Was it fear? These people were becoming like family; to think they might be afraid made Timothy feel horrible. Yesterday everyone had been bright and talkative; now no one would look him in the eye. That was normal back home, but what if healing Cavan made him an outsider again? Timothy didn't think he could bear that.

"Did Aenya mention that my grandmother is coming?"

"Aran sent word that her personal messenger delivered the official notice last night that she is on the way," Derval said.

"Have you all met her? What is she like?"

"Many of us have seen her, but usually from afar," she said. "Mostly we know of her deeds."

"Like?"

"Bardán would be the best person to tell you about them," said Ailill.

"I guess I should be on my way over there then," Timothy said. "Aenya, can I talk to you?" As he stood, everyone except Aenya hurried to their feet. Clearly, she wasn't affected by whatever everyone else was.

As soon as they were outside, he lowered his voice and asked what was going on. A small group of armed elves, like those from the night before, stood a short distance away. They took a step forward, but Aenya held up her hand.

"Nothing, Timothy," she said. "They're just trying to adjust to the reality of what they witnessed. It's one thing to hear from me what you've done, but it's quite another to experience it."

"I seem to be making them uncomfortable. I don't want them to feel that way."

"They're not uncomfortable with you," she said. "I think it has more to do with a better understanding of their responsibility. It became clear last night that you need protection. In a way, Cadwaladr did us a favor. His threat is out in the open."

"I don't know," he said. "And another thing, how is it that my grandmother is suddenly coming here? We've been in the country two days. How could she have known we were here?"

"Have you learned nothing? I bet she knew you were here by the time we landed on top of the train."

"When do you think she'll get here?"

"By tonight."

"So soon?"

The idea of a living grandmother was still new. It scared him to realize that he didn't know how to feel about it. He was going to meet a member of his family and, except for his mother, all he had to compare that with was a family member he hated. Why had she never bothered to find him and his mother, for that matter? Then a horrifying thought took shape. What if she was more like Seumais? He had to have gotten his rotten streak from somewhere. Just because his grandmother and his uncle had been on opposite sides didn't mean she'd be the same kind of loving person his mother had been. And what if she found out about his jump from the bridge? She'd know what a miserable failure he was back home. Forget that he'd healed a couple of people. When push came to shove, he'd tried to off himself. Would she find that pathetic or be the kind of grandmother who would show sympathy or concern?

Aenya circled her fingers around Timothy's wrist and zapped his anxiety.

"Have you noticed something?" Aenya asked.

"I've noticed too many things lately."

"That's true, but I don't think you've realized that you haven't ticked once since we fled your uncle's house."

Except for that brief instant of pressure after Cadwaladr had left, she was right. Before, with any kind of stress, he would have been ticking himself into jello.

"Let's hope I don't start again with my grandmother."

"Don't worry about her, I think this reunion will be one you enjoy."

She nodded to the escort, then raised her hand to Timothy in a gesture of goodbye. He reached for her hand. "Wait. Are they going to accompany me everywhere now?" He tilted his head toward the armed elves.

She nodded. "For your protection," she said, then left.

He didn't love the idea of being accompanied everywhere by armed elves. If anything, it drew even more attention. He would have preferred just to have Aenya come with him alone. Besides, he was starting to get the feeling he would know if something wasn't right anyway.

The few elves they passed stepped aside; every one of them gave a nod and turned their eyes downward, just as Derval had done. He hoped it wasn't because they saw him as some kind of freak.

Bardán was waiting by the fire.

"Morning," Timothy said.

He stood as Timothy closed the door, walked toward the fireplace, and sat right down. If there was a protocol to be observed in the presence of an elder, Bardán would let him know. The elder opened his mouth to speak, but Timothy beat him to it.

"I need to know some things."

He drew a deep breath. "I think so, too." Timothy was ready to start, but Bardán held up his hand for silence. "I have lived for more than eight hundred years, but last night was beyond anything I've encountered. Your abilities are far more powerful than I imagined."

"I remember the look on Donlan's face after he saw me heal Aenya. You look the same way right now, but the truth is, it doesn't seem so miraculous. I mean, you've lived all your life knowing the sídhe can fly, they cast enchantments, virtually talk to trees, stuff that would make a normal human freak out. So, how can you see what I've done as anything out of the ordinary? I just close my eyes and concentrate a little. I see the healing in a vision, and I feel the pulse passing from my body, but there isn't much more to it."

"Which is an extraordinary understatement. As you say, we have all these things and more, as you will learn, but to bring someone back from certain death?"

It was hard to admit, especially to himself, that Bardán was probably right. Timothy had never been anything special, so after a lifetime of feeling useless, it was tough to accept that he had a superpower.

"I need to know about my grandmother, and I certainly need to know more about Cadwaladr."

"I know."

"So what's the deal with him?"

Bardán shifted in his chair and stared into the fire. "King Henry II of England invaded Ireland in 1171, mostly to keep the Normans, who'd already invaded, from gaining too much power. He wanted to keep the kingdom for himself and his sons. Cadwaladr's father, Ruarc, bartered his services to Henry in return for a title and vast estates. He became the earl of McCrohan. By those days, the idea of elves had already passed into myth. Cadwaladr, who was born in the early 1400s, grew up enjoying considerable power. When his father passed away in the late 1600s, he embarked on a ruthless campaign to conquer Ireland for himself. He raised a sizable army of elves. It was his intention to create a new Alfheim with both elves and humans as his subjects."

"So what stopped him?" Timothy asked.

"Your grandparents," Bardán said.

"How?"

"They united Sídhlin, a large group from northern England and France, and confronted Cadwaladr. Fae from all around joined in the fight. None of us wanted to wage war, least of all with humans, not even the sídhe. If any of us had suffered persecution by humans, it was them. But even they stood their ground against Cadwaladr." Bardán smiled. "If you think an army of elves might be powerful, you have no idea what an army of sídhe can be like."

Timothy thought of how Aenya had dispatched the elves in the forest that night.

"Did they go to war?"

"Unfortunately, yes. There were several battles. Your grandfather was seriously wounded. He didn't die for some time, but he was never the same. Eventually, outnumbered, Cadwaladr ceased fighting, but he merely changed tactics. His hatred of the sídhe grew to an obsession. For several hundred years now, he's hunted them down and killed them."

"Why don't you arrest him, especially after what he did last night?"

"There were attempts after the war, but they led to further bloodshed."

"He has to be stopped." The image of his mother, helpless on the hospital bed, was more than enough incentive to press the issue.

"Timothy, I know this might not make sense to you, but you must remember that, at our core, we are a peaceful people. For us, the idea of warfare is detestable. That conflict was the last we fought."

"But in the meantime, he gets his way, murdering fae creatures like my mother with no consequence. I assume, since he just popped in last night to ruin Cavan's wedding, that he lives nearby?"

"Yes, some miles to the north and east. He lives in a moderate-sized human castle that was built by the Normans."

"Figures," Timothy said. "Is that why my grandmother doesn't live here in Sídhlin?"

"Yes."

"Is she afraid of him?"

"Your grandmother fears nothing. She has her own lands and chooses to remain there because she doesn't wish to put our people in harm's way. She knows well that if she were here, Cadwaladr would stop at nothing to kill her."

"You know her?"

"Of course. I've had the honor of knowing Tuathla my entire life."

"You must have fought those wars as well."

"Yes, the memories are horrific, even after centuries."

"If my grandmother is of Aylwen's line, why isn't she considered the queen?"

Bardán stroked his beard. "She's an informal queen. It was her wish not to serve in an official capacity. I think she felt she could accomplish more by guiding us from afar. To step forward as queen would have created tension between us and Cadwaladr."

"When I overheard Aenya and Donlan talking, I realized that if I'm the seventh son of my father, I have six other brothers somewhere."

"Indeed."

"Where are they?"

"I don't know. I understand you have a book dealing with your father's family. Perhaps we might look at it together and see what has become of them all. I can also ask the other elders what they may know of them."

"Any chance they're aligned with Cadwaladr, like my uncle?"

"It is possible."

Timothy got up from the chair to look at the tapestry of Aylwen again. On the plus side, he was part of something big, a descendent of a queen. On the negative side, things were getting serious. Life at school didn't seem so horrible anymore. Derek Hollister was nothing more than a cartoon creep next to Cadwaladr. The school bully might want to beat him up, but the big elf wanted to annihilate him and his whole family.

"So what now?" Timothy asked. "You and half the elfin population of Sídhlin know I can fix people just by touching them. What am I supposed to do?"

"That's not easy to answer," he said. "I don't believe the path you are supposed to take is clear. Hopefully, we will benefit from your grandmother's wisdom."

"In other words, take it one day at a time?"

"Something like that," Bardán said. "There are many things for you to learn and understand. As you do, it will become clearer."

Timothy was sure Bardán harbored some very specific ideas, but wasn't ready to share them.

"You know the guy who pointed me out to Cadwaladr was my uncle, right?"

"Yes. I know him," he answered in a soft voice.

"I hate him. I have no doubt he's the one who killed my mother, his own sister. I know he was expelled from here and that he probably turned on her in the end because it was what Cadwaladr wanted."

Bardán turned Timothy to face him, putting both hands on his shoulders. "I knew your uncle and your mother before they left the country. I also believe what you think. I was against your mother going with him, but it was also for her protection. Everyone felt that banishment from Sídhlin would end his treachery." He closed his eyes as if trying to summon the nerve to keep going. "Timothy, on the day of the last battle, he and I crossed swords, but the fighting was fierce. Our engagement broke off, and as I fought another, I saw him charge your grandfather's position. It was your uncle who stabbed his own father in the back."

Chapter 23

TIMOTHY REELED AS HE LEFT Bardán's cottage. His hatred of Seumais hit the stratosphere. He pounded his fists onto his thighs, and his growl sent a flock of birds into the trees. Slender branches of the nearby shrubbery fell away from him as if some invisible giant had just tumbled through the brush. He was glad that Aenya wasn't there like last time; he didn't want her to see him this way. His constant escort was missing, also. He was thankful for the opportunity to slip away quietly for a while.

He stepped off the pathway and ventured deeper into the trees. Timothy knew he needed to curb his anger and not let the wave of emotion carry him into doing something dangerous. His uncle needed punishing. Cadwaladr needed something even worse; after all, it was doubtful that Seumais would have killed Owein, except that it was part of Cadwaladr's larger plan.

No! Timothy sensed that was too little. He couldn't allow his uncle to hide behind the excuse that he'd been put up to murder. Seumais had made a decision, one of the most despicable kind. He betrayed family. He killed family. His racism had blinded him to love and loyalty. It was a disease that needed radical surgery. Timothy thought of the expression *cure the disease, kill the patient.* He was willing to be the scalpel. This is what he'd come to Ireland for.

But if I kill Seumais, what would that make me? He gripped the sides of a birch tree with both hands and rested his forehead against the bark. He was no history major but he knew that violence always led to more, with unending finger-pointing followed by more death. Revenge itself was a disease. Was one preferable to another? He felt out of his depth trying to figure it out. Only one thing was clear: he had to deal with Seumais and Cadwaladr.

By the time he returned to the cottage, Derval was alone by the hearth, making bread. He didn't stop to ask where everyone else was; he simply excused himself and went up to his room.

He puzzled once more how his uncle and mother could possibly be related. What scared him was that whatever genetic makeup was in his uncle was also in him. Was it possible he could turn as loathsome as Seumais? And Cadwaladr, yet another evil relation. What other dark secrets lurked in his family's history? Timothy wondered if all family trees had such diseased branches.

Timothy woke to Aenya gently shaking his shoulder. He had drifted off, exhausted from the anxiety caused by his meeting with Bardán.

"Come on, we must hurry to the forest," she said.

"Why, what's happening?" He tried to shake off the drowsiness. It was late afternoon, judging by the dim light outside the window. "Have I slept the whole day?"

"You needed it. Your grandmother is nearing the forest, and if you want to see, we need to go."

He followed her outside, and naturally, his entourage was waiting. He hoped he hadn't caused them too much worry for the time it had taken them to realize he'd returned safely to Ailill's cottage. They hurried deep into the forest and onto a path that took them to the Primal trees. The sunlight faded more the farther they went, replaced by the liquid blue that seemed to be the only color to penetrate the thick filter of the enormous tree branches. It reminded him of the murky depths of the ocean he'd seen in movies. But the fireflies were there, hovering around the trees, glistening.

The path crested the top of a hill that sloped to the foot of the Primals. A latticework bridge spanned the valley and ended on the face of the hill opposite theirs.

"Look," Aenya said, pointing to the far side.

At first, Timothy saw nothing but a glow, like the shine of a dim flashlight in the darkness. Then a pair of white horses stepped from the trees and onto the planks of the bridge. The sound took a second to reach his ears. More followed; then a single rider trailed by, an equal number of attendants on horseback behind.

"Is that her?" he asked. "In the middle, is that my grandmother?"

"Yes," said Aenya.

If ever there was a queen, he was seeing one then. She was a vision in white, and her horse was white. She gleamed. If Seumais and Cadwaladr were the dark side of his family, then he was witnessing the other. She was too far away to see her features clearly, but he could see how regally she sat in the saddle. He felt a sparkle of pride that she was family.

At the near end of the bridge, the procession turned right and into the underbrush, moving down the slope as if the forest were swallowing them from view.

"Should we follow them?"

"No, we must get ready for the feast. Everyone will be celebrating her return."

Aenya moved off, but Timothy stood looking into the trees. They were so big and he felt so small, yet he didn't want to leave. He'd now spent maybe ten or fifteen minutes in that part of the forest, but the sense he belonged there was consuming. He felt a connection, like if he put his hands against the trunk of one of the Primal trees, it would talk to him. He wanted to say this to Aenya, but she was beckoning him to catch up. He tore himself away.

The gathering was to take place on the same field as the wedding, but this time there were children. The girls were especially excited to see Tuathla, the boys less so.

"Do I really have to kiss her hand?" one boy complained.

"If you're lucky enough to meet her, you will do so without question, do you understand?" The mother was stern, and Timothy could sense the boy bridling.

"Many of the elves have never actually seen your grandmother, they only know her stories from the wars and her heroism against Cadwaladr, me included," said Aenya.

When they reached the outer circle, Timothy spotted Bardán and waved. He moved toward them, and Timothy's escort slipped away.

"We'll see each other later," Ailill said. He nodded his greeting to Bardán, then moved into the crowd with Oillin and Derval.

"This is a propitious occasion," said Bardán. He kissed Aenya on the cheek. "I think we should remain back here for the time being."

"Why?" Timothy asked. "Won't I be able to meet my grandmother?"

"Of course, but that will come later. Her duty to our people must come before anything personal. Many have waited their entire lives for this occasion."

"I guess I can say the same for myself," he said. "Except I didn't know it."

A single horn blew a long, trembling note. They were standing just high enough on the slope that they could see an opening in the crowd. A procession passed out of the forest and onto the field near the oak. Timothy was closer to his grandmother than before by quite a distance, but was still unable to see her clearly. One thing he did notice was that each of her escorts, though elegantly dressed in white as she was, carried a bow, had a quiver full of arrows slung over one shoulder, and had a sword strapped to the waist. This wasn't merely an honor guard.

She sat on a large wooden chair. The armrests and capping looked golden, but it was hard to be certain in the moonlight. Soft harp music began to play, and elves made their way forward to offer their greetings to the unofficial queen. Timothy watched closely as she spoke to all, frequently patting an eager child on the head. As they moved past her, they regrouped at the tables, once more laden with food and cheeses and breads.

There was no dancing, but the mood was festive. Everyone seemed to look at her arrival as a way to forget the events of the previous night.

Aenya took Timothy's hand and squeezed it, then moved off. He watched her weave through the elves to the harpist. The musician continued to work the strings with her fingers as Aenya leaned over and said something. The harpist turned to an elf next to her, holding his pipes as if ready to play, and nodded. The music stopped for a beat and then both began to play. As before, the notes were mournful, but beautiful. Aenya stepped a few feet from the musicians and began to sing.

Ere silver tassels of the moon,
shining bright upon the gloom,
fade forever from our eyes
to live no more, nor be reprised,
the halls of Alfheim shall be no more
and pass from legend into lore.

"What is she singing?" he asked, turning to Bardán.

Without taking his eyes off her, he said, "She is singing 'Aylwen's Lament' in honor of your grandmother."

"What is that?"

"It's a ballad that tells of Aylwen as she laments the loss of Arthur and the demise of Alfheim."

Bowers of Og and Idris fair
bend with sorrow; deep despair
for passing days too few shall be
the Connleodh sword submerged in Sláine.
Where is he, the elfin lord,
to turn the tide and thus restore
the ancient realm for one and all,
the oaks and fields of Alfheim?

Timothy watched the crowd. No one moved. Aenya's voice carried through the glen. He'd never heard anyone's singing sound so beautiful, perfect as the ping of the finest crystal.

He doth not come; forests sigh,
fowl take wing and fill the sky,
glory fades, mists conceal
what was once the elfin realm.
Through forests deep she walks alone,
elves and fairies far and gone;
she waits for he that cometh not
ere all that was has been forgot.

He heard sniffling. Several of the elfin women and a few of the men were moved by the sorrowful ballad. Children took the hands of their mothers. Tuathla, seated in her chair, had lowered her head.

Where is he, the elfin lord,
to turn the tide and thus restore
the ancient realm for one and all,
the oaks and fields of Alfheim?
Blessed be the queen who was,
Aylwen lovely whose time had come;
the days of lore shall never be
the time for elves and fair-haired Sídhe
silent now, gone forever
lost 'neath pastures of purple heather.

The silence was heavy as the last echoes of the pipe faded. Aenya clasped her hands in front of her. Tuathla stood from her chair and walked to her. She cupped her hand under Aenya's chin, lifting her face, and pulled her into an embrace. They spoke for a time and then parted. His grandmother made her way back into the forest, and Aenya passed through the crowd toward him.

As she strode up the incline, her face beamed. Timothy was forced to face a truth he'd been avoiding and not allowing himself to think about. By comparison, what he'd once felt for Melanie now seemed thin. Even as he recognized this, the emotion was taking root somewhere down deep. He knew from then on it would be impossible not to be with Aenya.

"That was…that was beautiful," he said. The words didn't come close to capturing what he felt.

Aenya gave a quick curtsey. "Why, thank you."

He wanted to hug her, but Bardán put a hand on his shoulder.

"It's time to join your grandmother," he said. It was hard to pull away from Aenya.

He expected the forest to be pitch black, but the fireflies and the light from the windows of the Primal tree cottages made the paths clear enough to follow. Timothy's escort followed at a distance as he walked with Bardán, though they looked more tense than usual. He supposed having both his grandmother and him to worry about was a bit more stressful.

It was hard to focus on what he was about to do. They reached the base of the largest Primal tree in the center of the forest and began the long climb. The ornately carved wood of the stairway wound around and around the impossibly thick trunk. Timothy recognized the familiar pattern of the interlocking circles connecting the stairs to the upper rail. Several smaller cottages, built from the sides of the trunk, dotted the length of the soaring stalk. It took some time, but they reached a wide landing near the top of the tree, which surrounded an equally large dwelling like a huge wraparound porch. There was no door, just an opening with ivory-colored silk billowing in the breeze. Timothy paused there, but Bardán leaned in close.

"You may go in, you are expected."

He wondered if Bardán assumed he was both afraid and eager to enter. The elder gave a reassuring nod and gently pushed him forward. Timothy slipped through the curtains into a warmly lit room. Candles were everywhere, reflecting off the windows. His grandmother stood in the center of the room. Timothy gaped. It was his mother standing there, an older but perfect image of her. When she smiled, his heart skipped a beat; it was the same smile. Timothy felt the weight of his mother's death all over again.

She held her arms open, and Timothy slipped into them. It was restoration of the love stolen from him, and all trace of anxiety melted away. He finally recognized the touch for what it was. Aenya had done it that first day in her cottage, his mother had always made him feel renewed, and now his grandmother had the same effect. It *was* a sídhe's unique gift.

"Sit with me," she said. "You must be overwhelmed." She sat on a small couch, as if waiting for him to find a place to begin. She radiated an incredible and subtle power and serenity.

"She looked so very much like you," he said.

Sadness spread across her face. "I grieve her loss. It was my fondest hope that we would be reunited one day."

"You never came to see her in America."

"No. I felt it was safer for her if I remained here. My movements are watched closely."

"Safer?"

"I understand Aenya and Bardán have helped you understand some of our history."

"Some. Did you know my father?"

"Yes." She took one of his hands in hers. She was going to talk about something difficult; he was becoming wise to the sídhe's methods. "When your father and his wife gave birth to his fifth son, there were some who felt his existence was dangerous. He went into hiding with his family, but they found him when his sixth son was born. He defended his family. Tragically, his wife and newborn son were killed. Your father nearly died himself. He was no longer a young elf, and his wounds took their toll. It was then that I had a notion of what might be.

"A seventh of a seventh is so rare that it occurred to me that a union between your father, even though he'd sired his first six sons by another mother, and the bloodline of Aylwen might give rise to someone unusual. I sent your father to your mother in the hope she would accept him."

"You sent him? Did my mother know the truth of who he was? She never said anything about any of this."

"I believe this was as much for your protection as his. You are very young. I am certain my daughter would have told you everything before long."

"Aenya thought she might not have known he was an elf and was waiting to see if I would turn out human."

"I cannot say for certain what your father may have told her, but there would have been no way for him to hide the fact that he was elf born."

"I do seem to have a gift."

"Of course," she said. "I had little doubt you would possess that, at the very least. What I didn't expect, what none of us expected, is just how extraordinary it is."

"If I had known then what I could do, I could have saved her."

She was silent, as if weighing her thoughts carefully.

"There are many causes in our lives for regret and second-guessing. We experience triumphs and succumb to tragedy, but you must always remember to seek out the good, the useful, in anything that happens. Your mother's death has given you a depth of empathy that no other lesson would have achieved. Empathy breeds great compassion. You will need that. It has also taught you to be on your guard and to choose carefully those in whom you place your trust."

"Before we left, another elf suggested that I might have something to do with the restoration of Alfheim and now the things you're saying to me…well…it sounds like there is some plan for me."

"There is no such thing as absolute predestination, it's a matter of choice. Your power comes from your parents, but if there is a role for you to play, you will have to choose it willingly."

"Depending on my choice, do you think it's the direction I'm heading towards?"

"I suspect so."

"How could I possibly help make that happen?" Timothy was doubtful. He was a suicidal kid from New Hampshire with poor grades who happened to have a knack for healing people. He couldn't see how that would be a benefit in the restoration of an ancient kingdom.

"In time, Timothy. We will speak of these things again, but first we must be more certain."

"Certain of what?"

Her hand moved to the side of his face, and she slipped her fingers through his hair. It was just what his mother had done when she was feeling sad.

"I have had a long journey and would like to rest." She turned to the curtain and beckoned Bardán to enter. "I would speak with him alone for a minute. You must feel confident in placing your trust in him, always."

They stood and she kissed Timothy on the cheek. "I am so blessed to have you in my life. You are truly my daughter's son."

Timothy moved to the curtains so Bardán could speak with her quietly. They talked like old friends, smiling and nodding as if sharing some funny memory. Then Bardán stiffened and stood to his full height. He was shocked and concerned about something. She put her hand on his arm and finished speaking. He lowered his head and nodded like he was giving in. Timothy didn't like the idea that he was probably the subject of their discussion. Bardán lifted her hands to his lips and kissed them, then turned and strode toward Timothy.

"Come," he said.

"What was that all about?"

"We are going on a journey; we leave at first light."

Chapter 24

"BARDÁN IS WAITING OUTSIDE FOR you," Derval said. Timothy could only imagine what time it was; the room was dark. He pulled on clothes, grabbed a cloak that she'd tossed over the back of a chair, and went downstairs. She pressed a satchel into his hands.

"There's bread and cheese to eat along the way."

Aenya pulled Timothy into a hug.

"Do you have any idea what this is about?" he asked.

"Yes," she said.

"Would you care to share a little with me?"

"No."

Timothy hated when she looked uncomfortable, as she did now, because bad things usually happened. She wanted to say something, but she didn't.

"Okay, then," he said. He walked through the door with a confidence he didn't feel.

Outside, Bardán and six elves sat on horseback as the horizon was getting light. One of them dismounted and led Timothy to a horse next to the elder's. The elf helped him up into the saddle.

"I've never ridden a horse before," Timothy said. "I just thought I should mention that."

"Well then, this is a good time to open your mind to possibilities," Bardán said as he kicked the horse's side and moved off. Timothy knew to grab hold of the reins, he'd seen enough cowboy movies, but he didn't have to worry about kicking the horse; it just followed the others without any help.

Timothy managed to nudge his horse up next to Bardán's.

"Would this be a good time for you to let me in on the plan?"

"We're going to take a little boat ride," he said.

"To where?"

"Wales."

"That's, like, part of England, isn't it?"

"It is. It's on the western side, about two day's journey."

"Couldn't we just fly there?"

"We're going by boat."

His temper seemed short, so Timothy let his horse fall back again. They stayed within the forest, except for where the trees gave way to rocky hills and small mountains. Several of the climbs took them up hundreds of feet. They skirted villages and towns, staying at a distance, so anyone who might have noticed their passing saw just a group of people out for a ride. It took a few hours to cover the ten miles to a tributary that fed into the North Atlantic.

They dismounted near a dock. An old vessel tied to it looked more like a museum piece. The wood, blackened with age, curved from bow to stern in overlapping slats. The upswept bow rose much higher than the decking and ended with the carved head of a unicorn. A tall mast rose from the center of the ship, and rigging lines tied off at several points. At the stern of the forty-foot vessel, a door led into what Timothy guessed must be a cabin.

An elf wandered up to them from a barn that he'd hardly noticed and started leading the horses to it.

"This is the boat?" Timothy said, afraid to ask if she was seaworthy.

The six elves took their packs and crossed a small plank to board her.

"I've heard of wanting to live in the past, but isn't this just a little extreme?"

"Were you expecting a motor yacht?"

"Well, now that you mention it…" he said, but Bardán had already boarded, so Timothy followed.

The boat was barren. Apart from ropes and several long oars lashed to the inside of the ship's sides, there wasn't much else to distinguish her from a basic, if oversized, rowboat. Within minutes, the elves had the sail unfurled and took positions along each side, three each, with oars in their hands. The elves on the dockside cast off the ropes, and those aboard pushed against the quay with their oars until the boat floated far enough out. Then they pulled up several deck planks along the edges of the boat, revealing hidden seats equally spaced apart, one for each elf. In unison, they passed their oars through holes in the walls and began to row backwards into the middle of the tributary. When the boat faced in the right direction, the elves retrieved the oars and lashed them down, ready to set sail toward the North Atlantic. One elf settled into his post on the right side of the ship, taking hold of a huge wooden handle that Timothy learned was the steer board, to keep her on course.

"Come, Timothy," Bardán said. "Now we will have the chance to talk."

They entered the cabin, and Bardán pulled open several shutters. Daylight streamed into the area, which was small, but comfortable. Several bunks, some chairs, and a table filled the room. A firepit for preparing meals dominated the center of the cabin. Somehow, starting a fire in the middle of a bunch of ancient timber didn't seem like the best idea.

Timothy sat in one of the chairs and opened the satchel Derval had given him. He offered to share the bread and cheese with Bardán, who dug right in.

"First, I apologize for the suddenness of our departure and for not taking the time to explain everything to you. I was more concerned with your safety than for adhering to rules of etiquette."

"I get it. I think."

"Thank you," he said. "I want you to know this voyage is at your grandmother's request." Bardán appeared nervous, or, if not nervous, troubled.

"Was there a reason for not telling me herself?"

"Maybe not, but I can understand why she is leaving it to me."

"Talk to me."

"As I said, we're going to Wales. It's believed that our destination was once part of the original Alfheim, but we cannot be certain. Over the thousands of years, most traces of the ancient realm have been lost, as you will have heard in Aenya's song last night."

"I'm afraid I was more focused on her singing than the lyrics."

"I understand," he said. "The point of the lament was that Aylwen, having lost her husband Arthur, wished for another to appear, one who would help her keep the realm together. In other words, there was no champion to protect her and the rest from those who wished to destroy Alfheim and take it for themselves."

"I remember something about a sword," Timothy said.

"Yes," said Bardán, as if he'd struck on the very thing the elder wanted to talk about. "The Sword of Connleodh. It was a gift from Arthur to Aylwen on the occasion of their marriage."

"Arthur gave his wife a weapon as a wedding gift?"

Bardán shook his head. "The sword is not a weapon, it's a talisman. Aylwen enchanted it as a way to ensure that whoever possessed it would be worthy of ruling Alfheim. When Arthur died, she had the sword hidden away in the care of a sídhe guardian until such time as one would come forward to claim it."

"You know, this story sounds kind of familiar," Timothy said. Bardán actually laughed.

"Humans are very fond of storytelling," he said, leaning back in his chair and raising a large cube of cheese to his lips. "Even to the extent that when they run out of their own tales, they'll borrow others' and claim them for themselves."

"You said Aylwen's husband was named Arthur. You don't mean like King Arthur, do you?"

"There never was a human King Arthur, and in Alfheim, Arthur wasn't a king. Yes, he was married to her, but his role was more of a protector, and the sword was given to a sídhe to guard, and she happens to live near water, but that's where the similarities end."

"So does that have something to do with where we're going?"

"I'm afraid it does," he said. The tone of his voice turned serious again. "There's a little more to the story."

"I figured."

"Your grandmother believes that you might be the one to take possession of the sword, that you might be the one who answers the dilemma of 'Aylwen's Lament.' I told you the other day that Arthur is the only other seventh of a seventh we know to have existed. I think your grandmother may be justified in her thoughts."

"But?" Timothy didn't like the sound of what he hadn't said. "I hear a huge but in the way you say that."

"There is one concern."

"And what would that be? If I try to take the sword from the stone, I won't be able to pull it out?"

"No. If you take the hilt of the sword as it's offered to you, and you are not the one, you will die."

Timothy put the piece of bread he was biting on the table. His appetite magically disappeared. Being the heir of an ancient queen was suddenly and potentially hazardous to his health in a completely new way.

"I will die," Timothy said. "Has anyone else ever tried to take the sword?"

"Legend tells us there have been two other attempts…both ended badly."

"So no one has rightfully held the sword since Arthur?"

Bardán shook his head, dropping his eyes. "Even in our world, it is sometimes difficult to separate legend from fact. We all believe in the existence of Alfheim and of Aylwen and Arthur. No one living has ever seen the sword, and none but a few would even know where to look for it. Since you seem familiar with the human stories of King Arthur, then I would equate the existence of the sword to something like the Grail. Since I am the keeper of our histories, and given my relationship to your grandmother, there is no doubt in either of our minds as to its existence and whereabouts."

"How can it be that in thousands of years, no one has been able to claim this talisman? Someone must have been good enough."

"There may have been, but no one has tried."

"So why should I then? My grandmother is willing for me to risk death just to check it out?" The elfin world was starting to make him nuts. That his grandmother thought he might be something special was great, but this was pushing things to a whole new level. The very fact he was buying into the story was weird enough. Two weeks ago, he would have written it off as a movie script. Only now, he'd seen enough to know that if Bardán said he could die by touching the sword, then he might very well die if he touched the sword.

"Bardán, I'm Timothy Brennan, a kid from New Hampshire who may or may not have an attention deficit disorder. A few days ago, I tried to off myself, only Aenya swooped in at the last minute to save me. I'm not some chosen one, I'm not the kid Donlan thinks is going to restore Alfheim."

"Perhaps not, but maybe you are."

"Do I have a choice in all this?"

"Of course. No one will force you to risk your life."

"Wouldn't it have made more sense to bring all this up before we left, then? Lately, I've been dragged around not really knowing what's going on. You say I have a choice, but then last night you just tell me we're going and the next thing I know, I'm on a boat in the middle of the North Atlantic. It feels more like force than choice. And you all seem to forget the reason I'm here is to do something about my mother's murder."

Timothy wished Aenya had come. He wished he could look into her eyes and ask if she thought he should do this. Then again, she knew where he was going and what they were asking him to do, and she had said nothing. What did that mean? He stood and left the cabin.

As they sailed along the tributary to the open ocean, the land on either side was drifting farther apart like the arms of the world opening to set them free. He studied the faces of the elves on board, but none of them would look him in the eye. Did they know what was going on?

Timothy looked at the bulging, fluttering sail. The flapping noise was like the voice of the wind pushing them through the water. The canvas was emerald green, emblazoned with a symbol he'd seen before. It was the same delicate pattern of interlocking circles on his mother's necklace and on the tapestry of Aylwen in Bardán's cottage. It was part of her standard, her symbol. He was standing on board her boat, the last of her line. *If that symbol was once hers, now it's mine to claim if I want to,* he thought. The chill he felt wasn't from the wind.

At the bow, he peered over the side, fascinated by how the water was sliced and folded back as they passed through the waves. His eyes followed the keel up the stem to the carving of the unicorn's head. The animal's expression was fierce, the eyes angry, as if daring the sea to throw the worst it had against the small ship. He could understand how sailors had been so keen on having the right figurehead for good luck. With everything else he'd experienced over the past weeks, he couldn't help wondering if unicorns existed, too.

He jumped as someone draped a cloak around his shoulders. One of the elves had come forward with the garment.

"I thought you might feel cold."

"Thank you," Timothy said. "How long before we reach open water?"

"In about an hour, we will tack to the east around the southern coast of Ireland. From there, we will sail northeast to Wales."

"Do you know why we're going there?"

"We all do."

He recognized the elf as the one who'd taken charge after the wedding. "I didn't know you were a sailor also."

"We do what is necessary and when it is necessary."

"What's your name?"

"I am Ruairí."

"You've been looking after me for a couple of days. Thank you for that."

"And we will continue to do so." He nodded and then turned back to his post.

Bardán stood in the open doorway of the cabin, and Timothy felt like a fool. He'd whined about taking a risk, offended that he was asked to tempt death to satisfy a whim. But everyone around him thought nothing of putting themselves in harm's way for him: first Aenya, then Ailill and his family, and now Ruairí and his men. What did they see in him? Something he couldn't see himself. Whatever it was, Bardán and his grandmother seemed to have the impression his choice would be to step up. Was it possible that by not making more of a fuss about following blindly, he was subconsciously making that choice already? But he just didn't see himself in any kind of leadership role. He wanted to punch Seumais's and Cadwaladr's tickets for killing his mother, along with anyone else who had a hand in it. If, in order to do that, he needed to deal with all this other stuff, then that's what he would have to do. He'd decide on all the rest when he got there.

Timothy went back inside the cabin. "So we have two days," he said. "That gives us plenty of time to work on my education, right?"

Bardán reached into his saddlebag and pulled out a thick leather volume. He dropped it on the table with a thud, heavy as a brick.

"What's that?"

"It's a summary of our people's history."

"That's just a summary?"

Bardán smiled and opened the cover. “Once upon a time,” he started.

It was going to be a very long two days.

Chapter 25

By the second day, Timothy felt tongue-tied and bleary-eyed. Elfin had a lot of awkward phrasing that sounded like lisping, but oddly, over the course of an entire sentence, it wound up flowing like poetry. Either way, he didn't understand a word of it. Learning to read the tightly woven script was yet another beast; the words all had the same appearance, some longer and some shorter. Every letter seemed to have a straight line with some number of curves attached. He was dismayed at the number of accent marks; he'd counted five in the first hour of lessons. An entire paragraph of script looked more like art than language.

"Maybe this would be better to tackle once we get back," he said. If I get back, he thought.

Bardán grunted, apparently in agreement, and all too quickly closed the book.

"Were you ever a teacher?"

"Of course, but it has been some years," he said.

Timothy sat back in the chair, thrilled at the reprieve from more lessons. "I never asked you, do you have a wife and children?"

"Yes."

Timothy waited for Bardán to elaborate, but he didn't; maybe bringing up the subject hadn't been the best idea.

Bardán had a way of lifting his chin when he was trying to decide what he wanted to say. Then there was no certainty that when he lowered it again, he was going to say anything at all.

"I am married to Sorcha, she is of the sídhe. I have had two children, a son and a daughter." Thinking about it obviously required some effort on his part, like a nerve had been touched. "My son was killed in the war. My daughter, Muirenn, lives with my wife in a Sídhe colony in Scotland."

"I'm sorry," said Timothy. "You said the war was horrific."

"For a people devoted to peace, we've experienced a good deal of violence."

"My grandmother told me that my father's sixth son and his wife were killed when some faction of elves discovered where he was, that they were intent on preventing him from having me… but that leaves five other brothers."

"Four; his fifth son was killed at the same time. But yes, that's right." Bardán seemed eager to turn the subject away from himself. "Why don't we have a look at that book of yours? Aenya put it in your pack."

"How did you know that?"

"I asked her to," he said. "She strikes me as quite an impressive young lady. She was a bit flustered when she learned where I was taking you."

Timothy stopped fiddling inside his pack, and his ears perked up. "Flustered?"

"I think she worries about you." Bardán winked. "But don't mind me, I could just be imagining things."

Disappointed, Timothy jammed his hand back inside the pack and felt for the book at the bottom. He pulled it out and put it on the table. Bardán took it and went to read it by the light of the window. Timothy drummed his fingers on the table.

"You know, people have been looking at me a little strangely since the wedding."

"And you're surprised because...?"

"I know, but it's sort of freaky. I can't tell if they want to run away from me or if they're fascinated."

"When one doesn't know the nature of something, it is best to be cautious at first, wouldn't you agree? I feel confident, however, that they don't loathe you. Ah, here we are. There is a summary of your father's offspring beginning in 1600 with the birth of his first son, Alastair. It's followed by Goban in 1624, Kyran in 1681, and then Darragh in 1732."

"Great, they were all born before my country was even a country."

"Gearalt in 1809 and Lonán in 1921 are shown as deceased," Bardán said, his voice lowered.

"It seems kind of weird that my father had children so many years apart. Is that normal?"

Bardán glanced up from the pages of the book. "Why, is there some rush to have them all at once?"

"Well, no, but—"

"If elves lived significantly shorter lives like humans, I imagine we would bunch them together, too."

"I'm only seventeen in human years. Aenya is one hundred and ninety, but she doesn't look any older than me. It's hard to figure out how that is, too."

"We tend to age at a much slower pace, obviously. In relative terms, even though you have a one-hundred-sixty-something-year gap, you and Aenya, given her even longer life expectancy, are actually considered peers."

Timothy wasn't sure why, but that felt good to know. Maybe just on the off chance he asked her out. Did elves date? He wanted to ask, but was too shy to open his mouth. He thought it would be better to ask someone like Derval.

"This is interesting," Bardán said. "Your father must have written this after you were born. I know you're called Timothy now, but according to this, your name was to be Tuathal."

"That sounds like my grandmother's name."

"And they have very similar meanings. Tuathal means 'ruler of the people.'"

"So is it possible that my mother and father knew what I might have to go through?"

"It's unclear what your mother might have thought, but it seems your father had some inkling."

"Is there anything in there that might tell me where my other brothers might be?"

Bardán shook his head. "After the war, thousands of elves left to make their own ways in the human world or to live in the forests of Europe or America. It was evident to many that the old ways were gone. Your brothers could have been part of that exodus."

"How will I ever find them?" Timothy stood and moved to the doorway.

Bardán came close behind and draped an arm around his shoulders.

"Perhaps they'll find you."

It wasn't a sídhe's touch, but it was comforting in a way he wasn't used to. The kindness on Bardán's face was so different from the sternness Timothy had come to expect. Thinking of the elder as strict didn't seem fair as Timothy got to know him better, and imagining him with sword in hand, hacking and slashing in a pitched battle, was almost impossible. It brought the notion of war one step closer to understanding it for what it was. It crossed the line from fiction to stark reality when you knew actual people who might die, like the six elves sitting on the deck a few feet from the cabin, sharing a loaf of bread and some cheese. War would mean risking their lives and parting from their families, possibly forever. Was it conceivable that he could ever play a part in changing the balance between murder and war and long-lasting peace?

Timothy squeezed Bardán's forearm, then moved free of his embrace and onto the deck. Slipping between Ruairí and another, he sat amongst the elves.

"Any more bread and cheese?" Timothy thought it was almost fun watching them exchange questioning looks, then hastening to break off a fist-sized piece of bread and hand it over.

They talked for over an hour, sharing stories. Timothy learned that all but one of the elves had a wife at Sídhlin; most had at least one child. The youngest elf, Eoghan, was only a few years older than him and fascinated by the story of his chase through the woods. Timothy figured if Eoghan were human, he'd be the kind to like movies where things blow up. He was an apprentice bow maker and sat with a yew stave across his legs, polishing the rounded wood of the longbow.

"How long does it take to make one of those?" asked Timothy.

"Depends," he said. "This particular piece was shaped from a thrice-split log that was left to dry for ten years. This one is going to be very pretty when I've finished." He seemed quite pleased with himself and obviously took pride in his talent. Timothy would never have thought of a bow as something pretty. "Funny thing about the yew; we make bows from it for hunting and defense, but one of the poisons in elfshot also comes from it."

"I'm familiar with that stuff," Timothy said.

"No match for you, it seems."

"I don't know, I think it came pretty close to doing its job on Cavan." Timothy moved back as Eoghan stood, put the stave between his legs, and bent it, testing the tension in the curvature. "Maybe when you've finished with it, you might show me how to shoot."

"Me?" The young elf seemed shocked at the idea. "I'm not the best shot, but it would be my honor to show you what I know."

"I look forward to it," Timothy said. He liked something about the elf. It would be good to make some real friends, if he survived the next day. The thought reminded him of why he was there in the first place. His stomach did a couple of backflips.

"Ruairí, how hard is it to learn to use one of those?" he asked, pointing to the sword attached to his belt. It seemed like a sensible question, considering how many times someone had tried to kill him over the past few days.

"That's determined by the aptitude of the student," he said. "It's one thing to learn how to wield a sword, it's quite another for the sword to become an extension of your arm. A good swordsman should be able to slice the skin from a grape using tip of the blade with as little effort as picking one up with your fingers. Of course, it doesn't always come down to technique, but tactics. In a fight, you just need to win, not to dazzle your opponent with a fine display of craft."

"A long time then."

"A lot of practice," Ruairí said, his face breaking into a smile. "My father had me striking an upright pole from side to side with a long sword until he could compute the distance between strikes with a measuring stick to make certain they were equal. It took years."

Who'd have thought? It looked so easy in the movies.

Timothy walked to the bow of the ship. This was yet another first, along with the plane and the trains. He'd seen maps of Ireland and England; on paper they were so close to one another, it was hard to imagine the boat was far enough at sea that there was no sight of land.

His thoughts turned to the next day. Tuathla didn't seem concerned with his touching the Connleodh sword; neither did Bardán. But he said that Aenya was apprehensive, which meant there was a chance of death. Two weeks ago, that prospect would have made him happy; now he wasn't so sure. Circumstances were different. *Will I have the courage to do it?* He'd jumped off a bridge, but was that the same thing? Countless men throughout history had faced battle knowing they could die, yet they went. Were they any more special because they found the courage to go, instead of turning to run?

Timothy guessed he would know soon enough.

Chapter 26

THE SUN HAD JUST CLIMBED above the British Isles as the ship approached the Welsh shoreline from the west. Sheer grey rock rose from the blue water, crowned with a layer of green. The prow of the boat slipped from the frothiness of the open sea to the glass-like surface of a river. The surrounding hills sloped to the water's edge, coated in soft green moss, like the carpet around the base of a tree in the forest.

Bardán came from the cabin dressed in black. The leather tunic cinched with a wide belt holding a short sword in its scabbard. A black hooded cloak circled his shoulders and clasped in front with a silver brooch. Dark gloves covered his hands.

All six elves were wearing swords; a stand of bows had been set near the mast, along with six full quivers of arrows.

"Are we expecting trouble?" Timothy asked.

"I don't think so, but it's no excuse to lower our guard," said Bardán. "I've left some clothes in the cabin for you."

They were just like his. The short tunic was thick and hard, as if designed to protect against an arrow or the slash of a sword. That didn't help his anxiety.

When he went back on deck, the ship was passing through a narrow opening in the rock face. The walls rose straight from the water to a height of several stories and were covered in moss and ferns. Small waterfalls cascaded down the rock and forced a mist to rise from the surface of the water. The moisture clung to his face. The waterway meandered ahead. Looking straight up, he could spot small patches of blue sky through the trees. At points, the rocky ledges closed over the chasm like a natural bridge. From the air, it would have been impossible to see the boat.

"We are near," Bardán said. His speech was hushed and reverent, like a sinner in church, not quite ready to let God know he was there.

The elves had secured the mast, and four of them were back at the oars, Ruairí at the tiller and Eoghan at the bow, watching above and ahead.

As in the Primal tree forest, Timothy could sense the magic and didn't have to ask if enchantments had been cast there. It was doubtful whether any human had ever or would ever enter the watery trail.

"Oars up," Ruairí whispered.

Ahead, Timothy could see a natural rocky landing extend from the wall. Beyond that, a path led farther into the labyrinth. Ruairí angled the boat so that it lay to the side of the outcrop. Eoghan vaulted onto stone, holding a tether in his hand, and secured the vessel. They tied off the stern and bridged the gap with a plank.

Bardán gave a nod and proceeded onto the rocks. Timothy followed. At times, the winding path narrowed so they had to pass one behind the other. The elves remained with the boat and were quickly lost from sight. After a while, they could no longer hear the soft waterfalls from where they'd come, only the rustling of braches and ferns high above. It was hard to see more than ten feet ahead; the moist fog that swirled had a rich, earthy smell. There was something ancient here, liked they'd stepped onto the first place on earth. All the magic that no longer existed in the world seemed to surround them. For the first time, Timothy felt the joy of not being human and yet the sadness of realization that humans had lost their way, no longer capable of connecting with this.

A new sound of water reached them from somewhere ahead; it grew louder as they turned another bend. All at once, the fog parted, and they entered a natural rotunda. A thousand tiny rivulets of water from high above cascaded over the branches and ferns into a crystal-clear pool. Thin shafts of sunlight shone on the water, and they could see the bottom of the pool wavering beneath the ripples on the surface. The stone pathway ended on a small round island in the center of the pool.

"This place is incredible," Timothy said in a hushed voice.

As they crossed over the slender finger of rock, they heard the fluttering of wings above them as three or four birds rose from the branches and disappeared over the rim of the chamber walls.

"What do we do now? We've run out of path." Timothy didn't mind the idea of staying there at all. He walked to the edge; the water lapped at the grey rock, and as he peered into the depths, schools of fish darted from one crevice to another. There was a small splash. A tree grew on a separate outcrop across the water, and a piece of fruit from it had fallen in. Several pieces floated around.

"Are those apples?" Timothy asked.

"If not, they look similar," said Bardán.

A swift movement under the water caught Timothy's eye. The fish had disappeared from view, as if something had startled them from below.

Bubbles started to rise, a few at first, then more and more until the water roiled. He stepped back, afraid of being cooked, yet there was no heat; the air was still cool on his face. Something radiant white appeared just below the surface, then rose into the air and stepped onto the small island before them. A woman in a flowing hooded white dress, bearing a wrapped bundle, took a step toward them. She was achingly beautiful, as Timothy had come to realize the sídhe were. She'd just come from the water and yet showed no sign of being wet.

"I am Aine, guardian of the Connleodh sword," she said.

"I am Bardán, Elder of Sídhlin. This is Timothy of the line of Aylwen."

"Welcome. You come to claim the sword?"

Timothy wanted to ask Bardán what to do. The elder met his gaze but said nothing. He couldn't tell if Aine thought he was doing the right thing or not, either. Her look was expectant but noncommittal. As Bardán had said, this was to be his choice and his alone.

"Yes," said Timothy, his voice shaky, which annoyed him. He didn't want to come off as some frightened young boy.

"Have you been counseled as to the penalty for not being worthy?"

"Yes."

Aine took a final step toward them. She moved the bundle and began to unwind the ivory silken fabric, turn after turn. At last, she revealed the sword. It was breathtaking. Shorter than he'd imagined, it looked more like the pictures of Roman swords, golden in color and polished bronze, not steel. The handle was tight strands of emerald-colored chord that ended with an intricate ball of Celtic knots. Engraved just below the guard was Aylwen's standard. Aine held out the sword with the handle closest to Timothy.

He couldn't take his eyes off it. If he lived, he would be the first elf to hold the sword in the thousands of years since Aylwen. If he died, the hopes of so many would vanish. It would play right into the hands of Cadwaladr, Aylwen's line would die out forever, and Seumais would celebrate over his grave. *How did I get here?* Bardán had said Timothy had a choice. He no longer believed it. Walking away would be nothing short of cowardice. He might not be much in a fight, but he wasn't a pushover, either. He remembered his uncle calling him a wuss and anger fueled his courage.

Timothy's right hand rose as if someone were pulling it up with an invisible string. His breathing was shallow as his fingers closed the distance. He started shivering, not from fear, but from curiosity of such intensity that he was trembling with anticipation. Death was inches from his fingers.

Cupping his hand under the sword, Timothy thought he could feel something charged, an energy, not unlike the healing pulse, but with a vast amount of power. A buzzing sound filled his ears, like a power line ripped from a transformer in a storm. Then it morphed to that of a hundred people whispering to him in words he could hear but not understand. The volume rose to shouting the closer his hand got. He couldn't quite close the distance, like the opposite ends of a magnet repelling each other. Was it a warning? Were the voices yelling at him to step away? Was the sword itself rejecting him? Darkness swirled around him; he could no longer see or even sense Bardán or Aine. He couldn't hear the waterfalls, just voices, screaming now. Suddenly, there was no air. He tried to gasp, but there was nothing. *Have I touched the sword? Am I dead?*

A single voice rose above the others. "Timothy, do not be afraid."

I'm not. The words were in his mind only; he had no breath with which to speak.

Something shimmered in front of him, slowly taking form. A figure cloaked in dark blue with long, flowing blond hair hovered nearby. A shining ring of gold circled her forehead like a crown. Timothy recognized her from the tapestry. It was Aylwen.

She nodded toward the sword, urging him to take it.

He closed his eyes and forced his hand forward, his fingers brushing the taut threads of the handle. With a final burst of determination, he gripped the sword and pulled it from Aine's grasp. The screeching, the violent energy, and Aylwen's figure all disappeared in an instant. He felt dizzy.

When he opened his eyes, the sword was there, in his hand.

He was alive.

"You have passed the test," said Aine. She stepped back and bowed. Bardán did the same. Timothy wanted to scream. *What does this mean?* But he couldn't find his voice.

Aine unfurled the fabric in her hands a few more turns and revealed a matching scabbard for the sword. She fastened it to his belt. "You are the true heir of Alfheim. Choose your path wisely," she said, her voice soft.

"Bardán?"

The elder stood to his full height. Timothy could tell by the look in Bardán's eyes that the exchange had affected him as well. The young elf realized how it must feel to have a legend that persisted for generations suddenly become reality before you. There was no way to prepare for that. "Will you help me?" He didn't know what to do next, but if anyone were to offer guidance, it was sure to be the elder.

"Nothing else I could do with my life would be more important," he said.

Timothy turned to say something to Aine, but she had vanished. The fabric that had wrapped the sword remained on the rock, fluttering in the breeze.

Bardán pulled him into an embrace. Timothy wanted to ask if he'd seen Aylwen, too. He wanted to tell Bardán that she'd appeared, that she had told him it was okay to take possession of the sword. But he couldn't. Not yet. He had to get his own head around it all first.

"Let's go home."

Reluctantly, Timothy turned from the serenity of the pool. He thought if he ever needed a break from the world, it would be a great refuge. Magic was there.

As they rounded the last bend in the path to the boat, the elves all stood. Eoghan was closest. When he saw Timothy, he smiled, but then his eyes drifted to the sword on his waist. The smile faded quickly.

All six elves knelt, lowering their heads as if by command. Timothy stopped in his tracks. How in the world was he supposed to react to something like that?

"Guys? It's just me," he said. It sounded lame, but he was out of his depth.

"Let's get underway," Bardán said. It broke through the awkwardness, and they scrambled aboard. In minutes, they were moving back along the chasm toward the Irish Sea.

"Bardán, I know this means something that none of you have had to deal with in your lifetimes, but wow, I don't want people reacting like that."

Bardán stood against the wall by the cabin and folded his arms over his chest. The chin moved up; he was thinking again.

"Timothy," he said. "There is something you must grasp here and the quicker you do it, the better off we'll all be."

"That sounds ominous."

"There is you, a young male elf with talents. Then there is that sword, an object of legend and myth for all living fae, except for Aine. Separate, both are noteworthy. Together, they mean something different. When you experience a reaction like that, it is not for you as Timothy, but for the hope of something yearned for after millennia. They offer respect to you as the bearer of that hope. You must meet it with grace. To the unworthy, such a gesture would fuel the ego; to the worthy, it's the acknowledgment of responsibility."

"Do you believe I possess that potential?"

"No one can even guess the full breadth of your capabilities yet, but yes, with all my soul," said Bardán.

Timothy turned toward the bow, not wanting to go inside, but he did notice the remnants of a smoking fire from the cooking pit. As Ruairí moved to the stern, Timothy noticed his lower face was covered in dark whiskers. He sat on the deck next to Eoghan.

"You guys had time to cook a meal?"

"Sure, why?" Eoghan said as he pulled back on the oar.

"Just wondering," he said. "Wasn't Ruairí clean shaven?"

"He hasn't shaved since we got here."

"You mean he grew a beard in two hours?"

"My lord, we awaited your return for a week."

Chapter 27

Aenya paced the floor of her room. With Timothy gone, she found herself on unfamiliar ground. In some ways, it gave her a better perspective for what he was going through. His world had been turned upside down, and now Aenya was feeling the same effects. A hundred years of virtual solitude had formed a much different routine of living. She'd come to enjoy the company of forest creatures, protecting them, as well as the trees, from human meddling, but that had not prepared her for dealing with her own kind. She felt guilty that she had pushed Timothy into a similar situation. But that was different. He was extraordinary in ways she still couldn't understand.

With each day that passed, her sense of foreboding grew. Bardán had expected the journey to last four days, five at the most. The eighth day had dawned with no word from any of them. She'd held off Darina and the other sídhe, even though they seemed anxious to have her join them. Aenya was reluctant to forge any relationships until she knew that Timothy was safe. If something happened to him, she wasn't sure she would remain in Ireland, despite the warmth and appeal of Darina's welcome. She wasn't certain she could change her whole life around and become part of a community after so many years of isolation.

Aenya wasn't used to spending so much time indoors, either. Sitting and worrying was driving her insane. Tuathla would know more about what was happening than anyone else. Aenya flew out the window and straight to the Primal trees in hopes that she might request an audience.

She stepped onto the platform of Tuathla's dwelling. The curtains were billowing open. An elf saw her and came rushing over.

"Greetings," he said. "May I help you?"

Aenya felt she was intruding. Her act had been impulsive and presumptuous, and she started to back away. The elf held up his hand.

"You're quite welcome here," he said. "All Sídhe are."

She hesitated and then spoke softly. "I was hoping to have a word with my lady, Tuathla."

Before he could say a word, she came into the room.

"Good morning, my dear. I was so hoping you would stop by for a visit. It saves the trouble of sending Labras here to find you."

"You wanted to see me?" Aenya said with no small surprise.

"You sang so beautifully at my reception the other evening."

"My mother taught me the ballad when I was a girl. It was always my favorite."

"Mine too, even if we fae tend to be a bit maudlin," Tuathla said. She had lowered her voice as if sharing a secret and put her hand on Aenya's arm. "Why don't we sit?"

"I'm very honored," Aenya said.

"Oh, nothing of the sort." Tuathla laughed. "We owe you a considerable debt. In the short time you've known my grandson, you've done more for him than I ever have."

"Timothy and I were curious about something."

"You want to know why he was kept in the dark and why we never came for him." Tuathla nodded and looked down. "It's entirely my fault. No one here in Sídhlin ever knew of his existence, except for Bardán. He has been a confidant of mine for centuries. We had begun serious correspondence about the idea of finally revealing ourselves to him. Unfortunately, or fortunately, circumstances proved otherwise."

"Do you know why it's taking them so long to return?" Aenya asked. "They should have been back days ago."

Tuathla held her gaze and smiled. "You have feelings for him."

"My lady, I would never presume—"

"Oh Aenya, believe me, I would not oppose such an arrangement. You share a unique bond. Each of you has saved the other more than once. But as to his safety now, I can assure you he's fine."

"How do you know? Touching the sword could kill him."

"While that rumor is true, Timothy would not suffer that fate. In a lapse of thought, I failed to mention to Bardán the peculiarities of Sláine. Time works a little differently there. Hours are measured in days."

"So you believe he is the true heir."

"Beyond all doubt," Tuathla said. "But I sense your discomfort about more than just Timothy."

Aenya wasn't used to being on the receiving end of perception, at least not since her mother. She looked at the intricate pattern of the carpeting to avoid Tuathla's eyes.

"I don't have a great deal of practice fitting into a social environment like this."

Tuathla sat back against the cushions of a settee. "You and I are not dissimilar," she said. "I have spent many years on my estate to the north, living very quietly, partly because I have reached a great age, but also because here I am a thorn in Cadwaladr's side. While I live, there is always the threat that those who oppose him will rally around me. We've lived by a delicate truce for nearly four hundred years. But you are young, and you should rejoin your kind. You would fit here very well."

"You're looking for Timothy to take up the fight?"

"I can only hope that he has the strength within him," said Tuathla. "I sense that he does."

"My lady, he is very strong in some ways and fragile in others."

"I am aware of his frame of mind, and that is why I hope you will be one of those who will help him."

"But how can I? I am no one in this world."

"And who here has such a connection to him as you do? The bond between you that I mentioned is stronger than you imagine. It's not the length of time you've known him, it's the severity of your shared experience."

"I wouldn't want to let him down." Aenya felt a sense of alarm sharpen her fear. There was no question about the task Tuathla was setting before her. She was used to protecting deer and rabbits and the occasional moose from a hunter's rifle or a trapper's snare. Protecting and advising Timothy, who had half the elfin world ready to kill him, was beyond her ability, she was sure.

"You won't, it's not in your heart to allow such a thing to happen. Trust in the instincts of an old sídhe. Open your heart to Sídhlin, and it will fill you. There are many of our kind here, and most of the elves of this realm are elegant and good-hearted—not all, but most. In fact, your perception will be all the more valuable because you are not familiar with this realm. And you haven't been tainted with the playfulness of the Sídhe. Your awareness is more serious and mature."

Aenya thought of how Éabha had cavorted in childlike pleasure with the fireflies. They seemed far more intent on games and mischief. She had never had that kind of opportunity and looked at the world for what it was, often painful and always treacherous. She doubted whether Darina's friends had ever felt the sickening anguish of the forests in time of war and death. The American Civil War had taught her many lessons on the subject of grief.

"Doesn't that mean we'd be using Timothy like a pawn? Forcing him into an impossible situation?"

Tuathla suddenly looked tired. She focused on the floor, as if weighing her thoughts carefully. When she spoke, it was like resignation.

"It is vital that whatever Timothy does is a choice that he makes. If he does not summon the passion to take up the cause, he must not be forced. There has not been someone like him in ten thousand years, no one has had the blending of blood and power that he has. So yes, I hope he will rally. If he doesn't, I fear that our world will take another turn toward its ultimate destruction."

"Is it so desperate as that?" Aenya asked.

"It becomes harder and harder to save the part of our world that we need to live. Humans encroach on the natural environment, but when there is rot from within, the task is all the more difficult. Cadwaladr is a poison. His desire for power can absolutely diminish the best part of our race, what is left of us." Tuathla stood and smiled at Aenya. "Didn't I tell you that we are prone to being maudlin? Please don't mind my ramblings."

Aenya stood also. She sensed her audience was at an end. Despite Tuathla's last words, she had no doubts about the reality of the situation. It was far more serious than anyone was willing to admit.

"When Timothy returns, I am going to have him stay here with me. As for you, my dear, I will arrange for your accommodations in the Primal tree just there," Tuathla said, pointing across to a dwelling in a neighboring tree.

"That's very gracious of you," Aenya said.

Tuathla pulled her into an embrace. At once, she felt what Timothy must have when Donlan hugged him: the kind of loving experience only another can provide.

* * *

Tuathla watched Aenya disappear into the trees, then turned back to her inner chamber. A thick pile of single parchment sheets rested on a desk of hewn oak; a newly sharpened goose quill and a beaker of black carbon ink waited for her. She still preferred the quill, and of course parchment instead of paper since the wood content wore down the nib too quickly.

"I like her," said a voice off to the side. Líle sat on a small ottoman.

"As do I," said Tuathla. "She has an inner strength and a powerful connection to nature."

"She's a little shy."

"I'll leave it to Éabha and Éadaoin to lighten her spirits." Tuathla took her seat by the desk, facing Líle. "I need you to do something for me. My time is growing short, rapidly so. These pages are a record of my life and a history of our people for the past thousand years. Timothy will need these, but he is not ready for them. First he must be taught to read our language, which Bardán is seeing to, and Timothy must have a better understanding of our world. I am asking you to safeguard this history until that time comes."

"Wouldn't the council serve as better curators, or even Bardán himself?"

"Bardán has always had my full confidence, and I would trust him with my life, but he is still only elfin. He cannot protect these in a manner consistent with the talents of the sídhe. I would have given them to Aine in Sláine, but I think it best they remain here for when they are needed. Aenya is strong, but is still unfamiliar with our world in some ways. No, my dear, it must be you."

"Then you may rest knowing that no harm will come to them," Líle said. "How will I know when Timothy is ready?"

Tuathla let her shoulders slump, the weight of knowing excruciating. There was no one to blame but herself for having let things pass unchanged for so long. The shortness of Timothy's seventeen years, a mere blink of an eye against the life of a sídhe, was a poor excuse. She had fallen into complacency. Worse, she'd turned a blind eye to the darker side of their world, and to elfin treachery; it had cost her daughter's life and nearly Timothy's. And, Tuathla feared, that might still come to pass. Her reluctance to break the tenuous truce with Cadwaladr had been a mistake. It had been her responsibility to put an end to his cancerous ruination of their world. Instead, she had allowed the idea that by holding back she was saving lives guide her thinking. By letting him live, she had virtually ensured Alfheim's final destruction.

"I sense terrible things ahead for him, tests that he must face and survive. There is no guarantee he will outlive them, but if he does, he will slowly acclimate to our culture. Watch him and become his counselor, then you will know when he is ready. Timothy must fully embrace his talents and use them in a genuine attempt to resurrect Alfheim. Even if he survives what faces him, there is no guarantee that he will not turn from who he is, from what he is."

"What if he does turn away?" Líle asked.

Tuathla could sense a deep-rooted fear behind the younger sídhe's stoic expression. It was like a stab to the heart. When the knowledge of the end is hidden, there is little to be afraid of. When truth is exposed, its horror will spread like a disease, unabated. It will consume and turn what was once beautiful to a rotting shell, grotesque.

"Tuathla?"

"If he turns away, the age of elves and sídhe will end."

Chapter 28

A HUNDRED MOUNTED ELVES WERE lined along the road beyond the dock.

"I guess word spreads fast," Timothy said.

"I'd have thought you'd learned that by now," Bardán said.

Two sídhe rode at the head of the column as the assemblage worked its way back to the forest. Timothy assumed they were there to avert the attention of local humans. His original crew trailed behind, and Bardán rode next to him.

"Is this the way things are likely to go from now on?"

"I'd say you'd best get used to a bit more attention."

"Great."

It was growing dark as they entered the forest and made their way to the Primal trees.

"Tuathla is waiting for you," said Bardán. Timothy looked forward to the day when he figured out how everyone knew everything that was going on without talking. When he reached the high platform of her dwelling, he slipped through the curtains and found her sitting on a comfortable lounge. She looked tired, but gave him a bright smile.

"You knew before I left, didn't you?"

"I did," she said, standing to embrace him. "It is important that everyone else comes to know. May I see it?"

Timothy slid the sword from the scabbard and held it out to her. "Is it safe for you to touch?"

"Oh yes, quite safe. Once the sword has been claimed by a worthy heir, it is safe to be handled…as long as you, or the heir who possesses it, are alive." She held it in both hands. "It is quite a remarkable thing, isn't it? No one living, except its guardian, has ever laid eyes on it."

"What comes next?" he asked. "Is there something I have to do?"

"You mean is there some ceremony? I imagine in the days of Aylwen there might have been. What happens from here depends on you. Tomorrow you will meet with the elders, and tomorrow night I will present you as Aylwen's heir. Despite the verbal claim, you now have undeniable proof."

"I'm pretty sure Cadwaladr won't be happy when he hears the news."

"No. The time is soon coming when he will have to be dealt with."

"It wouldn't be good politics to be introduced as Aylwen's heir only to have another war start."

"We will not be the ones to break the peace," she said.

"Does that matter when it comes to elves and fae dying?"

Tuathla smiled. "I think you are going to prove a worthy heir."

"I'm still not sure I can be, or should be, but Bardán has pledged to help me figure it out."

"You will have no better counsel."

"This is going to take time," Timothy said. The unsettled feeling hit him again. It was more of what people weren't saying. They kept talking about making choices, but everything was leading to an expectation; they were watching him as if the next move were up to him. He felt like he was playing a game without knowing the rules or even the object. Even in video games, the learning curve elevated your capabilities to the point where you could defeat the boss at the end of the level. This felt like he'd started the game in its advanced stages with no preparation.

"That is one thing you still have on your side. However, you must be tired and hungry."

"Now that you mention it, it's been a few days since I've had a good meal," he said. There'd been plenty of bread, cheese, and fruit aboard the boat, but a good steak sounded nice.

"I've arranged for you to reside here with me from now on," she said. "I hope you don't mind."

"Mind? That's awesome."

"We'll eat in a short while. In the meantime, I believe there is someone waiting for you just outside."

Timothy jumped up and went to the curtains, passing into the cool night air. Aenya rushed to him and threw her arms around him.

"I'm so glad you've returned," she said.

"Were you worried I wouldn't?" He was thankful she hadn't stopped to bow or anything.

"Not at all, I was never really worried," she said. "It's just things get kind of boring when you're not around."

"Thanks...I think."

"Your grandmother was kind enough to insist that I move to a dwelling just across the way," she said, pointing to a Primal tree some hundred feet away.

"So far?" Timothy had been getting used to having her in the same house.

"For you maybe, but not for someone who can fly." Aenya squeezed his arm.

"Are you going to eat with us?"

"No, I think you should spend time with your grandmother."

"I have to meet with the elders tomorrow," he said.

"I know. Pretty soon, you're going to be too important to talk to."

"Ugh. How did I get here?"

"Well, you don't get to pick your parents, do you?"

"You're a big help."

Aenya laughed and kissed his cheek. "Go on...get back inside. Maybe I'll see you tomorrow after you meet with everyone."

"I hope so."

The table was now laden with food, though he'd been outside just minutes. There was ham, the breast of some kind of fowl, bowls filled with carrots and greens, several breads, cheeses, and a beautiful decanter of wine. Tuathla poured some into a pair of crystal goblets.

"One wonderful thing about the Irish humans, they do have a way of creating beautiful glass objects," she said, admiring the goblet.

"Is that for me?"

"Why not?"

"I don't have much of a track record with alcohol," he said. Watching his uncle chug down beer was enough to put anyone off the idea of drinking.

"That's quite all right. A glass of wine is soothing."

Timothy took a small sip and was surprised how good it was. He filled his plate with food and they talked. He told her about his father's diary and that it had revealed the names of his brothers, but nothing as to where they might be. She repeated what Bardán had suggested, that in time, they might somehow find each other.

"I suppose I need to ask you of all people what you think is expected of me," he said. "You can't just put a sword into my hands and expect me to know what to do with it."

Tuathla stood and led him outside. Over the railings, a warm glow from the other dwellings and the ever-present swarm of lightning bugs cast shadows that moved in the darkness, making the forest look all the more alive.

"The Connleodh sword is a talisman that proves who you are, but it is also a symbol of what once was," she said. "You will find that possession of the sword itself will serve as a rallying point for our kind. It is not that I have any expectation of you other than your acknowledgment that you are the worthy bearer of it. Alfheim didn't exist because Aylwen chose it to be. It existed because all the elves who were a part of it imbued it with elegance and culture. Aylwen was the binding force. Everyone believed in her, they listened to her counsel and ideas. A strong leader doesn't achieve power from forcing others to do what they desire, but allows the best in everyone to surface to the benefit of all. Very soon, you will have to make a choice."

"What is it?"

"You will have to choose to relinquish the sword and return to your own life, or keep it and assume the role left vacant by the death of Aylwen so long ago."

"Does it make sense to have been tested and found worthy to hold the sword only to give it back?"

"There would be great disappointment should you choose to do so, but no one can ask you to give what you don't believe in your heart you are capable of giving. The very fact that someone who was worthy enough to possess the sword was able to step forward will give immeasurable hope for the eventual restoration of Alfheim. We have waited thousands of years. We are a patient people. Perhaps your path will be limited to your extraordinary healing powers alone."

"You don't believe that, though," Timothy said.

Tuathla held his eyes. She was intense, as if searching every molecule of his brain.

"You will face even greater tests," she said, her eyes turning back to the forest. "I am sorry you will have to endure them. Only then will you know."

He watched as his grandmother's shoulders went slack. She was very tired.

"It's late, Grandmother. Maybe we should both get some rest."

Inside, a young sídhe attended to her, aiding her down a hallway to her room.

"May I show you to yours?" An elf held up his arm, suggesting Timothy go up a short set of stairs that wound around the tree to a set of rooms above. In the center stood a huge four-post bed with beautiful pale-green fabric hangings on three sides. A small group of chairs surrounded a small table, and an assortment of candles illuminated the room. A deep chest of drawers sat against one wall. A quick peek revealed a full assortment of tunics and leggings. Timothy wondered if they had commissioned Derval to create an entire wardrobe for him.

"May I bring you anything?"

"No, thank you," he said. "This is amazing."

The elf bowed and left. Timothy undressed and climbed onto the bed. It was the softest thing he'd ever lain on. He closed his eyes, wanting to fall asleep, but one thing kept going through his mind: his grandmother's apology for the tests he had yet to face.

Chapter 29

TIMOTHY OPENED EVERY DRAWER AND growled in frustration. The elf who'd shown him to his room the night before came rushing in.

"My lord, is there something I can assist you with?" He looked petrified.

Timothy turned on him. "What?" he asked. "Wait…what did you just say?"

"I asked if there is something I might help you with, my lord."

Timothy threw up his hands and took a breath. "First, my name is Timothy. Second, I apologize for not asking yours last night."

"Labras, my lord. I am called Labras."

"Timothy," he said again, pointing to myself. "That would be inappropriate, my lord."

"I tell you what, when we're talking, you and I, can we just drop the 'my lord' stuff? Can we do that?"

Labras hesitated, as if Timothy had just asked him to solve all the world's problems in ten words or less.

"Okay?"

"I will try, my…yes."

"Good. Thank you. I need your opinion." Timothy turned back to the chest. "I have to meet with the elders this morning. What the hell are you supposed to wear for something like that?"

"Allow me," said Labras, practically pushing him away from the chest. He slid open the fifth drawer down and pulled out a pair of black leather leggings that were so soft they could double as a pillow, then a full-length tunic of royal blue. "This will be perfect, my…" Labras shook his head. "This material will allow you to wear the belt and sword without fussing up the fabric too much."

"I guess the elders are slaves to fashion?"

Labras looked dismayed.

"Sorry," Timothy said. "I'm still getting used to elfin clothing. Up till a couple of weeks ago, I lived in jeans."

"Jeans?"

"Never mind."

"Shall I help you dress?"

"No, I think I can take it from here, but thank you."

Labras bowed and exited the room. Timothy hoped he wasn't too much of a disappointment.

He went down to the main room, but Tuathla was still sleeping. There was a full spread for breakfast. Timothy ate slowly, wondering if someone would tell him the time for the gathering.

Before long, Ruairí stepped inside the curtains.

"Good morning, my lord," he said.

"Don't you start, too."

"Start what?"

"A week ago my name was Timothy."

"A week ago you did not possess the Connleodh sword."

"The sword has not changed me," he said.

"No, my lord. The sword has changed us."

"When am I meeting with the elders?" said Timothy in a voice bordering on defeat.

"They are gathered in the hall and waiting for you to attend them at your pleasure."

Oh boy. Timothy fought the urge to roll his eyes.

He followed the elf down the long winding stairs to find a horse waiting for him. He was shocked to discover that his usual detachment of six had grown to twenty. At least Eoghan was there, too.

Their procession made its way to the hall he'd seen that first day with Aran, who was, in fact, standing just outside to greet them. The last time the room had been dark. Now, light filled it from wall sconces and every candle on the chandelier hanging over the center of the table. Seven elves occupied chairs. Bardán gave Timothy a nod of greeting and encouragement. Another group of attendants stood behind the elders.

Aran guided Timothy to a chair on the opposite side of the table facing them, leaving two unfilled seats on either side. As he pulled out the chair, all seven elves stood. As they sat, Bardán remained on his feet.

"Timothy, I'd like to present the elders of our realm." At least someone used his rightful name. "Liam oversees our infrequent dealings with the humans—an ambassador of sorts. Cillian manages those who occupy our realm, Myrddin is our ambassador to other elfin realms around the world, and Dwyryd is our Elder

Druid." Timothy recognized him as the one who had performed the wedding. "Eirnin is the Elder Judge and representative from the Council of Judges, and lastly, Aldith looks after our military affairs. Of course, as you may recall, my duties include the keeping of ancient texts and the management of our forests."
"I remember," Timothy said.

"May I present Timothy, Aylwen's heir and holder of the Connleodh sword."

"Will you present it?" Cillian asked.

Timothy stood and pulled the sword from its scabbard and laid it on the table. Under the direct lighting of the candles above, the sword glistened as if on fire.

The six elves leaned in to one another and began to speak in Elfin.

Bardán cleared his throat. "I suggest that we continue our discourse in English, as Timothy has not yet mastered our ancient tongue."

Eirnin, the Elder Judge, stiffened, evidently uncomfortable at Timothy's lack of education. Timothy caught Bardán's eye, but he just winked as if to say he shouldn't worry about it.
"How are we to be certain this artifact is genuine?" asked Myrddin.

"I was there during its presentation," Bardán said. "I will vouch for its authenticity."

"Why was this mission to retrieve the sword not pre-authorized by us?"

"The voyage was carried out by request of Tuathla."

"Forgive me, Bardán," Myrddin continued. "While Tuathla has our greatest respect, she has no official capacity here."

"And none of us are of Aylwen's line. I believe it was well within her rights to commission such a voyage to test the worthiness of her grandson," said Bardán.

"Given the gravity of the outcome, there should have been a much greater force sent with you to retrieve it," said Aldith. "The sword is far too important to have been accompanied by a mere six men."

"You forget that it would have been lethal for anyone else to touch it."

"Until it had been claimed," Aldith insisted.

"I, for one, am not comfortable with an expectation that we relinquish any measure of control over Sídhlin to a boy who cannot even speak our language," said Eirnin.

"No one is suggesting anything of the sort," said Bardán, the volume of his voice rising.

"It has been thousands of years," Eirnin continued, his voice rising higher than Bardán's. "If we are tasked with the responsibility of restoring Alfheim, it must be done with great care and planning. Liam, you are most familiar with humans. I think you must take the lead in guiding Timothy to a greater understanding of our ways and see to his education."

"I agree, and in the meantime, I think the sword should be put under my protection until he comes of age," said Aldith.

"I disagree," said Bardán, who ran his hands through his hair. "First, we have not been tasked with Alfheim's restoration.

Second, the talisman belongs to the rightful bearer of it in accordance with its original enchantment."

Timothy had no idea what he'd expected by coming to the gathering, but it wasn't that. Eirnin's face was red as he turned to Bardán. Each of the seven faces, with one exception, showed tension, if not outright anger. Only Dwyryd, the Elder Druid, ignored the rest of them. He was gazing at Timothy as if watching for a reaction, studying him. Several of the attendants attempted to put themselves between the chairs of the elders, offering goblets of amber-colored liquid. It seemed heavier than mere wine, and Timothy figured it was something to calm everyone down. He was a little concerned about that. Alcohol would loosen their inhibitions to argue, not curb then.

The heated discussions fractured into separate debates, all related to what steps were to be followed now that the sword had made the transition from myth to reality.

"I think it is well within our rights to have the boy swear a fealty to the governance of this body until he proves himself worthy of a leadership role," Eirnin demanded.

"And it should be witnessed and seconded by Tuathla," Cillian added.

Timothy stood up. He reached over the table and took the sword, sliding it hard into the scabbard. The clang echoed through the room, and there was instant silence.

"I see some things in the elfin world aren't that much different from the human one. A couple of weeks ago, I didn't even know I was an elf, and now all of a sudden I have a legend for an ancestor and a sword that…well, I don't even know what it does yet. But it's kind of ridiculous for you all to be arguing like this. You sound like our Congress back home, and that's not a good thing." What was it with adults? It didn't seem to matter whether they were elves or humans, but put a bunch of politicians in a room and everyone becomes an idiot. Without a second look at any of them, Timothy strode around the table and through the opening.

"Ruairí, can I have my horse please?"

Eoghan had the reins in his hands and helped him into the saddle. Timothy was more than grateful so that no one would see his hands shaking. Taking the reins, he turned the horse around with a confidence he didn't have. He prayed he wouldn't fall off the beast and make a total fool of himself. Thankfully, he made good on his exit and breathed a sigh of relief.

* * *

Bardán had to force himself not to smile as he watched the faces of the elders turn from shock to indignation.

"He just walked out on us," Eirnin said as if he'd just witnessed something totally unimaginable. "The impudence!"

Myrddin leaned back over his seat to an attendant. "Go fetch him back, immediately."

"Let him go," said Bardán, letting his face relax with a laugh.

"You think this show of disrespect is funny?"

"Eirnin, I think you might question just who showed greater disrespect here," Bardán said. "One of the most important events in our history has just occurred, and you all sat there quibbling like a bunch of old fairies."

Myrddin's face puffed up like a fish, obviously insulted and trying to find words.

"Listen, all of you. There is only one thing clear: Timothy is Aylwen's heir. Beyond that, we have no claim over what he decides to do. It is not our right to assume that he will become a rallying point to address our concerns with Cadwaladr."

"Then what are you suggesting we do?" Cillian asked. "As you say, a historic event has happened, it has fallen into our laps. Are you suggesting we not seize the opportunity to leverage this to our advantage?"

"I'm suggesting that we give Timothy some time to digest what's happened to him over these last days and be his guides, not his surrogate parents. He has his own agenda, but I've spoken with Tuathla and to his friend Aenya. Both have confessed to me that they sense something in Timothy that is true and deep. You can't expect a flower to blossom if you grind the bud to earth with the heel of a boot."

"Well spoken," said Dwyryd. "I concur. Myrddin, you may not think that Tuathla has an official capacity here, but never forget that she saved our ass from catastrophe."

"I was only suggesting—"

"Save it," said Dwyryd, holding up his hand. "Tonight, she will present Timothy to the realm. Let us gauge the reaction of the people once they understand what we know, and let us serve as counselors to him instead of taskmasters."

Bardán was grateful, as always, for the voice of reason that Dwyryd offered. The time for doing nothing was over. But it was also a time where mistakes would be costly.

Chapter 30

Timothy cantered down the path toward his tree. He knew he was supposed to make the trip with his attendants but he was angry and didn't care about the protocol. *To hell with the sword,* he thought. None of that stuff was going to make any difference in terms of his settling the score over his mother. It was all a distraction; it had nothing to do with him. As far as he was concerned, if they hadn't figured out how to deal with Cadwaladr and take steps to restoring Alfheim over the past several hundred years, then his presence wasn't going to make any difference at this point.

He pulled gently on the reins, and his mount slowed. He was starting to get the hang of horse riding, though he felt the animal deserved more credit in knowing what to do than any talent on his part. Timothy swung his leg over the back of the horse and jumped to the dirt, then reached out a hand to its nose. Its nostrils flared, and its big brown eyes looked right at Timothy, as if the horse were smiling at him.

Aenya leaned against the railing of the stairs with her arms crossed.

"You're learning to make quite an entrance," she said.

"Thanks, but you should have seen my exit."

"Oh?"

"Yeah, what a bunch of stuffy old..." He didn't know what to call them. "They're like a bunch of bickering old women."

"Doesn't sound too good," she said. "What happened?"

Timothy related the events of the brief meeting and felt his anger drain away.

"So apart from them acting in a bad way, can you see what was really going on?" she asked.

"What do you mean?"

"I think it's important to look past their initial reactions. Obviously they're afraid of a major change."

"So you're siding with them?"

"Not at all, I think you were justified in walking out. Just take the higher road and understand what fueled their fears."

"I'm not sure."

"For hundreds of years, they've guarded the affairs of Sídhlin, and to their credit, this realm is the best and largest of its kind. The war with Cadwaladr notwithstanding, they've done a pretty good job."

"The war, that was a sizable ball to drop," he said.

"No argument, but they didn't create the conflict, it was brought upon them. Now you show up, demonstrate an amazing ability to thwart certain death, retrieve a sword that hasn't been held by anyone in thousands of years, and they see what they've worked so hard to maintain face a fundamental shift overnight. They're scared."

"You make it sound like it's my fault. I didn't ask for any of this."

"No, you dope," she said, cupping his cheeks with her hands. "Just recognize that something wonderful might be happening, and be the one who keeps the coolest head. Last I saw, you're the one with an ancient sword on his belt."

It took a few seconds for the fluttering feeling of having her hands touch his face to go away so he could find his thoughts again.

"You're right," Timothy said. "I hadn't figured it that way." Everyone seemed so ready to promote him for what they needed him to be. As far as he was concerned, there was only one goal. He had no idea what should come after that.

"Of course I'm right. Now go play, I promised to help your grandmother get ready for tonight."

"Go play?"

She pointed behind him. Timothy turned to see Eoghan standing a few feet away. He was holding a long bow in his hands, his eyes staring at the ground in front of him.

"Is that the bow you were working on during the voyage?" Timothy asked.

"I finished it last night and thought you might like to try it out, my lord."

"I would love to…on one condition," he said.

"Yes, my lord?"

He stepped close enough that only Eoghan would hear. "If you're going to teach me how to shoot, then while we're practicing, if I hear you say the word 'lord' so much as one time, I'm going to use you as a target."

Eoghan laughed. "Deal," he said.

They walked through the forest, guiding their horses while the rest of the troop followed close behind. Eoghan wanted to know more about what it was like to live in the human world. He asked Timothy question after question, though he couldn't imagine how freaky it must be to realize that you're no longer part of a species you once thought you were. He said he'd be devastated to find out he was human and not elfin. Timothy had to agree that a transition in that direction would be devastating. It turned out that Eoghan was the youngest member in his family's history to enter Sídhlin's small military, but his family had been bow makers for generations, which in the elfin world covered about an eon.

They went far into the fields outside the forest, through the pastures that weren't quite ready for the spring tilling and planting. Several bundles of hay were rolled and standing upright.

"There," Eoghan said. "Those will make good targets."

He showed Timothy how to string the bow by flexing the stave between his legs. The chord was so tight, plucking it produced a musical note.

"Now you nock the arrow with the odd feather up, then pull the bow on an angle like this," he said, demonstrating. "You have to stand with your target to the left side of you and turn your head to face it. Then you draw the nock back all the way to your ear, aim, and release." The arrow flew at blinding speed; the shaft buried itself in the dry straw. "Now you try."

Timothy pulled an arrow out of the quiver and nocked it just as he'd been shown. He pulled the bow up and drew back on the string. It wasn't as easy as it looked. His muscles strained trying to get it all the way to his ear. He pointed the tip of the arrow toward the straw and let go. A searing-hot pain burned the inside of his left forearm as the bowstring scraped along the thin material of his sleeve. There was a sharp twang and the arrow went up in the air, did somersaults, and fell harmlessly to the ground about ten feet in front of them.

"Damn that stung, what did I do wrong?"

"Ah, you have to sort of turn your wrist so the string flies clear of your arm. Not to worry, it's a common mistake."

"Any other common mistakes I should know about?"

"Nah, but it wasn't something I could tell you about; you have to experience that once or twice for yourself." Eoghan was grinning.

Timothy tried again. This time the arrow flew forward, but it went a good five feet wide of the target and buried itself in the field a dozen yards farther away.

"Not bad," Eoghan said.

After several more tries, Timothy managed to put one into the base of the haystack. By then his fingers were sore, and he could see blisters starting to form.

"All in all, I'd say it was a passable first lesson," Eoghan said.

"How long have you been shooting?"

"Since I were about four."

"It seems most elves know how to use a bow."

"Aye, but most don't spend the extra time to become a marksman like we need to be. Most master the basics so they can hunt."

"So how good are you?" Timothy asked.

"I'm a fair shot."

"How fair?"

Eoghan went to his horse, reached into a saddlebag, pulled out a small disk around six inches in diameter, and handed it to Timothy.

"We use those for long distance targets to qualify for service. Give it a toss in the air," he said. He stood there holding the bow in one hand.

"Don't you want to get ready first?"

"I am ready, go on."

Timothy curled his index finger around the disk like he was going to try skipping it over the surface of a lake and threw it high in the air.

Eoghan was a blur. In an instant, he drew an arrow, nocked it, aimed, and fired. The arrow came down about twenty-five yards away. They ran to retrieve it. The tip of the arrow had pierced the disk about an inch from the center.

"A little sloppy," he said.

"Sloppy?" Timothy was stunned.

"An inch could mean the distance between striking a man in the heart and letting him live."

"I'm impressed. I am also very glad you're on our side."

"If you ever want to see real fine shooting, watch Ruairí on one of his good days. He's terrifying."

"Good to know," Timothy said. It was nice to feel safe.

Chapter 31

"I'M AFRAID YOU HAVE UPSET some of the elders," Tuathla said. She slipped her hand around Timothy's arm as they reached the bottom of their tree.

"I know."

"Between them, they have several thousand years' worth of wisdom."

"That doesn't mean they're always right."

Tuathla laughed. "No, it doesn't mean they're always right." She leaned her head close to his. "Don't tell them I said this, but some of them are old windbags."

Timothy was coming to admire his grandmother more and more, and found himself wishing she had accepted being queen. She would have made a great one.

"You must never show weakness, but balance that with respect. You stung them today, and they won't forget it. That's a good thing because even though it made them angry, you have shown them you will not be one to walk over. It gives them something to respect in return."

"So in other words, make nice for a while."

"Quite right," she said. "I know what Aldith suggested. Never surrender that sword to anyone other than the sídhe in Slaíne."

"I promise."

The number of attendants for both Timothy and Tuathla had grown to nearly a hundred. It felt like travelling with a small army. As they approached the oak field, Tuathla pulled her arm back and stood straighter. A large crowd parted ahead of the first of the attendants, and Timothy stepped back to let his grandmother go first. She moved to the fountain under the oak branches.

Quiet spread through the gathering. It was the largest congregation of elves Timothy had seen yet. To one side, standing in front, were the elders, including Bardán, whom Timothy hadn't seen or spoken with since he'd walked out of the meeting. He hoped the elder wasn't upset. It was impossible to read what Bardán was thinking. Timothy scanned the crowd for Aenya, alarmed she wasn't there, but then he spied her standing with Ailill and his family.

"It is good to be with you all again so shortly after our last reunion," said Tuathla in a clear voice. "We are still under the influence of the Alder Moon, which is as it should be, for it is a time to recognize the potential of recent events.

"A short time ago, our lovely Aenya sang for us, reciting the words of 'Aylwen's Lament' and reminding us that we still look to the day when Alfheim will exist once more. It is a source of great joy that the cause for her lament may soon be past. The Connleodh sword has been restored to us."

A buzz flared through the crowd like fire over dried kindling. Hundreds of heads turned to each other with looks of astonishment. In hushed whispers, they repeated the phrase of the lament: *who is the elfin lord*?

Tuathla waited for everyone's attention to focus back on her.

"Many of you either witnessed or heard of the events at the wedding. Cadwaladr nearly killed the bridegroom, Cavan, but he was miraculously saved by a young healer. This healer is, in fact, the seventh son of a seventh. Only twice have we known of their kind, and this one is only the second to Aylwen's beloved Arthur." Tuathla paused, making eye contact with several in the crowd. "This young healer is my grandson and a direct descendent of Aylwen and Arthur."

There was a collective gasp, as if everyone had taken a breath on cue. "Where is he?" someone shouted.

"Is he with us tonight?"

"Can this be true?"

Tuathla raised her hands. She waited for everyone to quiet, then held out her arm. Timothy reluctantly stepped forward, terrified to stand before these hundreds, if not thousands, of elves. He was nothing compared to the enormity of their hopes. Thousands of years of waiting now seemed to center on him. Everyone had said he would have a choice, but stepping forward seemed like a clear statement of intent. Was Tuathla simply setting him up for the challenge, or was it something else?

As he moved beside her, Timothy could feel the expectation, like gravity. What could he possibly give them? The idea of a speech was ridiculous; public speaking was never one of his strengths.

The sword, he could show them the sword. It was what they most wanted to see, the talisman that fueled their belief in a different future. Timothy drew it from the scabbard; the metallic ring echoed into the branches over their heads. Then, like the ebb of a wave on the beach, the front rows of elves knelt to the ground, the effect rippling backwards until the whole field had followed their lead. One remained standing. It was Aran. He watched and then turned into the trees on the far side of the field. Even the elders had taken one knee. Aran's reaction struck him as very peculiar.

Then the oddest thought popped into Timothy's head: Derek Hollister, the captain of the ice hockey team. Timothy wished the bully could see him now.

He slid the sword back into the scabbard.

Tuathla embraced Timothy in front of all. A tremendous cheer struck him as their way of signifying the expectation that he was to rise to a position that would oversee the restoration of Alfheim. Even the elders seemed to have spent their anger and came up as a group to acknowledge him and put themselves at his service. When Timothy mentioned that he hoped to serve them just as well, Bardán looked ready to burst with pride.

Cavan and Mairin found him afterwards and were ecstatic, especially in light of whom he was to them now. Ailill and Derval expressed how glad they were to have been the first to host him in Sídhlin.

The evening went on for hours, and every elf greeted Timothy, sometimes twice. Every boy wanted a look at the sword and incurred, without exception, the wrath of their parents for having dared to ask. One boy of no more than four or five years of age had large blue eyes, puffy cheeks, and red hair. His request was so genuine that Timothy couldn't resist. He knelt down and pulled the sword out quietly. The boy's eyes went wide, and he broke into the biggest grin.

"Thank you," he said.

Timothy put a hand on the boy's head and took a minute to enjoy how happy he was just to see it.

By the time Timothy and Tuathla returned to the dwelling, all were exhausted. She was beyond tired but also looked content. He stepped onto the platform outside his quarters. It was farther around the turn of the tree than Tuathla's and at a level higher, but he could still make out Aenya's dwelling across the way. He hadn't seen her for more than a second and wished he could catch her attention, but all was quiet on her side. He guessed they'd catch up the next morning. He was anxious to talk with her about the night, how being in the spotlight would change things now that everyone knew who he was. Virtually every elf Timothy met after the announcement had left him with the impression that they believed the thousands of years of waiting for a return to their golden age was about to end. It seemed more of an opportunity to disappoint thousands in one shot the instant they realized he wasn't what they thought. He felt more like an impostor than a leader.

"Good evening, my lord," said Labras. "Can I bring you anything?"

"I thought we weren't going to use that term," he said.

"Things are a little more official now, my lord. It would be inappropriate for me not to adhere to the correct form of address."

"You have my permission," Timothy said.

"Thank you, my lord."

It was a losing battle.

"I don't suppose you could make hot chocolate, could you?"

"Of course. I shall bring you some at once."

Timothy returned to his room and changed into a pair of soft leggings and a linen shirt, placing the sword on top of the chest. He sat on the foot of the bed to wait for Labras, trying to think of the last time he'd had a hot chocolate.

The sound of tree branches and leaves rustling outside reached his ears, as if a great wind had kicked up, but the curtains didn't move. It was odd; then he remembered the wedding just before Cadwaladr arrived. There was a creaking sound outside, and the tip of a shadow spread across the open deck.

"Labras?" There was no sound. Timothy wondered if Aenya had flown across and was waiting outside to see if he was still awake. "Aenya?" He took a few steps toward the opening, but had a bad feeling, like the one on the plane after the flight attendants had opened the door.

A scuffling noise came from behind, as if someone were dragging a heavy object across the floor, then gurgling. A jumbled shadow appeared from the hallway. Aran slithered into the room and the light. He was holding Labras, pushing him forward with a dagger drawn across his throat.

"Aran, what are you doing?"

"Cadwaladr sends his greetings," he said. "He apologizes for not making a personal appearance this evening." Timothy felt the hair on the back of his neck tingle. He wanted to kick himself. He'd never felt comfortable around Aran and now he knew why. Hadn't he always heard it was the quiet ones you had to keep an eye on?

"Cadwaladr's the last person I would have expected," Timothy said. Labras was struggling, but doing himself more harm than good. Small trickles of blood rolled down his neck as Aran kept the blade close. "Let him go, Aran."

"I'm afraid he's seen me."

"I'm obviously the reason you're here, you don't need him. Deliver your message and go."

"Message?" Aran smiled. "There's no message."

"Why are you doing this?" Timothy asked. "How can you betray your people?"

"My people?" Aran said with disgust. "My people have languished for millennia, waiting for some miracle to give them back what was lost. It is well past the time for elves to restore sanity to the world, and people like you and Tuathla merely interfere with great leaders like Cadwaladr. You once asked if my parents were proud of me. The answer is no, because they think I have given my life to those who oppose Cadwaladr. The elders shunned my mother and father because they attempted to broker an alliance with him. But they will be proud now, when they learn of my contribution to his ascent...to the position he deserves. What we all deserve."

Labras yanked down hard on Aran's arm and sank his teeth into the side of his hand. The elder-servant cursed and shoved him away, drawing back to strike, but Labras ran into the hall, yelling to the elves posted at the base of the tree, far below. Aran looked torn between giving chase and doing what he'd come to do. Timothy backed toward the outside opening, but froze as Aran raised his arm to throw the dagger. It whizzed past his face and struck the curtain behind, skittering harmlessly to the floor and out through the opening. Timothy ran to grab it, but pulled up short. Scruffy, the elf from the airport, was standing there, his face conveying the satisfaction of a hunter whose prey had just run into a trap.

"Well mate, aren't we glad to be seeing ya again? This time, we're gonna finish what we started back home now, won't we?" He pulled his own dagger. Timothy lunged at him to put himself inside the attacker's reach. He thought he was doing something right by the look of surprise on Scruffy's face. Timothy gripped the forearm of the hand holding the blade with all his strength and circled the fingers of his other hand around Scruffy's throat. The elf pushed back hard, forcing him up against the wall near the opening. Timothy's head bounced off the solid wood; a blinding pain rippled through his body. Somehow, he'd managed to keep a grip on Scruffy's wrist, but the point of the dagger was driving toward his face. Timothy had forgotten how strong the elf was. He pulled his head to one side just as the dagger buried itself in the heavy oak. He smashed the elf's nose with his forehead and felt the soft squish as cartilage moved in a direction it wasn't meant to go.

"You bloody bastard!" Scruffy screamed. As he brought his hand up to his face, Timothy ducked out of his grip but managed only two steps toward the stairs before someone yanked him backward. Timothy sprawled onto the deck as Aran picked up his dagger and sprang forward, but Scruffy was having none of it. Blood streaked his cheek. He shoved Aran out of the way, obviously angered to the point of wanting the victory all to himself.

He grabbed Timothy by the front of the tunic and lifted him onto his feet, driving his lower back against the railing of the platform. Timothy thought he was going over the side, but Scruffy jerked him forward and then slammed him onto the wood a second time. The railing bowed outwards, and he heard a crack. Timothy hoped it was the wood and not his spine.

"Hurry up," Aran shouted.

"Just pipe down and give us a minute, will ya?"

There were voices from far below, and the sound of boots racing up the wooden steps.

"Timothy!" Aenya's scream echoed through the trees, and then a very sharp crack. The railing gave way, and Timothy fell into space. Scruffy pawed at the crumbling wood to keep from going over himself. Timothy saw a branch just inches from where he'd been pinned to the rail. If only he'd been able to grab it. Falling, he reached toward it.

Everything stopped. As if he were floating, the distance between his hand and the branch started to close.

Ruairí led ten men through the last turn of the stairs and rushed onto the platform. They took in the scene and then froze as they stared at him. He expected Aenya to be holding him, but she wasn't, there was nothing but air below and around him.

"Timothy?"

He turned to the sound of Aenya's voice. She was hovering twenty feet away, her face a mask of shock.

At the railing, Scruffy was whimpering for help. Timothy thought of grabbing him by the neck, and then it was happening. He yanked the elf back from the edge; that broke through everyone's confusion. Ruairí's elves took hold of Scruffy and seized Aran, who was trying to slip back inside.

Ruairí ordered four elves to Tuathla's rooms to check on her as Aenya landed on the platform next to Timothy. If he hadn't felt so shaken and angry, he might have laughed at the look on her face.

"You flew," she said. "You were flying."

"I guess I did."

"Elves don't fly."

"It's better than the alternative," Timothy said, looking past the broken railing and down at the ground.

"I would have caught you."

"You might not always be there."

They descended the stairs to Tuathla's rooms and met Bardán as he finished ascending them, breathing heavily. He herded them inside, where Tuathla stood as one of the elves wrapped a bandage around Labras's neck. She looked stunned, but her features relaxed when she saw her grandson enter the room.

"Are you all right?" she asked.

"I'm fine," Timothy said. "Just a little sore."

"That was Aran they were dragging down the stairs," Bardán said. "I cannot fathom the depth of his treachery. He has served the elders for over three hundred years."

"It would seem the dangers are more real than I feared," Tuathla said, "or closer than I thought possible."

"He flew," Aenya said. Tuathla and Bardán stared at her. "How is that possible?"

"Who flew?" Bardán asked.

"I did." Timothy said.

"I don't understand."

Before he could say a word, Aenya recounted the struggle. "The railing broke and instead of falling, he flew upward and then straight at the elf, grabbing him away from the edge. How is that possible?" she asked again.

"Could it be the sword?" asked Bardán.

"I don't believe so," said Tuathla. "But, as you said, no one knows the full extent of a seventh's powers. We know more of Aylwen than Arthur, perhaps by design."

"What will be done with Aran?" Timothy asked.

"Eirnin, the Elder Judge, has been summoned. Both of them will be held and indicted for treason. Aran has a lot to answer for," said Bardán.

Tuathla was flustered, but her stoic bearing suggested everything was all right. Timothy was more worried about Aenya. She was reserved in a way he'd never seen, as if deep in thought and uncertain what to make of this new development. For that matter, it hadn't truly sunk into his head. He was just glad not to have become a permanent part of the foliage below. The fear of falling, mixed with the sudden realization he could fly, all within the span of five seconds, made him dizzy.

Another thought crossed his mind: he had just survived the fourth attempt on his life in a matter of weeks. Back home, he'd only been beaten up two or three times in his whole life. So much for living among a peaceful species.

The adrenaline rush had passed, and Timothy felt exhaustion drain what little energy he had left. Before long, they all decided to get some rest. Aenya walked Timothy back up to his room. Her serious expression gave him the sense that she needed to talk. He wanted to talk too, but wrapping his head around every new thing was becoming harder and harder. It should have been getting easier, but it was impossible to get a grip on what he'd been through: seeing Aylwen, taking the sword, and suddenly finding out he could fly. He felt a little squirmy with Aenya, like she was somehow angry that he'd been hiding his superpower. He felt embarrassed, which was ridiculous.

In the end, it seemed that neither could find a way of talking about anything. They stared at one another, too shocked or just too unbalanced to make any sense of what they were feeling. Exhaustion didn't help. Timothy flopped onto the bed, just to rest his head on the pillow and close his eyes for a minute.

* * *

Timothy started snoring lightly. Aenya was glad, because she needed to sort things out. She settled into a chair opposite his bed and stared at him. Every day brought another revelation, and they weren't little ones anymore. They were life-altering, changing everything she ever knew about her own kind.

As she watched the gentle rise and fall of his chest, she felt something quirky take hold that she couldn't quite label. Clearly, it was something else new. Was it pride? She'd saved him and, considering all the developments, the ramifications of that act were staggering. It dawned on her that diving into the river was mostly likely going to be the defining action of her life. Aenya couldn't begin to understand where all this was heading, but whatever happened, it was going to be something far different than she could ever have imagined.

There was something else. When she'd seen the elf forcing Timothy over the railing, her reaction hadn't simply been a sense of alarm. She'd felt a panic like nothing else she'd ever experienced. And it wasn't because he was important to their world; it was a direct assault on her well-being. She recognized her attachment was personal.

And he could fly.

How was that possible? No male-born elf had ever done that. Some had the gift of healing, but Timothy's ability was on a completely different plane. It was like the gentle exterior everyone saw was a shell that hid unexplored and unknown talents.

Aenya felt tired but was too wired to fall asleep. Her thoughts kept replaying the last three weeks, which only served to increase her anxiety about not knowing what role she needed to play, if any at all. Tuathla had made a convincing argument that Timothy might need Aenya. But she recognized on some deeper level that she didn't want to be anywhere without him. Aenya wasn't familiar with that kind of need.

She walked to the side of his bed. For someone who had just survived yet another murder attempt, his face was surprisingly free of concern. She brushed her fingertips over the wisps of hair lying across his forehead.

"I'm here," she whispered.

Chapter 32

Seumais's mount cantered through the portcullis as he held the reins of the two horses carrying empty saddles. Aran and Sorley hadn't come back, and that didn't bode well. Cadwaladr was going to be angry. Seumais had waited three full hours before giving up and leaving Sídhlin.

How bloody hard was it to kill a boy? He seemed to have the charmed life of a cat, but Cadwaladr wasn't going to see it that way. Seumais had organized four groups of elves to do away with him, and each time it had failed, three times by the help of the stupid fairy. He was personally accountable and debated not telling the master of his failure. He was beginning to think he should turn around, sneak back into the realm, and take care of it himself, along with the girl. Cadwaladr would be extra appreciative if he took her out in the bargain. He would never allow Seumais to lead any of the elves into the attack if he didn't prove himself now.

An advance group of sixty would arrive from Poland within the week. The plan was to have Sídhlin in turmoil before then, weakened by the deaths of Timothy and Tuathla. There would be no one to stop them from overrunning the forest and crowning Cadwaladr as king. Then he and his followers would start to build a real Alfheim from the ashes of the old realm, one that was strong and ready to renew ties with the world of men. The weakness of humanity would soon yield to the prowess of elfin knowledge and strength. Cadwaladr had worked for over a hundred years, quietly building connections with small groups of influential men in the major countries of the world: America, Russia, England, France.

Seumais had waited centuries to return home. He wasn't about to let a child, even one of his own blood, prevent him from standing with Cadwaladr as they reaped their rewards. His time with generations of humans would be of great use to Cadwaladr as they moved forward.

He led the horses to the stable and dismounted. Seumais kicked the boot of a sleeping stable boy who jumped up, frightened to be caught sleeping, even though it was late in the night.

"Sorry, my lord," he said. "I was just resting my eyes."

"See to these mounts," Seumais said with a grunt. "Tell no one of my return. I am leaving again."

"At once, my lord."

Seumais untethered a quiver of arrows tipped with elfshot and the bow from Sorley's saddle. He attached them to his own mount and then swung into the saddle. The horse trotted back through the portcullis and onto the open field; then Seumais kicked the animal into a full gallop. He wanted to be ready before sunrise.

Chapter 33

WARM SUNLIGHT CAST A GOLDEN glow through Timothy's closed eyelids. It felt like a Saturday with no school, and he wanted to roll over and slip back into a carefree and hopefully dreamless sleep.

"I thought you'd never wake up."

His eyes flew open, and he sprang to a sitting position. Aenya was slumped in a chair on the other side of the room.

"How long have you been sitting there?"

"Since last night."

"Why?"

She just shrugged her shoulders. She looked tired.

"After last night, I'm sure no one is going to get near the tree, let alone up it," Timothy said.

"And who'd have thought Aran would be allied with that creep?"

Timothy was secretly thrilled she was sitting there. Labras appeared as if on cue.

"Good day, my lord, and good day to you also, Aenya."

"Labras, what are you doing here?" Timothy asked.

"Where else should I be, my lord?"

"Resting. That was a nasty cut on your throat."

"I'm fine and I assure you I rested very well last night."

"I never had the chance to thank you for what you did."

Labras lowered his eyes as if he were undeserving of the words. "I should have done much more," he said. "I left you with two assassins, you could have been killed."

"It would have been worse if you hadn't called Ruairí. They might have tried to kill Tuathla, too. Without your help, we'd probably both be dead."

"Thank you, my lord, I am most grateful." His shoulders rose and his chest puffed out. "Can I bring you both anything?"

"I'd love some fruit," Aenya said.

"Right away."

"Is my grandmother up yet?"

"Not yet, she is still resting. But a note was delivered this morning from the counsel. They would like to know if you would be willing to meet with them later in the day."

After walking out yesterday, he wasn't thrilled with the idea of seeing them again so soon, but then they'd been agreeable at the gathering. "I guess that would be all right."

Labras bowed once and hurried from the room.

They ate a breakfast of berries and melon. Aenya was still very quiet. Since the day he'd awoken in her cottage, she had never been so gloomy. It was unnerving. *We need a day off.* Timothy was almost sorry he'd agreed to meet with the elders.

He went into the bath chamber and changed his clothes. When he returned, she was standing outside by an unbroken section of railing.

"I have an idea," he said.

"What?"

"Let's play hooky."

"We're not in school."

"No kidding, but we need a break. Things have been a little tense."

She laughed, but it seemed forced and without a smile.

"Besides, I need to explore this flying thing."

"Timothy, I don't think..."

He didn't wait for an answer. He walked to the edge of the platform where the railing had fallen away, dove into thin air, and plummeted straight down. The shock of it kept him from screaming. He came within fifty feet of becoming ant food before Aenya swooped under and caught him.

"Are you crazy or just stupid?" She was angry.

This time, he laughed, but it sounded more like crazy.

"Both?" His voice shook.

"I would say so," she said. Her eyes flashed with rage, and Timothy half expected her to drop him out of frustration. "Flying isn't like diving into water."

"What did I do wrong?" he asked as she started to pull him up higher.

"What was going through your mind last night when you stopped falling?"

"Well, when I started to fall, I remember thinking there was a branch right there that I could have grabbed. I guess I sort of reached for it."

"Exactly," she said. "You have to use your mind to fly. The power comes from reaching for something and pulling it toward you with your mind. You don't just float around."

"You mean like I could be sitting on the couch and drag the TV remote to me?"

"Technically, yes," she said. "But you have to be very precise or you'll find yourself flying headfirst into a wall. I'd wait a while before trying something like that."

"Gotcha."

"But there's more," she said.

"Isn't there always?"

Aenya rolled her eyes.

"Yes. You repel with the same power you use to pull something toward you. It's how you land. But you must be very careful with that. You must control it. If you use it in anger, you might release a pulse that is lethal."

"Wait…so that's how you pushed Derek Hollister without touching him and how you knocked out those elves at the airport." She nodded. Then a thought struck him and made him shudder. "I've had this power all along," he said, more to himself than Aenya. "That night when my uncle made me so angry, I went to my room ticking like a fiend…when I woke up the next morning, I realized that a glass on my desk was broken and I couldn't remember how it had happened. So all the time when I thought it was my ADD kicking in and making me tic, it was this thing inside my head."

Timothy looked to the tops of the trees. "How concrete does something have to be in order to grab for it?"

"What do you mean?"

"I mean, I can pull at a branch of a tree, but what about a cloud in the sky or a star?"

"Yes, any of those things. You simply reach for air and you'll be carried along. Move your body or refocus on something in another direction to guide yourself. When you want to set down, you just give a little push with your mind and step out of it."

He set his eyes on the tip of a thin branch at the top of the forest and mentally pulled at it. He felt his body slip from her arms as he began to rise through the air. Glancing to the side, he saw a couple on the platform of a tree-dwelling looking on with wonderment as they witnessed the impossible—an elf in flight. At the tops of the trees, a small flock of birds perched on a branch flapped their wings and backed away in shock. Timothy couldn't keep from laughing out loud. Then he broke through the trees and soared above the forest. His stomach rolled as if he'd just dropped straight down the world's fastest roller coaster, and a tingle electrified his spine as the earth opened at his feet. Flying came with a total sense of freedom.

Aenya came from within the trees, her arm stretched toward him, looking concerned that he might drop at any second. He smiled at her and turned to the west, toward the fields he had walked with Eoghan beyond Ailill's cottage. From the air, the ground was like a painting: rich green hues of the trees and grass, brilliant yellow gorse, and patches of purple where early spring plants were beginning to bloom.

"Is that heather?" The cold air blew past his face and smelled clear and perfumed from the warm air that rose from the ground.

"No, it's too early in the season. I think it's bog rosemary."

Timothy didn't care, it was the most beautiful patchwork quilt ever created. Birds were the luckiest creatures on the planet. Well, maybe no longer.

"Let's try a landing," Aeyna said. "Over there, the earth looks soft." She was pointing to a flat and level patch of grass.

"Okay." Timothy focused on the field and felt his body turn toward the ground. It started to come up fast, too fast.

"Push with your mind," she said, taking hold of his arm. He held out his hand and pretended to push away. He did feel himself start to slow, but then he ran out of air and landed hard, rolling over and over in the grass, sprawling onto his back. She landed daintily next to him.

"Are you all right?"

He wriggled his feet and hands. Nothing hurt. "I guess so. How'd I do?"

"Not bad," she said. "You'll get the hang of it."

She took his hands and pulled him up, then held his waist as he wobbled to keep him from falling off to one side. Her face was serious, and their eyes met. In the next instant, her lips closed on his, and her arms pulled him tight against her. Their bodies melded into one as he pressed his lips to hers in return. The thoughts he'd just had about flying were gone, replaced by the sensation and pure joy of her kiss. He felt like laughing and crying at the same time. Timothy wanted to scream aloud so that every creature in the world would witness the most stunning event of his life. Her lips were soft, and strands of her hair tickled his neck as the breeze carried them fluttering around his head. He was sure nothing before and nothing after would ever feel as good as that, except maybe more kisses from her.

They took a breath, and Aenya smiled at him. She held his hand and walked in the direction of the purple carpeting. She almost seemed shy.

"I should say I'm sorry I sprang that on you, but I'm not." There was music in her voice. It was as magical as the touch she'd used to drain his anxiety away that first time.

Timothy was afraid to say anything, afraid he'd ruin it somehow.

"You just did what I've wanted to do since the night I heard you sing 'Aylwen's Lament.'"

Aenya gave a throaty laugh. "I thought there was something different about you after that." Her smile faded. "The next day, when I heard you were going to be put to the test of reclaiming the sword, I wanted to…well…I was a little worried."

"When Bardán told me what would happen if I wasn't the right one, so was I."

"But there was a part of me that knew you would come back with it, and for what it's worth, Tuathla never doubted it for a second. I'd swear she's capable of seeing the future sometimes."

"If so, I wish she'd been able to warn me about my uncle and what would happen to my mother."

"I know. I wish that could have ended differently."

"You know, I think I'm glad you pulled me out of the water."

"Something tells me I'm always going to be pulling you out of the water."

"Well, I promise not to jump off any more platforms without checking with you first."

"That would be very kind of you, and besides, no one knows what to expect from you, so I think you're going to need extra help figuring it all out."

"So I take it you're signing on for the job?"

"Haven't you figured that out by now?"

"It's starting to dawn on me."

Aenya stopped and planted herself in front of him, serious again.

"Timothy, there are many who are going to put a lot of pressure on you to do things you may not be ready for. A month ago, you didn't know any of this existed. I want you to promise me that you'll take this one step at a time. Remember you have a choice, you must think about your actions." She raised the palm of her hand to his cheek. "Promise me."

"I do promise, Aenya." It was his turn to kiss her, and she responded with even more passion than the first time. There was so much to think about, but with her near, he felt there was nothing he couldn't do.

They lay back on the grass and spent hours kissing, holding hands, and talking, watching the sun move through mid-day and into the afternoon. Suddenly, listening and sharing the tinier details of their lives was fun, like filling in the background of a painting and adding color. He told her what he remembered of his father, though there wasn't much, and how his mother would spend hours reading and watching movies with him. Aenya related stories of life in the early nineteenth century and how saddened she'd felt when her father had gone off to fight in the Civil War. Then she told him of the sídhe she had met by the oak tree, and that she was actually having to learn how to fit in, just like he was.

The longer they stayed away, the more he thought how wonderful it would be to go back to her cottage in the woods of New Hampshire, away from Cadwaladr and his treachery, away from the promise of swords and Alfheim, to lead a simple life like Ailill and Derval. Would it even be possible to turn away, now that he knew about all of this?

"We should be getting back so you can change before you meet with the elders," she said. Timothy made no attempt to hide his disappointment. She gave him a quick kiss and then launched into the air.

"Come on," she said. "Last one back is a screaming banshee."

As they flew back, hand in hand, he couldn't help asking, "Are there such things?"

"Of course not," she said with a laugh. "Any more than fairies have wings."

"Yeah, how come fairies are always pictured with wings?"

"I don't know. Someone in Queen Victoria's time started painting us that way. Who were we to argue with human art?"

They landed back on the platform to find that most of the railing had been fixed. Bardán and Tuathla were waiting inside. He stood with a scowl and fists on his hips. Tuathla was resting on a couch behind him. Timothy let their clasped hands fall away under his withering stare.

"Where have you both been?"

"I was learning how to master flying," Timothy said.

"Do you have any idea the anxiety you have caused me, the elders, and your attendants? Not to mention your grandmother?" Over his shoulder, Timothy saw her shrug as she gave him a wink.

It hadn't dawned on him that anyone would be worried since he was with Aenya, but now it seemed pretty stupid in light of the previous night.

"I apologize. I didn't think that one through very well. It was sort of...spontaneous."

"I see. Well next time, please don't wander off without your attendants and let someone know where you're going."

"Understood." So much for feeling like the promised leader of the elfin world.

Bardán turned and walked toward the curtain. "The elders will be expecting you within the hour," he said. His voice was deep and gruff.

Aenya reached for his hand and gave it a gentle squeeze, as if to remind him what they had talked about. The gesture didn't seem to escape Tuathla, and she smiled, but it was sad just the same. Did she know something, or was it just his imagination?

Chapter 34

THE MOOD IN THE MEETING hall was far different than the first time. The empty chairs that had separated the elders from Timothy were gone; there were just eight chairs now, and they were evenly spaced. The elders stood as Timothy walked in and waited until he sat. He felt awkward by the change.

"First, we are all quite thankful that you came through the night unscathed," said Eirnin. "Furthermore, we must confess our extreme embarrassment over Aran's betrayal."

"I'm sure he was one of the few Ruairí would have let up the stairs," Timothy said.

"Indeed," said Aldith. "Ruairí has been tasked to tighten his vigilance, and Cillian is preparing a list of anyone who might have allegiance to Cadwaladr. We humbly request that you avail yourself of their protection."

"Bardán has already talked to me about that," he said. The scowl was still on the elder's face, but he gave a curt nod. "I received your message this morning that you wanted to meet with me, again."

The elders turned to one another as if questioning who was going to begin. At last, Myrddin spoke.

"I think we didn't make a good beginning yesterday," he said.

Timothy didn't really want to admit that, so he said nothing and used his best poker face.

"And after hearing Tuathla speak at last night's gathering, I think things are a little clearer. We thought it best to start again."

"Thank you," Timothy said. "I would like that, too."

"Bardán has given us a much better understanding of you," he continued. "We thought we might suggest, at least for now, that we continue with our duties and responsibilities governing Sídhlin while you are tutored in our culture."

"That sounds like you expect me to take over or something. To be honest, I'm not sure what I'm supposed to do yet."

"We all recognize this is way too sudden to make a meaningful decision of any kind," said Eirnin. "There is much for you to think about and many choices you must make."

"There's only one thing I know that has to be taken care of," Timothy said.

"And that would be?"

"Cadwaladr." Bullies came in all shapes and sizes, but Cadwaladr was the poster boy for them all, and this was something Timothy had experience with. "I don't know what your laws are, but he's the one responsible for my mother's death. He may not have been the one who poisoned her, but whoever it was, and I think I know who, did it under his orders. There have also been four attempts on my life, and he nearly murdered Cavan right in front of our eyes. He started a war several hundred years ago, but he's still walking around like he owns the place.""He is a formidable opponent," Eirnin said. "We feel as you, that he has been the cause of many deaths, not even counting those who perished in the war. But in order to try him on charges of murder, he must be in our custody, and we have no actual direct evidence to prove that he has committed such crimes, as much as we realize he's responsible."

"That sounds like an excuse," Timothy said.

"It is our way."

"Then it's the wrong way."

The elders' body language changed instantly, but they held their comments.

"What would you suggest?"

"Kill him. If you don't, more elves and sídhe will die."

"By taking such action, we would be no better than he," Eirnin said. "You have been too long in the human world. Life is much cheaper there. In the elfin world, we hold ourselves to a much higher standard. To cause someone's death is the most egregious act and requires the clearest of reasons."

"Clearest of reasons?" Timothy felt a small tightness in his chest. "You think it's better to let him do whatever he feels like? When will it finally be too much? He started a war, that's reason enough to put him on trial. Aldith, with guys like Ruairí and Eoghan, I can't believe you wouldn't be able to take him by force. Is there a penalty in our society for murder?"

"Yes. Death," Bardán said. "There are two capital offenses in our world. Murder is one, and the willful destruction of oak trees is the other."

"We have been at peace for four hundred years," said Eirnin. "There is value in that."

"Tell that to my mother."

"There is one thing we must consider," Aldith said. "Timothy, this may be difficult for you to hear, but Tuathla is old and nearing her time." He directed his attention to everyone at the table. "Once that comes to pass, I believe Cadwaladr will risk coming against us. He knows Timothy, who is young and untested and poses little threat, has claimed the Connleodh sword. If Cadwaladr succeeds in killing him and destroying the sword, he will be free to do as he pleases." Aldith looked back at Timothy. "I don't think you realize, or that Tuathla or Bardán realized, that when you took that sword in your hand, a line was crossed."

The Elder Council was quiet. Timothy felt good that by bringing up the subject, something they seemed determined to ignore, he might have made his first contribution.

"If Aldith's words are true, and we cannot hope that Cadwaladr will remain inactive, then we face two choices. We must take him into custody or go to war again," Eirnin said, as if echoing Timothy's thoughts.

"There must be another way," said Dwyryd, the Elder Druid. "Maybe if he agreed to lifelong banishment."

"Why would he agree to such a thing?" Eirnin asked.

"He did not prevail in his last war, perhaps he's lost his taste for it."

"If he kills Timothy after Tuathla passes on, morale will collapse, and for little risk he will reap a great reward," said Aldith.

"And how many will die protecting Timothy and Sídhlin?" asked Dwyryd. "We must consider that."

"The fight is coming, whether we do something or not."

Timothy was forced to realize that things weren't as simple as he wanted them to be. He wanted revenge for his mother, but hundreds if not thousands of lives would be at risk, if they weren't already. If Aldith was right and conflict was inevitable, would there be any other way around it? Was Cadwaladr a lunatic like Hitler or Stalin? How did you deal with a lunatic? He wracked his brain trying to remember his history lessons; he wished he'd paid more attention in class.

"Aldith, does he have the resources to attack us? Does he have an army or something?" Timothy asked.

"He has two or three hundred elves loyal to him here in Ireland. In the last war, he enlisted a couple thousand elves from eastern Europe."

"Has there been any sign he might be preparing to do something like that again?"

"Not as yet."

"Then before he does, we need to draw him out," Timothy said. "We need to capture him. Then we can put him on trial for war crimes. If nothing else, he needs to be put out of commission. If we don't want to kill him outright, then he should at least be put in prison for the rest of his life. Do we have jails?"

"Of course," said Eirnin. "However, we have had little use for such things. At least until last night," he said, lowering his voice. "Aran and Sorley have been detained at the top of one of the Primal trees under heavy guard."

"Well, you might need to make some more room," Timothy said. "My uncle Jim, Seumais as he's called here, is most likely my mother's actual murderer, her own brother."

"Do you have any proof of this heinous act?"

"I don't, just call it a strong intuition. But I bet if you push him a little, he'd be happy to admit it."

"Cadwaladr is nothing if not careful," Bardán said.

"Then let's throw him a curveball." The elders turned to one another, looking a little confused.

"What's a…curveball?" Eirnin asked.

"It's a baseball phrase."

"Baseball is a form of human recreation, a sport," said Liam. "I think what Timothy means is to offer some kind of surprise."

"Such as?" Bardán didn't look happy about whatever Timothy was going to suggest.

"Since he keeps trying to kill me, maybe he'd like an easier opportunity. Something like a meeting, you know, to talk things over. If we went prepared, we could arrest him."

"That's insane." Bardán stood.

"Think about it," Timothy said. "He knows about the sword, thanks to Aran. I'm sure he's itching to see whether it means anything at all, whether having it makes me more of a threat to him than I was before. I threw my mother's death in his face at the wedding, and he didn't look happy about it. Telling him I want to meet might be too much to resist, he might come out in the open again. And don't forget, his last words to me were that we'd talk again."

The elders leaned into one another, grumbling and talking. Bardán looked opposed to even considering the idea. Only Aldith sat silent, looking at Timothy. One corner of his mouth lifted in the slightest hint of a smile.

"Our young elf may have a good idea," Aldith said. "We have not committed an overt act of aggression toward Cadwaladr in four hundred years. He's no one's fool, but he might not suspect a trap. What Timothy suggests would be, as he said, a curveball."

"The idea is meritless," Myrddin said, his fist smashing down on the table. "The risk is too great. Aldith, there is no way for you and a hundred of your men to protect Timothy from an outright attempt on his life. One well-shot arrow would eliminate, in an instant, all that we've hoped for."

"Maybe I can even the odds," Timothy said. He locked his ankles around the legs of the chair. Concentrating on an empty goblet in front of Dwyryd, Timothy pulled at it with his mind. He felt his body start to rise but held on tight, and the goblet flew into his hand. All seven elders jumped to their feet in such haste that several of their chairs tipped over backwards. It was a cheap trick, but he wanted to show them that maybe he had more to offer than just a bit of attitude.

"I'm not sure how things are run here, but I remember reading something in school about parliamentary procedure and thought committees decided questions by a vote," he said.

"Indeed," said Eirnin, and he stared at Timothy while the elders collected themselves and righted their chairs. Eirnin's eyes narrowed. Timothy would have sworn that he was trying to figure him out. Then Eirnin shrugged and looked to either side of him.

"All those in favor of sending an invitation to Cadwaladr for an open meeting under a flag of truce, please signify." Eirnin lowered his voice and leaned closer to Timothy. "Where do you think Parliament got its rules of order?"

Aldith, Eirnin, and Cillian raised their hands.

"All those opposed?"

Dwyryd, Myrddin, and Liam raised their hands in opposition.

"Bardán, you have not cast your vote," he said.

He leaned back in his chair, clearly not comfortable with the idea.

"Bardán, you told me I was going to have to make choices. You didn't say they were going to be easy ones," Timothy said.

The elder rose to his feet. Timothy was afraid Bardán would be angry for setting him up. It scared Timothy a little that he might have jumped in over his head.

"Very well. I will vote in favor, but I want my reluctance noted. However, as a condition, I insist that a significant troop accompany you. Superiority of numbers is mandated."

"Myrddin, please send the invitation to meet," said Eirnin. "Aldith, make your preparations so we'll be ready to take the advantage on the field and arrest him. Doing so under a flag of truce will be a technical breech in etiquette, but given the circumstances I think we have ample justification."

"Thank you," Timothy said. "It's time we put an end to this monster." He bowed to the elders and felt, for the first time since Aenya had figured out his mother was murdered, that he was forcing something to happen, that he was making a decision for himself. He left the building praying he hadn't made the wrong one. Half the Elder Council would come down on him with vengeance if it went badly.

Chapter 35

"EOGHAN HAS SENT WORD THAT your horse is ready, my lord," Labras said.

Timothy finished strapping the sword to his belt and took a deep breath. "Is my grandmother awake?"

"Yes, she is resting in her chamber."

Cadwaladr had taken no more than a day to respond to the invitation. The downside was that he insisted the meeting take place on the open fields of his estate. Ruairí wasn't keen on it, preferring to have him come to Sídhlin. He expressed concern that Cadwaladr might set a trap, but thought that Bardán's mandate would even the odds, at least.

"Let's go then." Timothy went to his grandmother's room and parted the curtain to her chamber. Tuathla gave a weak smile and waved for him to come.

"You're on your way," she said.

"Yes, Grandmother. I wanted to see how you were before we left."

"A little tired."

That was an understatement. Dark patches pooled beneath her eyes, and her face was pale. If Timothy hadn't seen the swift change in her appearance over the past few days, he might not have been as concerned. He put a hand on her forearm and closed his eyes, but no vision appeared. She had a faint aura, but nothing like the ones he'd seen in Aenya or Cavan. It wasn't pink or blue, but pale golden yellow. Timothy could only assume the recent attempts on his life had caused her more stress than he'd thought.

"Don't try to heal me, Timothy. There is nothing to heal," she said. Then her eyes hardened. "You must take care today. Cadwaladr does not play by the same rules we do. I know you hope to lure him into an arrest, but he will be expecting this. Still, my wishes go with you for success. I approve of your goal of holding him accountable for his actions. Killing him outright, though he deserves it, would be the wrong thing."

"Eirnin explained that to me, but my mother deserves more," he said. "Except for his campaign to rid the world of the sídhe, she'd still be alive. He must be stopped."

"You are right, of course." Tuathla closed her eyes and let her head fall back into the pillows. "Come to me when you return and tell me how you fared."

"I will." Timothy watched her drift off to sleep and then made his way to the stairs. Eoghan was standing beside his horse, holding the reins. Aenya, already mounted, was next to Ruairí. Eoghan helped boost Timothy up into the saddle. Aenya leaned over and gave him a quick kiss.

"I don't think my grandmother is too hopeful for today," Timothy said so only she could hear.

"I'm not too happy about this venture myself," Aenya said.

The four of them rode through the forest to the western shore of the lake. As they emerged from the trees, a troop of about two hundred elves and sídhe sat on horseback, waiting. Timothy noticed a stern-faced sídhe nod in Aenya's direction.

"Do you know her?" he asked.

"That's Líle. They're the group I told you about. I don't know them very well yet, but Líle certainly has your back. She's the serious one of the group."

Timothy wore the heavy black leather outfit that Bardán had given him the day he'd claimed the sword. Half the troop moved out ahead of them, and the rest behind, sheltering Timothy, Aenya, Ruairí, and Eoghan in the center. Timothy had always pictured a leader riding at the head of the column, but he didn't figure they were going to allow that no matter how much he objected. He didn't feel like a real leader anyway, and they weren't really going off to war, even though he imagined this was what it must have looked like, back in medieval days.

Cadwaladr's estate was some distance away, which took them through several open fields and hills, through more forest, and over rocky crags. The sídhe spread through the whole assembly and kept the few humans they passed from noticing. Two older men cutting patches of bog appeared to sense something. They stood up straight and turned their heads as if trying to locate a sound, but without any visual evidence, they shrugged and went back to digging. It was interesting to think about the hidden things that no humans even knew about. Whole territories and a race of people existed under their noses, and only a few seemed to believe. It was pretty cool being one of the insiders.

Finally, they passed from the trees onto a vast field of green grass. Huge oak trees grew about the grounds. It seemed more like a golf course, but in the distance, a tall stone castle rose from the ground in the shape of a hexagon, a tower rising from each point. Birds circled above, chirping and singing as if paying no attention to what went on below; the sun was warm on Timothy's back. The pastoral setting made it hard to think that it all belonged to a monster like Cadwaladr. The path to hell was decorated with beauty.

As they crested a hill and passed onto a meadow spreading outward from the castle, Timothy saw a red-and-white striped pavilion. It reminded him of the medieval tents they used for jousting tournaments in the movies. A short distance away, between the tent and the castle, stood a cluster of about twenty elves. They didn't appear armed or threatening, which seemed odd.

Ruairí called a halt twenty yards from the tent. Cadwaladr emerged with a smile, his arms opening wide in a gesture of welcome. An elf followed from behind with a tray holding a carafe and two goblets, and placed it on a table in the shade. There were two chairs.

Timothy nudged his horse through the ranks and reined in next to Ruairí. Aenya followed like a shadow.

"I bid you all welcome," Cadwaladr said in a loud voice. "Timothy, I am honored by your visit, come join me."

"Does this seem right to you?" Timothy asked Ruairí in a low voice.

"Not really," he said.

"If he twitches, he'll get the shock of his life," said Aenya.

"Let's play it out a little," said Ruairí. "I've sent some into the forest to see if there are any surprises out there."

"Should we just arrest him now?"

"Not yet. I want to make sure nothing else is going on."

"Give me a heads up when you think the time is right," Timothy said. "There are only twenty or thirty elves. I can't figure why they're just standing there like that." He peered across the meadow to see if there were any stirring branches, but everything seemed normal. Timothy dismounted. Taking a deep breath, he walked across the grass to where Cadwaladr stood waiting.

"Welcome to my estate," he said. "That must be the Conn-leodh sword by your side. May I hold it?"

"No," Timothy said.

"Ah, you possess it as a king would bear his crown. So you are the boy who would be king?"

"I don't know about being a king," he said. "I only know it proves my lineage to Aylwen."

"Well, if the legends are to be believed, it means more than that. The legend suggests that the bearer of the sword is the one to rule over us. Do you deny your entitlement?"

"I haven't made any choices yet."

"Spoken wisely," said Cadwaladr. He took hold of the golden carafe and poured into the goblets. "Would you join me in a toast to your possession of the sword? Surely you are old enough to drink some wine?"

Timothy was starting to feel out of his depth, again. This was the sort of thing politicians and negotiators dealt with; he had no idea how to respond. He glanced at Ruairí and Aenya, but they sat silent and vigilant on their horses. He took the goblet filled with dark-red liquid and could smell the fragrant wine without even raising it to his lips. Cadwaladr held up his goblet. "Well done on passing the test, I know the risk was death," he said. He looked at Timothy as if waiting for him to take a sip. "Will you not drink to your own success?" he asked. Then he smiled. "Ah, you are afraid I have poisoned your cup." He raised his goblet and took a long drink. "See? I would be a poor host to plot your death in so crude a manner as that."

Raising the goblet, Timothy let a small trickle of wine pass over his lips. The taste was fruity and heavy, but pleasantly so.

"Excellent," he said. "Come, sit." He lowered his large frame into one of the chairs and rested his goblet on the table. "I am glad you asked for this opportunity to meet and talk," he began. "I was impressed with your display of healing power and have thought much of you since. And, of course, you now possess the sword. Do you feel it gives you added power?"

"The sword is just a talisman. It was enchanted to keep it from those who were not worthy to possess it, that's all."

"You are wrong," he said. "Possession of it is a symbol. It says to those in our world that you are the one to lead, the one to obey. Allegiance will follow whoever possesses it."

"I think you overestimate its value."

"And yet, you wouldn't allow me to hold it for even a moment," he said.

"Is there a point you're trying to make?"

Cadwaladr laughed. “It’s refreshing to talk with a child. They are more direct than wiser and older elves, or humans. Children are less devious, even if your true intention today was to kidnap me.” Timothy tried to keep from looking surprised. “So you don’t deny it,” he said. “That’s all right, I don’t hold it against you.”

“That’s very kind of you.” That his grandmother was right didn’t make him feel any better. In fact, his sitting in the open and outnumbered with such calm worried him. Actually, it was terrifying. Cadwaladr knew something, and that was disturbing.

“To answer your question, Timothy, yes I do wish to make a point.” He poured more wine into his goblet and drank from it. “When one is patient and waits, the world turns. You must learn to bide your time and prepare so that when it does turn in your favor, you are ready to take advantage. Your grandmother is ancient and failing, your grandfather is dead, you have extraordinary healing power, and you now possess the sword. My time has arrived.”

“What are you talking about?”

“You mentioned a short time ago that you have choices to make. I am going to give you one now.”

“Such as?” Timothy asked.

“You will surrender the sword and swear allegiance to me in front of your army, and then escort me to my castle.”

“And why would I do that?”

“To avoid war, of course.”

“I think you’re outnumbered.”

“In a fight, it’s not about size, it’s about cunning,” he said.

"I think it's time to end this," Timothy said.

"Is that you making your choice then?"

"Yes."

"Seumais, if you'd be good enough to join us," Cadwaladr said.

The flap of the pavilion opened. Timothy's uncle and three armed elves came out and surrounded them. Timothy looked to Ruairí. Every elf nocked an arrow and took aim at either Seumais and Cadwaladr or at the group of elves nearer the castle, the sídhe rushed into the air above, and Aenya held her palm facing outward. Cadwaladr remained calm and raised his hand.

The distant group of elves parted, leaving a gap in the center. Three figures knelt on the ground, bound and gagged, an elf standing behind each with a dagger against the captive's neck. It was Ailill, Derval, and Oillin.

"Now you have yet another choice to make. You can accomplish what you came here for, you can kidnap me, or you can witness the death of your friends. You might even get both, so it will be an interesting way to measure your resolve."

"Bastard!" Timothy said.

"That would be inaccurate. Either way, make your choice now, or I will start with the young one."

Timothy's brain was paralyzed, yet desperate to think of a way to change the course of the simple deception. Scruffy's friend, whom he had fought at the airport, was standing behind Oillin, a grin on his face, as if praying for the sign to kill him in front of Timothy.

"Finn, cut him," Cadwaladr shouted.

"Wait!" Timothy yelled. Finn had pulled up on Oillin's chin, pressing the blade across the boy's throat, but he relaxed his hold.

"Wise choice," Cadwaladr said, looking smug. "Seumais, escort our young pretender to the castle."

Timothy felt his uncle step behind. He draped an arm over Timothy's shoulder, a long, sharp dagger clenched in his hand.

"I suppose you'd like to kill me just like my mother, you freak."

"It would give me the greatest pleasure."

"You are all free to return to the forest," Cadwaladr shouted, with the calm of a host offering dessert. The elves and sídhe were powerless to do anything. The troop was silent; only the sounds of horses snorting and pawing the ground gave any indication of how agitated they were over the sudden outcome.

"Timothy!" Aenya yelled.

"I see you're still hanging with that broad," Seumais said, his hot breath in Timothy's ear. He tried to twist around to see her, but Seumais shoved him hard. Ailill, Derval, and Oillin were being dragging back toward the castle, too. Timothy knew once they were inside, it would be over. That had been Cadwaladr's plan, to reveal his surprise and get them off the field as fast as he could before anyone had the chance of figuring out what to do.

They crossed a small stone bridge that spanned what once had been a moat and went under a portcullis into a rectangular courtyard. The huge iron gate closed behind with a whirring sound. It was motorized. Timothy's idea that the castle had electricity was confirmed as soon as they entered the great room. A huge flat-screen TV hung on the wall above a massive stone fireplace. It was broadcasting CNN. Seeing that in an elf-occupied castle was surreal.

The modern look of the great room gave way to the medieval as they passed through a narrow door and down a steep set of stone stairs. The temperature dropped below ground. Seumais led them into the darkness of the tunnels beneath the castle. At the bottom of the spiraling stairwell, Seumais forced them apart: Ailill and his family to the left with two guards and Timothy to the right. The sparse number of light fixtures, bare white bulbs hanging from the ceiling, offered barely enough light to see. The space in between almost faded to black. The eerie glow from one showed an ancient iron sconce on the side of the wall. A dark patch above it was evidence of the flames that once lit the passageway and permanently blackened the stonework.

They reached the end of the tunnel, which opened to a larger chamber. A curtain wall of black iron latticework cut the room in half. There was a single door in the center of it.

"Open," one of the elves yelled.

The lock on the door clicked back. It was also electrical.

"Welcome to your new home," Seumais said. He shoved Timothy inside. The door closed and locked automatically.

"This doesn't seem much worse than the dump we lived in back in New Hampshire," Timothy said.

Mounted on the back wall were two short lengths of chain with rusted iron cuffs dangling from the end. A single cot with a worn-looking blanket stood to one side. A rickety table and a single wooden chair occupied the middle of the room.

"I still prefer the atmosphere of a dungeon the way it was in the old days," Cadwaladr said. "I remember when we still had water in the moat. The moisture would weep through the walls and mingle with the tears of the tortured."

Timothy wanted to add his own moisture by spitting in his face, but his mouth was too dry.

"Don't worry, we won't let you starve or die of thirst. However, I must insist that you remain here until you decide to do as I've asked."

"What about Ailill and his family?"

"They'll be taken care of…for the time being," he said. "Although at some point, I will have no more use for them." The other elves had gone, and it was just Cadwaladr and Seumais. "I will take my leave and let you consider things. Come, Seumais." He turned his back and drifted toward the tunnel. His uncle waggled his fingers and moved off behind him.

Timothy didn't know how or when, but Seumais was going to pay. They both would.

Chapter 36

Aenya watched Bardán's face as Ruairí related the events to the Elder Council and Tuathla. His eyes had widened and then his features went rigid. She could sense regret coming off him like waves of heat.

"He played us like fools," Ruairí said. "I thought anything he might spring would come from a position of strength, not this."

"It doesn't matter how he did it," Bardán said, his voice feral with rage.

"They could all be dead by now," said Cillian.

Dwyryd waved his hands in the air. "It's possible," he said. "Had he chosen to do it on the open field, he knew he'd have been rushed and killed himself. With Timothy safely tucked away, I suspect he will re-examine his options."

"What options?" Bardán asked.

"You said that he demanded Timothy hand over the sword and swear allegiance. If he controls Timothy, he controls the sword and by extension carries the standard of the elfin people. If Timothy swears his oath, then Cadwaladr also gains a personal healer without equal. So I don't think he will be in a rush to harm the boy. Ailill and his family might be a different matter."

"Then we have to get him out of there," said Aenya. "All of them."

"That would seem impossible," said Tuathla. "The simple threat of killing them, which was sufficient to get him off the field this morning, is equally as powerful in keeping us at bay. Also, you are forgetting that if Timothy dies, the sword will be rendered deadly to touch once again. Timothy must yield it willingly. It's the only other way for someone to take possession of it."

"The boy is untested," said Eirnin. "He will capitulate before morning. One night in the dungeons, and he'll be ready to do anything to save his neck." It was all Aenya could do not to fly across the table and slap him.

"Have you so little faith?" asked Tuathla.

"I'm sorry, my lady, but are you aware of his actions before he came to Sídhlin?"

"If you are asking me whether I am knowledgeable about his attempt to kill himself, then yes, I am aware. That was an unfortunate action by someone who had not the least idea of who he was. I believe you will find that the only thing he succeeded in killing that night was the weaker part of himself."

"What would you counsel, Tuathla?" Bardán asked.

"I doubt you will be hearing from Cadwaladr until he is ready to make a demand. He will be unable to do so until Timothy has either submitted or been killed. We have little choice but to wait. Of course, we could demand an accounting of his condition, but that sounds far too impotent on our part." Tuathla sat up taller in her chair. Aenya could tell she was masking her fear, and doing it well. The young sídhe doubted that an elf would see anything but optimism in the unofficial queen. "I suggest we wait and that you question Aran about what he might know of Cadwaladr's plans."

"He hasn't been very forthcoming," said Eirnin. "Sorley, on the other hand, is willing to say anything, only he has nothing valuable to contribute, as far as we can tell."

"Don't count Timothy out." Aenya spoke for the first time at the gathering. "It would be a mistake to underestimate him, and I'm betting that Cadwaladr is making a big one."

"Cadwaladr is ruthless," said Cillian. "Timothy has no experience against something like this."

"No one sitting here knows what Timothy is capable of. I'd rather not be on his wrong side when he finally gets pissed off," said Aenya. "For my part, I'm going back to the castle to wait nearby."

"That might not be safe," Bardán said.

"I won't be alone."

"We'll be just inside the forest across the meadow from the castle, too," Ruairí said. "We'll back you up."

Aenya grasped Tuathla's hand. "This is going to turn out fine, I know it," she said. "He has your blood in him." The old sídhe gave her a grateful nod and smiled; then Aenya turned to Cillian. "And for what it's worth, don't forget that he has some of the same blood in him as Cadwaladr, so let's just see who winds up being more ruthless."

Chapter 37

TIMOTHY'S EYES ADJUSTED TO THE dimness. What light there was came from several feet inside the tunnel. There was none inside the chamber itself. A dark, shadowy spot against the third wall, the one opposite the cot, caught his attention. It was an alcove built into the stone. At the base of it was a four-inch stub of thick candle, a small box of matches, a single pewter plate, and a matching cup with a broken handle. The thickness of cobwebs binding the objects together offered an idea as to how long it had been since the cell's last inmate. The thin cardboard box felt damp to the touch and smelled of mold. The matches inside were dry, so Timothy managed to light the candle. There were about twenty matches left.

He went to the back wall and studied the cuffs and chains. If they'd used them on him, sitting would have been impossible. What a nightmare. Once the legs gave out, the iron manacles would have sliced into the wrist and chaffed the skin away. Sleep would have been impossible until exhaustion overpowered the pain.

Timothy sat on the chair and put the candle on the table. There was a cracking noise. He stood carefully and hoped the cot was in better shape. He shook out the woolen blanket; a cloud of dust swirled around. A large mouse or small rat scurried from under the bed and ran through the iron bars into the darkness. The lump of something that resembled a mattress was thin and covered in dark canvas. It was also damp and smelled like mold. He tossed it into the corner and sat on the flat boards.

Timothy pulled his legs to his chest, wrapped the blanket around himself, and leaned against the wall. He wished he'd eaten more at breakfast. Closing his eyes, he tried to picture what everyone had done after they'd dragged him inside with Ailill and his family. Had they all left the field and gone back to Sídhlin? He was worried about what Tuathla was going to think. This wouldn't do her any good. He didn't want her to take a turn for the worse; she was fragile enough as it was. And Aenya? Timothy imagined her either being pissed off at him for having come up with such a stupid plan or worried enough that she might do something dangerous. He'd never felt more helpless.

For the first time in his life, he wished for a watch. There was no way of gauging if the time that passed was a minute or ten, or if it was day or night.

Timothy slid the sword from its scabbard, surprised they had left it with him. Wasn't it customary for a prisoner to be weaponless? It was clear that Cadwaladr wanted him to surrender it as a sign of submission, but he'd rather die first.

The thought occurred to him that if the castle had electric door locks and a television, then there might be cameras in the dungeons. He took the candle from the table and searched every inch of the cell and peered into the gloom of the chamber outside. If there was one, it would have to be hard wired; there was no way a wireless connection would penetrate all the stone.

"Ailill, Derval, can you hear me?" Timothy shouted into the chamber, but the walls and the darkness swallowed the sound. "Oillin?" The fact they were in this mess because of him was infuriating. Cadwaladr didn't have a good track record for compassion.

Would Bardán and the elders come up with a rescue plan? Cadwaladr already had what he wanted, so there wasn't much they could offer in exchange. There was no way the elders who had voted against this plan would let him forget it anytime soon, assuming he got out of this. Were they right? Storming the castle was out of the question. How many stories had he read about armies laying siege? It took months, and who knew what action Cadwaladr might already have taken to fill his ranks with mercenary elves again? This treachery was his declaration of war. Maybe it was on their part, too; Cadwaladr could blame his response on the plot to grab him. Timothy knew that while he sat in a cell, Cadwaladr could take all the time he wanted to scheme. His heart sank as he realized that the only sure way to avoid a war was to surrender. Would that be the right thing? Everyone had lived in relative peace for hundreds of years until he'd come along. They had tried to end the stalemate his way, and it failed. It was up to him to get them out of this mess, to give in for the good of the rest.

No.

That was the wrong choice. He would have to find a way out himself, but not by giving over to Cadwaladr's demands. It was true they'd been devious in trying to arrest him, but the monster had brought that on himself. As of that morning, incarceration would have been enough. With this, he had made his intentions clear. There was only one way to put an end to his threat, and that was to kill him. Timothy knew his mother deserved it, and so did the people of Sídhlin.

So how to break out of a cell?

Timothy didn't know how to pick a lock, or short circuit one, either. What did he know how to do? Healing people and flying didn't seem all that useful. Or were they? What was it Aenya said? That the power to repel is the reverse of trying to fly?

Timothy went to the alcove and brushed off the pewter cup. He put it on the table and stood back several feet, then focused on the cup and tried to pull it. His body jerked forward and the cup shot to his hand, but the table shuddered and started sliding toward him. He let go, afraid he would crash into the table, or it would come crashing into him. When he'd done it in front of the elders, his legs were wrapped around the chair. Timothy put the cup back on the table. Focusing on it, he tried to push it the way Aenya had taught him to push back on the ground to keep from smashing himself to bits, but nothing happened.

He tried to remember how Aenya had done it with Derek and with the elves in the airport. Her hands; she had used her hands to direct the energy. And just a little while ago, out on the field, she had her hand poised to do it again until everyone realized Ailill's family was in danger. Timothy raised his palm to face the cup and focused once more, trying to push out, but still nothing happened. *Why can I pull but not push*? He'd pushed at the ground, and he did manage to land pretty well after his first try.

"Concentrate, damn it."

Timothy closed his eyes and pushed with his mind. He imagined the cup moving, but that was all. There was no release of energy. He was so frustrated; he just wanted to grab the cup and hurl it against the wall. Then an all-too-familiar sensation came over him: the pressure inside his chest, the prelude to involuntary ticking. Not now, he thought, this is not happening now.

"Just forget it," Timothy yelled and waved his hand at the cup. It slid to the edge of the table and went over, clattering onto the stone floor.

"Whoa."

He picked it up to try again. When he waved his hand at it, nothing happened. Did he have to be angry to make it work? He tried to think of a memory that would irritate him. Closing his eyes, he heard Seumais say it would give him pleasure to kill Timothy, virtually admitting in the same breath that he'd killed Owein. Timothy's chest tightened and for the first time in his life, he was glad of it. He let the sensation build, concentrating harder and letting his hatred for Seumais fuel his anger. Then he opened his eyes and thrust his hand toward the cup. It flew half the distance to the wall before crashing to the floor. It was nothing like the power Aenya could summon, but she'd been doing it for more than a century.

With sudden awareness, he realized that the ticking had always been his body's way of channeling energy. Instead of releasing it or directing it outward, the result had been head tics. That was how the glass in his room had broken, but the key, at least for now, was based on anger. Until he became more familiar with his body and how it worked, he would have to settle for that.

But he still had to deal with the locks. Timothy put his hand through the bars and felt for the locking mechanism. There was no obvious keyhole, so there had to be a switch somewhere near. He would have to watch when someone came to the cell.

The candle on the table had burned down an inch, and there was no telling if he'd be given another one, so he blew it out and sat on the cot. There was nothing to do but wait.

Chapter 38

TIMOTHY'S HEAD DROPPED AGAIN, AND he had to shake himself awake. He was starting to feel hungry, and he had a powerful need to use a bathroom.

On a whim, he peeked under the bed and saw something metal. He wasn't too keen on reaching under after seeing the rat run out, but he had an idea what the item was for. The wooden pot had a metal band binding the slats together. It wasn't the most modern toilet, but it served just as well.

More hours passed. Timothy discovered the length of the cell took twelve full strides to cross, and it took almost as many from front to back. There was plenty of room in which to get bored and hungry.

He tried to sleep, if only to avoid feeling hungry. A scuffling noise came from the tunnel. Timothy used the best angle to look down the dark passageway. He half expected the rat, but as the sound grew louder, he knew it was footsteps. A minute later, the large elf, Finn, stood at the opening of the chamber. He pulled something like a credit card from a pocket in his tunic, swiped it in a mechanism that wasn't visible from the cell, and the lock clicked open.

"Sit on the cot and don't even think about movin'," he said. He pulled the door open so it clanged against the metal bars. Timothy followed the instruction and sat while Finn put a bowl of food on the table, as well as an orange and a plastic bottle of water. "Compliments of the 'ouse."

"A real feast," Timothy said. "You were on the field today."

"Aye, and I nearly gave your mate a new smile, what?"

"Yeah, I was wondering how you were feeling, though. I remember the first time we met you were in some pain." Timothy made a kicking motion with his foot.

"You watch your mouth if you know what's good for ya."

"Or what?" He wanted the elf to get pissed off, hoping it would spark his own anger, though he wasn't stupid enough to think the plan might not backfire.

"If you wasn't something Lord Cadwaladr was takin' a keen interest on, I'd step on you like a cockroach," he said. A small fleck of saliva drooped from his lower lip, making him look more ogre-ish than elfin. He was by far the largest elf Timothy had seen. "But that doesn't mean I couldn't have me some fun with them down the other end now, do it?"

The pressure started to build in Timothy's chest. It was interesting, though disconcerting, to realize that even in the elegance of the elfin world, there were bullies like Finn.

"You'd best be a good boy or Cadwaladr might punish you," he said, trying to wind him up even more.

It was dim in the cell, but Timothy was sure the elf's face turned a shade darker. He picked up the bowl of food.

"I hear the stew's a little bland," he said and spit into it. "There, that should make it right tasty and all."

Hoping it was enough pressure, Timothy thrust out his hand and pushed hard with his mind. Finn staggered back a step and then righted himself.

"'Ere now, what you playing at?"

Timothy sucked in a breath; he was going to need a lot more practice—if he survived the next couple of minutes. Finn was in the range of three hundred pounds to his one hundred seventy. Rushing him would be like a fly hitting a moose. Then Timothy smiled as he realized that one hundred seventy moving at fifty miles an hour was altogether a different thing. He focused on the elf's face and pulled with all his might. His body yanked forward as Timothy hurtled through the twenty feet between them, his head connecting with the elf's nose and driving him against the wall. Finn's skull bounced off the stone as Timothy pivoted and dropped to the floor next to the big elf, feeling pain along his entire right side. Finn slumped to his knees and moaned. He started to stand.

Timothy knew if Finn regained his footing, it would be over. Timothy jumped to his feet and drew the sword from its scabbard, flipped it so the blade was in his hands, and swung it at the back of Finn's head. The spot where the blade, the guard, and the hilt met hit bone with a crunch. The elf staggered forward and collapsed onto the table, crashing through the rotting wood like cardboard. He groaned and then all the tension left his body, though he appeared to be breathing from the look of the bits of dust that puffed away from his nose and mouth. Timothy was sure he'd given Finn a concussion. The bronze sword was better than a baseball bat.

"I know, Bardán, the sword's not a weapon," he said. "Well, it is now."

After sheathing it, Timothy grabbed the blanket from the cot and tore it into strips, using them to tie Finn's hands behind his back and his ankles. Timothy wadded a piece of wool, shoved it into the elf's mouth, and tied a gag around his head. He would have loved to use the manacles suspended from the wall, but there was no way he could move the elf's dead weight over to them, let alone hoist him up to fasten them around his wrists. They probably wouldn't fit anyway.

Timothy took the access card from Finn's tunic and hoped it was the same one for Ailill's cell. He went to the door and then rushed back to the alcove, grabbed the plate, and searched the floor for the box of matches. He found them and tucked them into his pocket, then slammed the cell door. The lock reset. Just beyond the entrance to the chamber was a small keypad with a place to swipe the card along one side.

He'd spent enough time in the gloom that navigating the tunnel wasn't hard. There was just enough light from the electric bulbs to see the passage without running into a wall or tripping over something. He followed it, making several right and left turns and passing a number of empty chambers, some of them so small a prisoner would only be able to stand up in them. The passage must have snaked under the castle for hundreds of feet. No wonder Ailill and his family couldn't hear his yelling. Panic grabbed hold, and he started worrying that Cadwaladr might have done something horrible already. Timothy stopped to listen, but heard nothing. He put his hand against the wall; bits of stone and grit flaked off and peppered the floor.

Timothy moved on, not wanting to waste time. He had no idea how long it might be before someone came to check on Finn. After another left turn, the run of lights ended and the tunnel went dark. He went slowly, cursing himself for not thinking to bring the candle. There was no way of knowing how much farther the tunnel went, and he couldn't afford to use all the matches. He'd need some for the return trip. After fifty feet or so, he decided to use one to see as far into the tunnel as he could and get some bearing. The match flared, but did little to penetrate the blackness.

Timothy heard a gasp in the distance, then a woman's voice. "What was that?"

"Derval?" he called.

"Yes, who's there?" she answered.

He walked forward, cupping his hand in front of the match. The flame was starting to burn his fingers as he came even with the iron wall of their cell.

"Derval, Ailill?" Timothy said in a low voice.

"Yes, we're here, who are you?"

He struck another match, and Derval cried out when she saw who it was. "Timothy, how did you get here? How did you get free?"

"I had a little run-in with our friend Finn."

"Yes, so did Ailill. He's not feeling too well."

Timothy saw him lying on the cot. His face was bruised and bloody. Oillin was sitting next to him looking devastated.

"I'm so sorry about this," he said.

"You're not the one to blame, my lord."

"Come on, we're getting out of here." He tossed the spent match aside and lit another, looking for the keypad. It was on the opposite side of the passageway. He lined up the mag strip and swiped it. Nothing happened. The faded green diodes on the readout flickered like there was a faulty connection. He tapped it with the palm of his hand and it glowed steadily. As he swiped again, the bolt snapped open. "Oillin, come on, I'll help carry your dad."

"How are we going to get out of here?" he asked.

"The same way we came in."

"But we'll have to get past his men, the great room, the courtyard, and I don't know how we're going to get past the portcullis."

"First, they're not going to be expecting us to escape, and second, I'm counting on it being dark outside. Third, I'm betting that we'll have help as soon as we get beyond the walls." Timothy helped Ailill up from the cot. The injured elf laid an arm heavily over their shoulders. "Derval, here are some matches. We have to go maybe a hundred feet before we have enough light to see by."

They all followed the winding tunnel, slowly at first. Ailill perked up and stumbled along with less help.

"Come on, my love," said Derval. "We'll have you home before you know it."

"When did they come for you?" Timothy asked.

"This morning. They came before sunrise," she said.

"I'm sorry," he said again.

"Nonsense," said Ailill. The right side of his face was puffy, and he sounded as if someone had stuffed his mouth with cotton. "You're not to think in such a way again."

They reached the point where Timothy had brushed his hand against the wall; there was extra dust on the stone pavers. "I think we're about halfway to the bottom of the stairwell." They rounded the next corner. A lone elf was striding down the passage towards them.

"Oy, Finn is that…bloody hell. How did you…" He turned and started to run back in the other direction.

"Damn, he'll bring a whole castle down on us," Oillin said.

Timothy pulled free from Ailill and grabbed the pewter plate stuffed in his waistband. Gauging the elf's distance and speed, he pulled his arm back and snapped it forward, flinging the plate at him. It struck at the base of his neck, and the elf went sprawling in a cloud of dust.

"How did you do that?" Oillin asked, his mouth hanging open.

"I'm pretty wicked with a Frisbee," he said, suddenly grateful for all the hours he'd spent in the park with his mother tossing it around.

"What's a Frisbee?"

"Never mind, I'll show you sometime."

Timothy used the card to open one of the small cells, and Oillin helped him shove the elf into it. Making sure he had come to his senses enough to see what was happening, Timothy focused on the plate lying on the floor about ten feet away and pulled it. The elf's eyes opened wide as Timothy caught it in midair. They opened wider when he drew the sword and rested the point of the blade against the elf's throat.

"Tell me where the portcullis controls are," he said. "I won't ask twice." He pressed the sword a little harder against his skin.

"It's in the tower to the right of the gate," he said. Timothy was amazed the elf was buying the act. If he had any idea just how little Timothy knew about what he was doing, the elf would have told him to get lost.

"I want you to sit here quietly. If you don't, I'll be back just for you." Timothy slammed the cell door and wrapped his arm around Ailill's waist. "Let's go."

They made it to the bottom of the stairwell and started the climb. Timothy didn't remember seeing a place to hide in the great room, so he hoped his instinct that it was night was accurate. Ailill sat on the stone stairs to rest.

"Stay here for a minute," Timothy said. "I'm going to take a look up there and see what's what."

When he reached the top, he closed his hand around the solid metal ring of the door handle. He twisted it and pushed so slowly, it would have been hard to notice. The hinges were well oiled and didn't make a sound. There wasn't a soul in the great room. Still, Timothy's fear was cameras. If not in the dungeons, he assumed Cadwaladr would have a security system around the castle. He was still surprised there wasn't one below.

A wooden-framed gallery ran along three sides of the second story of the great room. Timothy ran under it to keep hidden. He needed to see what was going on in the courtyard.

Glancing out the window, he could see the sky beginning to turn a deep shade of purple. They had to hurry. Timothy rushed back to the dungeon entrance just as his friends were climbing the last stair.

"We have to go, now," he said. "When we get outside, I want you to go straight to the portcullis. I'll go to the control room and get the thing open."

"I don't know how far we're going to get on the open field," said Ailill. "They'll be right behind. There have to be sentries out there somewhere."

"Don't worry, I'll shut the gates and find some way of breaking the controls. That should slow them down."

"But then how will you get out?" Derval asked. She looked horrified.

"Don't worry about me. I've got that part covered." Timothy gave her a smile. "Come on, let's get out of here."

He took a chance of being seen by moving straight across the hall to the main door. He should have checked first to make sure it was unlocked, but it opened right up.

The early morning air was cold, and a slight breeze was blowing across the courtyard. There were no obvious signs of a sentry, and he couldn't see any cameras outside either.

"Go," he whispered. Ailill hobbled forward with Oillin and Derval's help. Timothy ran straight for the tower. There was a heavy oaken door with iron straps on the side. He pulled it open and looked back. They were almost halfway to the gate. He slipped inside and found six computer monitors illuminating the room. They did have cameras. One swept the courtyard, one focused on the portcullis, and four switched through a sequence of locations from the great room to the security posts on top of the other towers. As they scanned, Timothy's heart jumped; there was a sentry on each, and they were all awake.

"Oh shit!"

Frantically, Timothy searched the room for a switch or button. The camera showed that they were standing in front of the gate. With the door open, Timothy heard a shout and then another. Glancing at the monitors, he saw that all six sentries were looking over the crenellated sides into the courtyard. One of them had a cell phone to his ear.

On the wall a few feet from the door was a metal box with a conduit running up into the darkness. A green button was labeled "up" and a red one was "down." He stabbed the green one with his finger. The walls vibrated. He fist-pumped the air as he watched the heavy iron structure lifting up. As soon as the three had ducked under, Timothy punched the red one. The gate stopped and started rumbling down.

He pulled the sword, held it with a firm grip, and hacked at the metal box. It took several swipes before the mangled fixture clattered to the floor, severed from its wires. The sword was getting a hell of a workout.

Timothy saw the sentries on the three towers closest to the field pull their bows and nock arrows. He launched outside into the courtyard and yelled as he raced to the center.

"Cease fire," he screamed, hoping they'd hesitate at a voice coming from behind them.

All three sentries appeared at the tops of their towers. Turning, Timothy saw the three from the backside of the castle do the same. Several elves poured from the castle doorway.

"Kill him," someone shouted. "Shoot him." Timothy knew that voice anywhere. Seumais was joining the chase, but this wasn't the time to confront him.

If nothing else, Timothy had taken attention away from Ailill and his family. He raced for the cover of the portcullis. It was easier to hit a fixed target than a moving one in the darkness. If any of those archers had the same skill as Eoghan, he was dead anyway. Four small thuds came from behind, and arrows started raining down around him. The sound was sickening. Above him, two sentries aimed at him, about to release. Timothy raised his hand and attempted to push a ball of energy, and though it didn't stop them from firing, he was shocked when the arrows glanced off and landed harmlessly to the sides.

An eerie sound rose through the air, coming from everywhere. At first it was like the lower register of a cow mooing; the bass reverberated in Timothy's chest. Then, with the escalation of a siren, the sound intensified from a moan to a wail so painful he had to cover his ears. He dropped to his knees and stared at the sky. The archers were doing the same, as were the troop of elves in the courtyard.

Seven sídhe flew over the castle walls. The air in front of each warped and every elf fell flat to the ground. Then one of them rushed at Timothy.

Aenya scooped him into her arms, hugging him tightly. He hugged her back with a wave of relief.

"You're all right," she said.

"I am, but we have to get Ailill and his family to safety."

"It's okay, we have them."

"What the hell was that noise?"

"Have you never heard the legends of the banshee?"

"Yeah."

"Well, now you know where it comes from." She grabbed Timothy's hand. "We have to go."

"What's wrong?" he asked.

"Your grandmother," she said. "You must go to her."

Chapter 39

THEY FLEW STRAIGHT FOR THE Primal forest, leaving the other sídhe to follow the elves on horseback surrounding Ailill and his family. Timothy didn't like the tension in Aenya's voice. They didn't talk on the way; he was too afraid of the reason for their haste.

As they passed over the trees, she took hold of his arm to guide him through the branches, probably still worried that he might hurt himself on landing.

They stepped onto the platform outside Tuathla's chambers. A number of elves stood outside, and as Timothy and Aenya entered the living quarters, all of the elders stood facing them, their faces grave. Bardán moved away from the rest and walked up to Timothy. He thought the elder was going to scold him for the mission having failed; instead, he pulled Timothy into a fierce embrace.

"Thank the heavens you're all right," he said.

"They roughed up Ailill some, but I think he's going to be okay."

"He'll be well taken care of, but you must attend your grandmother."

Timothy opened his mouth to ask what was wrong, but it was obvious by the looks on their faces. He turned toward the curtained doorway of her sleeping chamber. It was hard to put one foot in front of the other, to control the sick feeling in his stomach.

At first, he thought it was too late, but then he saw the rise of her chest as she drew a breath. He sat on the edge of her bed. Someone had brushed her hair; it lay about her shoulders in a soft cascade of white. Her face, though washed of all color, was serene, as though all the cares of the world had been brushed away also. He wanted to lay his hands on her, to fix her, but she had said there was nothing to heal. It was clear there were definite limits to what he could do. When the time was right, death became the master. He just didn't want to allow another family member to die without doing everything in his power to help.

Tuathla's eyelashes quivered and parted. She stared at the ceiling, as if trying to sense where she was. Then her eyes found Timothy, and a smile lit her face.

"I've been waiting for you," she said. Her voice was little more than a whisper. There was no surprise or concern. She had known he would return unharmed. Maybe Aenya was right, maybe she did possess a sense of what would be. Timothy slid his fingers under her hand.

"Are you ill? Isn't there something I can do?" His mother had slipped away with no help from him. Timothy felt that he should be doing something, or asking something, anything to make the minutes count. Tuathla squeezed his hand, and the terror washed away.

"It is time," she said. "You must not grieve, you must look to your own life. The people of Sídhlin will stand with you and be there for you."

"I have so much more to learn."

Tuathla smiled and shook her head. "Your heart already possesses all that I could have taught you. As long as you consider your actions, as long as you search your feelings for the right answer, you will not stray from the path. In this, I have faith in you."

"But why must you go now?" Timothy's voice cracked.

"I must prepare," she said.

"For what?"

"To help you…" Her voice trailed off and her eyes closed.

"Help me how?" He didn't understand. How could her death help? He needed her alive more than anything. It wasn't fair to lose her so soon after finding her. He had thought his only remaining family was his uncle, and Seumais was no excuse for family. To learn of Tuathla's existence was a gift, and now Timothy was going to be alone again; a loss equally horrible as, if not worse than, that of his mother. Some part of his brain took comfort in knowing Aenya was there.

"Grandmother?" Timothy needed to understand what she had meant by what she had said. It made no sense.

She lifted her arms, and Timothy slid into them for the last time and kissed her on the cheek. She held him for several precious minutes, then kissed him on the forehead.

"Go now and be with those who love you," she said.

She lay her hands together on her chest. Her eyelids drooped. She took a deep breath and looked back up at the ceiling, as if something had caught her attention. A smile crossed her face. She exhaled a long, slow breath and was still.

Timothy stayed with her. He knew the instant he left the room, the stark reality of his new life would take over. He wasn't ready for it. As long as he sat with her, time was frozen. If only it were possible never to leave the room, to have eternity arranged the way he wanted it.

But, she was not his to keep. For hundreds of years, she had been the beloved, if unofficial, ruler of the elfin world. He felt guilty for hoarding her to himself. He stole a last look, studying every feature of her face, her hands, memorizing every detail. He should have had a lifetime to learn them, yet it had been only a matter of days. He wanted to burn every facet of her presence into his brain.

Reluctantly, he turned toward the curtain.

Everyone rose with expectant looks. Timothy just shook his head. Labras stood by the door. He had spent much of his life in her service; he covered his face and turned away. Aenya gave Timothy a hug and took his hands in hers. He knew what she was trying to do and pulled them back gently. This time, he needed to feel the pain, to accept it, not to hide from it. She must have understood. She nodded and stepped back.

"Bardán, what are the customs here? What will be done with her?"

His face was the expression of pain. He put his hand on Timothy's shoulder with a gentle squeeze.

"Normally, our remains are cremated and spread among the oak trees," he said.

"Normally?" Timothy asked.

"Your grandmother has chosen something unusual. She ordered that her body be taken to Slaíne, to be immersed in the pool."

"Why?"

"We don't know, but we will see to her wishes. Aine has already been summoned."

"How will word be spread?"

"Cillian will see to it that all in Sídhlin are told, and Myrddin will send word to the other realms."

Timothy felt so tired. He hadn't eaten in a full day and hadn't slept all that much either. Looking outside, he noticed the sun had risen. Each of the elders offered their condolences before taking their leave. Bardán was the last to go. Aenya and Timothy were alone.

She sat on the couch and patted the cushion next to her, then hugged him, and they lay back together. Timothy felt her hand brush through his hair. She wasn't trying to suppress the pain, just trying to comfort him. He thought it might be her way of taking comfort herself. It seemed that helping others was a way of healing all by itself.

"There was never a question of tomorrow or the day after," he said. "Now, there's this dense forest I can't see through. I'm lost. How do I find my way?"

"Don't think too much on it right now," she said. "We'll take one step at a time."

Timothy rested his head on her shoulder, grateful for her presence. He closed his eyes and fell asleep, free from exhaustion and grief, at least for a while.

Chapter 40

TIMOTHY HAD EXPECTED MORE FANFARE with Aine's arrival the next morning, but there was little. She presented herself at the dwelling as if she knew her way around Sídhlin. The group of sídhe who had befriended Aenya accompanied her.

She paused by the curtain of Tuathla's chamber and held out her hand to Timothy. He felt a pull toward her, like she was commanding every cell in his body. Seeing her among her own kind, Timothy recognized there was something different about her. Though beautiful and youthful in appearance, there was a quality of age and power that set her apart from the other sídhe. He walked to her, certain he wouldn't have been able to resist, anyway. The curtain closed behind them, leaving them alone with Tuathla's shrouded body.

"You have been given yet another test," she said.

Timothy glanced at Tuathla, then held Aine's eyes.

"She said there would be many."

"Are you ready?"

"Yes…no…shit, I don't know." Timothy slid his fingers back through his hair. Aine nodded and went to Tuathla's form and put her palm where her forehead would be. "Bardán told me that we're usually cremated and sprinkled around the oaks. Why did my grandmother ask to be taken to Sláine?"

"There are many facets to Sláine that few even know. It is best that way. But in time, you will come to know its secrets."

"I know, like time is different," Timothy said. "And when I was there, being tested with the sword, I would have sworn that Aylwen called out to me and encouraged me to take it. Did you know that?"

"Do you believe that she did?"

"Well...yes, it felt pretty real."

"Then it does not matter if I knew of it or not. In the end, you took the sword."

"But Aylwen's been dead for thousands of years."

"Must someone be living in order to influence your thoughts?"

Timothy wished for someone like Omar to slap him on the back and tell him to *keep it real, dude.*

"The memory of my mother influences me, not an ancestor from the dark ages."

Aine's face softened with the hint of a smile. It was her eyes that caused Timothy to hold his breath. For a moment, the room around her seemed to darken, and the aura he normally saw glow with the injured made her look about to combust. Had he angered her? Timothy took a step back. She was powerful, more powerful than any of the other sídhe he'd met, including Aenya. It was no wonder she was the guardian of the Connleodh sword, and had been for millennia. Then everything returned to normal, like the pressure escaping from a slow leak in a balloon.

"In order to understand Sláine, you must be ready to put aside what you assume the world to be. You cannot comprehend it with what you think you know, with what your eyes have seen and your ears have heard." Aine looked down at Tuathla's form and said, as if speaking to her, "He is not yet ready." She looked at Timothy again. "We will meet again, and next time you will be better prepared."

Timothy wanted to ask what she was talking about. Instead he slipped back beyond the curtain and stood with Aenya, Bardán, and Dwyryd, the Elder Druid, as Aine prepared Tuathla for the journey. Why it was that Aine and his grandmother found it necessary to say things that only led to further confusion was beyond him.

Labras had been very quiet, but dutifully appeared when Timothy had woken in his own bed. Aenya must have carried him up to his rooms at some point, and he'd slept without waking. Labras brought fruit and cheese, and then dressed Timothy in a long azure tunic. Labras's eyes teared as he adjusted the belt and scabbard on Timothy's belt.

"You must feel her loss worse than me," Timothy said. She had been his grandmother, but he'd been her companion for centuries.

"There was never a creature so fair as your grandmother," he said.

"What will you do now?"

"I haven't given much thought to it, my lord."

"Do you have a family somewhere?"

"I have no mate or children," he said. "A brother and sister to the north, but that's all."

"Maybe you'd like to stay with me," Timothy said.

He couldn't quite read the elf's expression and thought he might have upset Labras, that he might find it too painful to stay in a place where his mistress had died.

"Timothy, it would be my honor to remain with you."

He didn't know what to feel more: shocked that Labras had referred to him by his name for the first time or touched by his willingness to stay.

"Thank you," Timothy said. "I'm grateful."

Finally Aine appeared, carrying Tuathla wrapped in a silken cloth of brilliant white embroidered with an intricate pattern of Celtic circles. It was their family pattern from the days of Aylwen. They followed the sídhe to the outside platform. Timothy glanced over the railing. There'd been no fuss at Aine's arrival, but her departure would not go as unnoticed. Thousands stood at the base of the tree and throughout the forest. They had come to witness the last of Tuathla.

Dwyryd stepped in front of Aine and laid his hands on Tuathla's body. He closed his eyes and spoke in soft tones using the elfin tongue. It reminded Timothy that he needed to learn their language, especially since Tuathla had mentioned that she was leaving him her diaries, full of passages relating to his family and especially about his mother.

"May she go from us to a place of peace to join Aylwen and Arthur, and may she always look over us and guide us in the days and times to come," he said.

Aine nodded once as Dwyryd stepped back. The fairies lifted from the platform and rose through the branches into the clear blue sky. They lingered for a few seconds and then were gone.

Dwyryd stepped to the railing. He held out his hands and spoke to all assembled below. "Go in peace, and may we all come together in Alfheim."

Timothy watched for nearly an hour as the crowd mingled, drawing comfort from one another before drifting from the forest floor. There was no wailing or crying. They left in silence.

"Do you wish me to stay?" Bardán asked as he came outside.

"It's okay," Timothy said. "I'm all right. I was thinking I'd like to see how Ailill is doing."

"I'm sure they would be touched," he said as he turned to go, leaving Aenya and Timothy alone on the platform.

Timothy took Aenya's hand. "Will you come with me?"

She moved close and kissed him. It was like a message, telling him she was there for him. The simple joy of feeling the softness of her lips was like the perfect medication.

"I'm afraid you're stuck with me," she said when she pulled away.

He kissed her again and wondered if it was addictive. He had a feeling it was, very.

"Come on," she said. "Let's go see Ailill and later we can take a walk."

They went down the stairs together and met with Eoghan and his men at the bottom. The group passed from the Primal forest onto the road to Ailill's cottage.

Derval bolted down the path as they passed through the small gate in the fence. Timothy thought she was going for a tackle as she flung herself at him.

"How is he?" Timothy asked.

"He's resting upstairs, thanks to you."

"If it wasn't for me, it wouldn't have happened at all."

"Shush! Come inside," she said. "I am so sorry about Tuathla."

"Thank you."

"Are you hungry?" she asked, always wanting to be the mother.

"I'm fine, but I don't know about Eoghan and his group. I have no idea how long they were posted below us."

"I'll take care of them while you visit."

Timothy and Aenya went up the stairs to Ailill's room and knocked on the doorframe. He opened his eyes and tried to push himself to a sitting position, but he grimaced in pain.

"Easy," Timothy said. "No need to sit up, rest. We wanted to see how you were feeling."

"Much better," he said. "Just some bruising, I think, though the healers said some of my ribs were broken, thanks to Finn."

Timothy sat on the edge of the bed and laid his hand on Ailill's ribcage. He jumped at the touch. Timothy closed his eyes, and the vision came without effort. Ailill was standing in the field across from his cottage. It seemed that the condition of the person in the vision reflected how easy the cure would be. He opened his eyes and saw aural redness on the left side of his ribs and in his left shoulder. He let the energy flow into Ailill's body and felt the satisfaction of seeing the redness fade to blue.

Timothy pulled his hand away and the vision closed; his aura dissipated.

"Is that better?" he asked.

Ailill pushed his side with his fingers, then harder. He lifted his left arm with no trouble.

"That is truly amazing," he said.

"If we hadn't been in such a rush to get out of the castle, and if I'd had the sense to think of it, I could have taken care of you right in the cell."

"That was not the first priority," said Ailill. "You should have escaped without us. You should not have risked yourself any further by coming for us, though I will be forever grateful to you for saving my wife and son."

Timothy was touched by his thoughts, but he knew if he ever began to feel as though Ailill was right, he would give up the sword and go home. Thinking that anyone should consider a leader as more important than everyone else angered Timothy.

"In the eyes of your family, there is no one more important to them than you. You all were no less deserving to be saved than I was."

Aenya slid her hand onto Timothy's shoulder.

When they all went downstairs, Derval's mouth hung open in shock, and Oillin jumped up from his chair.

"Father?" He broke into the widest grin. "I didn't think I'd see you up for days."

Ailill smacked his side to show he was good as new. Derval put her hand to his face, amazed that the bruising under his eye had all but disappeared.

Eoghan and the elves swallowed platefuls of eggs and bread and rose quickly to be ready to leave.

They left Ailill and wandered out into the bright sunshine. The day was warm, and the breeze smelled like flowers, a perfect spring morning. Timothy had that sense of optimism that comes with the warmer weather, like wonderful things were on the way, despite all the trouble. He pulled Eoghan aside.

"We're going to take a walk in the fields," he said. "I know you're going with us, but I was wondering if you could hang back a little…you know?" Timothy nodded toward Aenya. "For a little privacy."

Eoghan pulled himself up to his full height, the request clearly not sitting well with him.

"My lord, considering the events of the past few days…even though we're far from Cadwaladr's estate, I'm a little worried."

"I know," Timothy said. "I'm not saying that you shouldn't stay close, just not that close."

The elf looked conflicted, but gave a sharp nod in acceptance.

"Thanks." Timothy couldn't imagine that Cadwaladr or Seumais would dare step foot inside the realm after kidnapping him. He took Aenya by the hand and walked down the gradual slope into the field. There were so many things to think about, he wasn't sure how to work his way through them all. Maybe it was best not to try yet, but just to enjoy time with Aenya. After all, they had hundreds of years ahead of them to work everything out.

They came across a small stream that gurgled its way through the fields, tripping over small rifts in the ground and forming crisscrossing rivulets as it bent around the larger stones. He dipped his fingers in the cool water and cupped a small amount to his mouth. It was as cold as ice, sweet, and refreshing. They paralleled the water upstream until they came to a rise in the bank and sat down.

Aenya pushed Timothy onto his back and practically lay on top of him. She kissed him and he circled his arms around her. Her hair fell forward and created a curtain around his face. He could feel her shoulders and back, and the rise and fall of her chest as she breathed.

"Can I tell you something without you getting mad at me?" he asked.

"Go for it," she said.

Timothy looked up into her eyes. The insanity of the past weeks ran through his head, but the best part of it all was Aenya. Despite the fear and anxiety and loss, she was there. Was it possible to feel so strongly about someone that it actually hurt? That was the way it seemed to him right then.

"I love you," he said. He thought she might stand in a huff and charge away because he had ruined the moment, but instead she smiled.

"I love you, too." She laid her head on his shoulder. Under the sun, in the grass, all thoughts disappeared, and his tension went, too. Relaxation filled him, such that it felt like dozing.

An occasional soft breeze ruffled her hair so that he had to push it away from tickling his nose.

"Sorry," she said with a gentle laugh. "Maybe I should cut my hair shorter."

"Don't you ever," Timothy said.

"Come on, I know you think I'm a tomboy."

"Well, duh. You're still stronger than me, too."

"Not for long I bet," she said. "You seem to be more sídhe than elf lately, so I'm sure it won't be long before I'm not."

"Good, then maybe you won't worry about me so much."

"I doubt that. You seem to have a knack for finding trouble."

"I think it's just that trouble comes looking for me."

"Well, here's some more trouble," she said and reached to kiss him again.

Timothy heard a loud rustling in the branches of the oak tree a few yards from the bank of the stream. When he didn't feel a gust come with it, his eyes flew open. He looked over her shoulders and twisted his head. The branches waved as if caught in a gale. He pushed her away and jumped to his feet, turning and looking in all directions.

"Something's wrong," he said.

"I know." She was alert now, too.

Timothy could only think that they'd let their guard down, concentrating only on each other. He drew the sword, though he didn't know what he was going to do with it. Four elves appeared over a crest in the hill beyond the tree, bows at the ready. Seumais was in front and pointed at them, a signal to the others.

"Eoghan!" Timothy yelled, wanting to kick himself for not letting them stay closer. The three elves raised their bows, taking aim. Timothy cocked his arm and threw the sword at Seumais just as the elves released their arrows. Aenya pushed him to the side and yelled.

“There they are,” someone bellowed from the opposite side of the stream. It was Cadwaladr himself with another group of elves.

“Kill them!” he said. They raised their bows at once.

Timothy’s rage was hot; it seared the inside of his chest. The pressure was so tight he thought his very bones would crack under the strain. As if to ward off the inevitable, Timothy raised his hands and screamed.

“No!”

The air in front of him warped as they released their arrows. It was like looking through an expanding bubble as it rolled off his fingers in slow motion like a blob of mercury in a petri dish. As the arrows met the leading edge of energy, the wooden shafts shattered into thousands of pieces, rebounding in the direction of the elves. The tiny fragments peppered them like buckshot, and Timothy saw Cadwaladr’s body punctured with a hundred bloody holes as he fell backward, writhing in pain.

Somewhere behind Timothy, Eoghan shouted.

“Fire!” The resulting screams told him the elves behind his uncle had met their fate. From the trees on the other side of the stream, four or five of Cadwaladr’s elves came running forward. They grabbed his arms and legs, dragging him away. He was moaning and yelling in pain, but he was alive.

Timothy ran to see if Seumais and his group posed any further threat, but they all lay on the ground. His uncle’s body was bucking and squirming, the Connleodh sword protruding from his chest. His eyes were wide, and a small river of blood flowed from the corner of his mouth. His breathing was rough and fragmented, his fingers clutching at the blade. Then his eyes set on Timothy with a venomous stare that conveyed his intense hatred.

Timothy grabbed the hilt of the sword and yanked it from his chest.

"That's for my mother," he said. He felt no pity as Seumais coughed up a plug of blood. He'd heard that killing someone was an intensely emotional ordeal, but standing there looking down at Seumais, Timothy felt nothing. If anything, he felt as if he'd just yielded some of the need for revenge he'd been carrying in his heart. It wasn't enough.

"My lord," Eoghan called, his voice laced with distress. They had come within yards, but stopped. Then Timothy saw why.

Aenya lay on the ground with three arrows in her stomach and chest. Unlike Seumais, she was motionless. Timothy dropped to his knees next to her, tossing the sword to one side.

"No, no, no…"

Timothy grabbed at his hair; her eyes were half-open and staring sightlessly. Seizing her, he shut his eyes, summoning a vision. A field of red and yellow flowers and heather stretched before him. A strong breeze bent the flowers as it passed over the ground. But Timothy was alone. He poured energy into her at a rate that made his body tremble. The ground began to sway, as if in an earthquake. Every nerve ending in his skin sizzled like the sting of a thousand wasps.

He grabbed at the shafts of the arrows and worked them free, tossing them blindly away.

"Aenya, please wake up." He covered the arrow holes with his hands, and his fingers grew slick from the blood. Timothy searched for an aura, but there was none. He poured harder into her, willing her to enter his vision, but she didn't come. "Aenya, not you, not you." He pulled her close, praying it would meld them together, and increase the power flowing into her by using his whole body.

"No, no," he heard himself sobbing as he rocked her, her arms falling to the ground behind her, lifeless. The flowery field remained empty and began to fade. A sharp pain closed around his head like a vise. He was losing focus. He tried to hold his grip, but it was failing. A shriek rose from the ground so loud that it hurt his ears. It was a long time before he realized it was the sound of his own screaming.

Chapter 41

TIMOTHY WOKE ON THE FIELD with Eoghan leaning over him, tears flowing down the elf's face. Someone had turned the sound off in Timothy's ears, along with the nerve endings in his body. He had a flickering thought that he'd damaged himself beyond repair in trying to save her. He heard Eoghan's voice only in muffled tones, and it was impossible to distinguish the words he was saying. A hundred mounted elves surrounded them in a vast circle. Horses reared their heads and pawed nervously at the ground, but he heard none of it. He knew they were trying to lift him to his feet but was certain that standing was out of the question, and he was right. They carried him to his horse and lifted him into the saddle.

Timothy saw Ruairí bend over to pick Aenya from the grass. He tried to yell and then dismount, but several hands kept him from moving off the horse. Somehow, he managed to make it clear that she was to be taken to Tuathla's chamber, though he never heard the sound of his own voice.

He didn't remember the ride back to the Primal trees or going up to the dwelling. Sometime after seeing Ruairí pick her up and his horse starting to move, he lost consciousness again. He didn't know how he stayed in the saddle or even if he did.

Timothy woke to someone touching him and he yelled.

"Shh." Hands pushed him back into the pillows of his own bed. It was Derval. "You cried out in your sleep," she said.

The memory of what happened came flooding back, and Timothy felt ready to collapse. If Derval hadn't been there, he might have been able to stand it without falling apart. Instead, she put her arms around him, and he broke down and cried against her shoulder. When Aenya had tried to ease his pain from Tuathla's passing, he had refused. He had needed to feel it. This pain was worse than anything he could have imagined.

"Where is she?" he asked, trying to force himself back to a state of self-control.

"She's in your grandmother's chambers, as you ordered," she said. "No one has wanted to do anything until we were sure you were all right."

Timothy didn't know how to respond to that. He didn't know if he would ever be all right.

"Eoghan?" Timothy asked.

"He has resigned from service. He blames himself for failing you."

"And Ruairí allowed him to?" If Eoghan hadn't come as fast as he did, they both would have been killed. Then again, maybe that would have been better. He wasn't sure he could have recreated the energy he'd thrown at Cadwaladr, and there were obviously more elves at the scene than just the ones who'd appeared. "I must speak with him, with both of them."

"Bardán is in the main chamber downstairs. So are Ruairí, Labras, and Ailill. I hear the elders are beside themselves," she said. "Timothy…I want you to know…" Derval was struggling to find a way to say what was on her mind. "I want you to know how much we thought of Aenya. We're so sorry."

"I'm in love with her," he admitted.

"I know. We all knew as soon as we saw you both together. She was in love with you, too."

Timothy forced himself from the bed as he felt another swelling of emotion threaten to make him lose control again. Light-headed and dizzy, he went into the bath chamber and washed his face, then made his way down the stairs to the lower level. Derval followed behind.

Everyone in the room wore the same expression—one of sadness and concern. Each started to say something and move toward Timothy, but he held up his hands. If everyone he met acted the same way, he would never be able to stand on his own two feet again.

"Please," Timothy said. "There are some things I need to take care of."

Everyone stood, though Bardán looked the worst. Labras was the first to speak.

"I'm going to prepare something light for you to eat, my lord. You look rather pale."

Timothy didn't want to tell him that if he was pale, it had nothing to do with hunger, but he thanked him anyway, not wanting him to feel badly.

"Ruairí, I want you to tell Eoghan that I will not allow him to resign his position. He saved my life, and it was my own foolishness that…" He couldn't complete the thought and instead took a seat. "I will need you both to come with me to Sláine," he said. "Please have the ship prepared."

"On what errand?" Bardán asked, alarmed.

"Aenya has no family. I wish to take her body there."

"Why?"

Timothy thought about that, but couldn't come up with an answer. Something told him it was the thing to do.

"Because that's what must be done," he said. The alternative was unacceptable. He could never allow for her cremation or for her ashes to be sprinkled around the great oaks. "Ailill and Derval, can you build a litter to carry her and fashion a burial shroud for her?"

"At once, my lord," said Ailill. "We'll have them by tomorrow." Derval quickly agreed.

"Thank you," he said. They seemed reluctant to go, as if afraid to leave Timothy alone, so he went through the curtains into her room.

A dark cloak covered Aenya's body, probably from one of the elfin guard. Only her face was exposed, her head placed on a pillow. She could have been sleeping. *Isn't that what everyone thinks when they see a dead body in a casket?* If only it were true.

It had been a day, just one day, since he'd said goodbye to his grandmother in that same spot. He wanted to feel something, but everything was numb. He slid his fingers through her hair, a simple gesture he'd been looking forward to doing for centuries more.

He pulled back the cloak. The blood on her gown, which had seeped from wound to wound across her chest and stomach, had dried to a dark brown. The palm of his hand followed the contour of her body, and he could feel that her wounds had healed, superficially at least. If Cadwaladr hadn't distracted him, he might have been able to save her. Why hadn't they sensed that something was wrong? How had Seumais been able to get so close? *Were we that hyper-focused on one another that we just missed the warning signs?*

Timothy put his hands on her face and closed his eyes. Like he'd tried to memorize every detail of his grandmothers' face, he wanted to remember the feel of Aenya's in his hands. It was going to have to last a lifetime.

Before dawn, Labras helped him dress in the black clothing he'd worn to Sláine and to Cadwaladr's estate. He waited in the main hall of Tuathla's chambers for everyone to arrive. Eoghan was the first, and he appeared distressed. He refused to look Timothy in the eye.

"Eoghan," he said. "We must understand one another. I know you blame yourself for what happened, even though it was me who asked you to hold back. I get that. However, I need you. I need you right now because I trust you, and there are so few people I feel that way about."

Eoghan looked at Timothy like he'd lost his mind.

"Please…help me." Timothy could see the conflict swirling in his head.

"I'm at your service, my lord," he said in a quiet voice. It wasn't exactly an enthusiastic response, but it was good enough for now.

Timothy clasped his shoulder. Bardán, Ruairí, Ailill, and Derval all arrived at the same time. Ailill had created a beautiful litter with white silk sheeting and two oak poles, the ends carved in ornate patterns of cloverleaf. He must have worked on it through the night. Derval had embroidered a white silk shroud, with each corner bearing a matching pattern of clover.

The four men went into the chamber and moved Aenya's body onto the litter, carrying her carefully from the room and down the stairs. Derval walked by Timothy's side, holding his arm. At the base of the tree, an armed troop of elves and fairies were mounted and waiting. One of the sídhe had tears streaming down her face. They placed the litter in a carriage. Timothy mounted his horse and took a position behind her. He supposed he might have carried her to Sláine as Aine had done with his grandmother, but he couldn't bear to hasten the inevitable.

Bardán clasped Timothy's hand. "May your voyage be swift," he said.

"Thank you, Bardán."

The passage to the river was slower to avoid jostling the carriage too much, but they managed the trip in just a few hours. Timothy never took his eyes from Aenya's form lying under the shroud, hoping against all odds that she would suddenly wake and fly.

At the dock, the elves carried her aboard and put the litter onto a frame that Ailill had made just for the voyage. Several elves, including Ruairí and Eoghan, boarded—twice as many as on the first trip.

There was a strong wind in the Irish Sea, and the trip took less time than before, arriving near sunset of the second day instead of dawn the following morning. Timothy didn't sleep much. He spent most of the time at the bow staring at the mesmerizing rhythm of the waves. He cared little for the spray that washed his face and soaked his clothing. It caused a chill, but it reminded him that he was alive, though he wasn't sure he wanted to be. The stars that night were brighter than he'd ever seen them, as the moon was waning.

Every time he thought of her lying in the cabin at the rear of the ship, loneliness yanked at him, leaving him breathless and feeling like it was all a bad dream. He wanted to feel her against him, his lips on hers. The joy of kissing her was so new, and now it was gone forever. No one on board dared go near Timothy. He figured they all sensed he wanted to be alone, that they could not cure what he was suffering from. They were right. The numbness he'd felt while looking at her in Tuathla's chamber was wearing off, and he was afraid of the pain that was sure to come again. He was afraid it would twist and warp his thoughts until he became a babbling lunatic with a pretty sword. Standing at the bow of the ship, he could blame the seawater for the wetness on his face.

They made their way down the narrow chasm that led to the hidden pool of Sláine late in the afternoon of the third day since she had died. Two of the elves tied off against the rocky outcrop and four more negotiated the tricky chore of carrying the litter safely off the ship. They were prepared to carry her down the narrow footpath to her final resting place, but Timothy held up his hands and had them lower her to the ground.

"I'll take her," he said. He pulled the shroud back from her face. Her features were smooth and, as with his grandmother, someone had brushed her hair. Probably Derval. He pulled her body close so that her head rested against his shoulder, then turned and walked onto the long path that led from the river.

The sun must have been getting closer to setting over the sea. Shadows spread along the path, but he moved forward, careful not to let her feet scrape against the walls of the chasm. Finally, Timothy heard the sound of water ahead. He stepped onto the narrow path that led to the tiny island of rock in the center of the pool.

Aine was waiting.

She was dressed in the same flowing white gown she'd worn when he'd claimed the sword. His breath came in ragged gasps, and Aine's form grew fuzzy through the tears that filled his eyes. She held out her arms and took Aenya from him.

"We will care for her," she said. Her voice, though gentle, was powerful. It resonated in Timothy's chest, and his anxiety disappeared. He took one more glance at Aenya's face, knowing it would be his last. He brushed her lips with a kiss. They were soft, but cold. Aine looked at Aenya's face. A frown creased Aine's forehead and her eyes narrowed. Timothy thought it was a strange look, but when she raised her chin, she smiled at him and nodded. He turned and started away.

"Timothy, look to your dreams." The words echoed in his ears in a way that made him uncertain if they'd been spoken or if he'd imagined them. He turned back to question Aine, but she wasn't there.

Aenya was gone, too.

The walk back to the ship was the longest of his life.

Chapter 42

As soon as the boat turned up the river in Ireland, Timothy stepped on deck. It was late in the afternoon, and a dull grey had settled over the countryside with low-hanging clouds and a mist that rolled in from the sea. He called Ruairí and Eoghan over and told them he was going on ahead. They both looked at him with concern, especially Eoghan. Timothy believed it was the elf's intention never to let him out of his sight again. But Timothy simply couldn't bear the hours it would take to reach Sídhlin on horseback.

Timothy had come to think of them more as friends than protectors. He embraced each in turn. Then, with a wave and thanks to the others on board, he lifted from the deck and disappeared into the mist. There was little chance of having a human see him. He was grateful for the turn of bad weather.

He had a general sense of where he was going and ducked only occasionally low enough to get his bearing and continue. Dusk was beginning to settle as he touched down on the soft grass in front of the great oak by the stone fountain.

He wasn't ready to go to the dwelling. He didn't know what to say to Labras. He wasn't sure what he was going to say to anyone, for that matter. Ignoring the moist grass, he sat in front of the fountain, listening to the gentle lapping of the water as it slipped from one tier to the next. The sound was just enough to blot out any other noise and gentle enough not to interfere with his thoughts.

If he closed his eyes, he could still imagine the resonance of Aenya's voice as she sang "Aylwen's Lament" just feet from where he was sitting. He didn't think he would ever forget the clarity of her voice and the effect it had on him. That had been the first time he'd recognized being in love with her. He remembered his mother once telling him how she'd felt when his father had died. She said when you lost someone you loved, it was only a matter of time before you were able to embrace living again. That the agony of existence shrank just a little each day, until you found it was bearable once more. He wondered how long it would take before he just felt like breathing.

"You've returned," Bardán said. "I wasn't certain you would."

"I am not certain I should have," Timothy said. Then again, where else could he go?

"Have you given it much thought?"

"I try to think, but it's hard to focus."

The elder sat on the ground next to Timothy, and they faced the massive trunk of the ancient oak. Timothy saw him look down at the sword still attached to his belt. He had the feeling Bardán was worried he might have surrendered it to Aine. It occurred to Timothy that, had he thought of it, he might have. He released the clasp of the scabbard and laid the sword on the ground in front of him.

"It's kind of ironic," he said. "I am at the same point in life where I was just minutes before Aenya saved me. It's like I've come full circle. I wonder if all would have been better off had she let me drown."

"Do you believe that?"

"It feels about right." She was dead, Tuathla was dead, people had suffered. Cadwaladr was still alive and probably plotting an attack. The coincidence of Aenya's death occurring at almost the same instant he'd killed Seumais was gnawing at him, too. He'd partly avenged his mother, which had been his aim from the minute he learned of her murder, but was Aenya's death the price he had to pay for that revenge?

"And what of your time together? Do you consider it wasted?"

"No," he said. "The time we had was best of my life."

"Then her saving you was the right thing. That time, short as it may have been, was meaningful to both of you. Sometimes it's not the quantity of your experience, but the quality of it. Be grateful for it."

"It's become clear to me that it doesn't matter what decision a leader makes, there will always be consequences. I thought I was making the right decision in going after Cadwaladr, and innocent people almost died. If I made no decision at all, sídhe like my mother and elves would have died anyway. I don't know if I have the stuff that makes me worthy of possessing that sword. I don't see how I'm worthy to step into the shoes of my ancestors."

"You have doubts."

"Of course I have doubts. Cadwaladr lives, I saw his men drag him off the field. Aldith was right, with Tuathla's death, he'll step up his war, and with me here, it will only fuel his desire."

"What will you do?" he asked.

"I don't know, go home, I suppose." Timothy sensed he didn't even know what that meant. He wasn't sure he would recognize what home was anymore. There was nothing back in New Hampshire. His parents were dead, his grandmother was dead, and now Aenya was gone. Life just didn't seem worth it. But he knew he wasn't the one to pull it all together. If he left, maybe things might return to normal, at least as normal as they were before he got there. Maybe Cadwaladr wouldn't feel so threatened if he disappeared. It would certainly be easier for the elders to negotiate with him.

"Everyone has doubts, it's part of living," Bardán said. "Try to think things through and listen to your heart."

"Those are my grandmother's words. I have no heart."

"What would Aenya tell you to do?"

"That's not fair," Timothy said, anger flaring in his chest. He was hurt Bardán would throw that in his face. But as soon as the words came out, they felt wrong. How many times had Aenya saved him, rebuked him for being irresponsible? Then there was Tuathla's faith in him. What had they seen that he couldn't see in himself? They were wrong. Sídhlin would be better off without him. It was time to cut and run.

Timothy stood up and reached for the sword. He turned to hand it to Bardán and froze. He'd been so caught up in his thoughts that he had failed to notice the hundreds of elves who now stood on the field behind them; more were drifting from the trees. Bardán seemed less surprised.

He scanned their upturned and expectant faces. It was easy to imagine their concern for the future now that Tuathla was dead. All their hopes rested on an unproven young boy who couldn't even speak their language. If he failed them, life would return to what it was. No, it was worse; it would come without the hope of Alfheim ever becoming a reality, since he was the last of Aylwen's line. Worse still was the probability that the new Alfheim would be a distorted version of the enlightened realm it once was. Cadwaladr would poison the very notion of what was best of the elfin world. That monster would continue to hunt the sídhe, hunt them to extinction. His mother and Tuathla and Aenya would have died for nothing. He had taken vengeance for his mother with Seumais's death, but that was of little consequence to these people's futures.

Was simple hope enough to bind the elfin world together? Was their faith, and that of Tuathla and Aenya, enough to recreate what was lost? Timothy's arm, the one holding the sword, dropped to his side. They must have read it as a sign that he'd given up. The essence of their hope dwindled. Shoulders drooped, and faces looked downward. One by one, they turned, making their ways back to the trees.

Timothy knew he didn't have the right to take that hope from them. The image of Aenya's disappointed face appeared before him, and he couldn't bear it.

"Wait!" he called out.

The crowd of elves hesitated and then turned back toward him. They circled around, forming a large ring around the stone fountain. Bardán walked down the slope and joined them.

Timothy drew the sword from its scabbard and held it high for all to see, then drove it into the earth. In a voice that trembled, he spoke to them all.

"From this day forward, and with your help, we'll build a new Alfheim from under this oak. I pledge this to you as long as you'll have me."

There was a moment of hesitation, and then for the second time, the entire assemblage dropped to one knee; only this time it was for him alone. He realized that nothing else could have made him feel the weight of the responsibility he'd just claimed. He prayed to wherever Aenya and Tuathla and his mother were that he would live to be worthy of that pledge. For an instant, Timothy thought he felt Aenya's hand on his shoulder, and he was glad.

Chapter 43

SHE FELT COOLNESS ON HER cheeks, and tiny waterfall sounds were like lullabies in her ears. It was an unexperienced state of being, like floating on a cloud, rested but not wakeful, peaceful without so much as a hint of discomfort. It was perfect. She opened her eyes to a paradise, all shades of green and broad-leafed yellow flowers, red and purple buds, and petals cascading down the surrounding sheer cliff walls. And water, threading its way around the ferns and flowers, lightly feathered as it went into freefall to the crystal-clear water of the pool far below.

A deep breath carried a dizzying fragrance that pulled her into a euphoric place. A movement caught her eye; a radiant shimmering white was moving closer to her.

Her eyes adjusted to the intensity of the light, and then she was surprised as her vision cleared and focused. It was Tuathla.

"Greetings, Aenya. We have so much to talk about."

End of Book One

Acknowledgments

A NOVEL BEGINS WITH A tiny breath of life; like the gentle puff on the spark that lights the tinder. A solitary venture at first; but before too long it passes out of the hands of the writer and into a larger world. Many thanks must go to many people.

From my earliest memory, my mother, Enid, read the Bobbsey Twins to me, especially on those occasions when I was home sick in bed. It cultivated an indelible connection between books and imagination.

Decades later, while toying with my need to write, Rance Crain of the Crain Publishing empire read my first novel and gave me a thumbs up; it was the encouragement I needed from a leader in the world I wanted into.

To my sons, Alex and Ian, who often suffered my absence as I wrote and went to school to hone my craft. Thanks go to Carol and Jerry Garrett, who accepted me into their family and became my earliest fans.

I owe much gratitude to the faculty and students of the Southern New Hampshire University MFA program, especially my mentors: Katherine Towler, Robin Wasserman, and Jo Knowles, each one a gifted novelist, and to Diane Les Becquets, who accepted me into that perfect writer's bubble.

To all the young people who took the time to be my first audience by reading the earliest version of *Alfheim* and the feedback they offered: John Allard, Kate Ball, Eric Besanceney, Melanie Blackmore, Harrison Cullen, Brianne Donahue, Brian Haldenwang, Jaclyn Hansen, Jess Hassell, Valerie Lamberson, Joseph Priolo, Amanda Tyrie, and Ashley Vanderwaren—I thank you all.

To my incredible editor, Susan Kennedy, who poured through the manuscript twice—first for structure and content, and finally line by line and word by word, helping me polish the final draft; and my amazing publicist Wendie Appel, whose guidance breathes life into the book.

Lastly, and most importantly, thanks to my beloved Nancy, the first to tell me I needed to do this. Without her, nothing that followed would have begun.

Pronunciation Key

Character Names

Aenya: EN ya
Ailill: AL yil
Aine: AWN ya
Aldith: AL dith
Aran: Ah ran
Aylwen: AIL wen
Bardán: BAR dawn
Cadwaladr: Kad WALL a der
Cillian: KILL e an
Darina: da RE na
Derval: DER val
Dwyryd: DOO'EE rid
Éabha:AY va
Éadaoin: A deen
Eirnin: AIR nin
Eoghan: O in
Gormflaith: GORA mith
Heulfryn: HALE vrin
Iúile: LU ile
Labras: LAU rahsh
Líle: LEEL

Muirenn: MUR in
Myrddin: MIR thin
Oillin: ULL yeen
Ruairí: ROH ri
Ruarc: ROO ark
Sorcha: SOR aka
Tuathla: TOO uh la
Tuathal: TOO a hal

Other Words

Connleodh: KON leh
Sláine: SLAW nia
Sídhlin: SHEE lin

About the Author

Gary A. Nilsen is a writer and a blogger. His career as a financial professional spans nearly four decades. He lived in Saudi Arabia for five years, helped on the initial excavation of a 1500-year-old shipwreck off the coast of Africa in the Red Sea, and has lectured on underwater archaeology and novel writing. He earned his MFA in Fiction with Southern New Hampshire University and currently resides with his girlfriend, Nancy, and their two Old English Sheepdogs, Nana and Harry. Visit him at garynilsen.com